Ashby Jones

The Little Bird

HISTRIA
FICTION

Histria Fiction

Las Vegas ◊ Chicago ◊ Palm Beach

Published in the United States of America by
Histria Books
7181 N. Hualapai Way, Ste. 130-86
Las Vegas, NV 89166 USA
HistriaBooks.com

Histria Fiction is an imprint of Histria Books. Titles published under the imprints of Histria Books are distributed worldwide.

Library of Congress Control Number: 2024931092

ISBN 978-1-59211-476-4 (softbound)
ISBN 978-1-59211-484-9 (eBook)

And when love speaks, the voice of all the gods

Make heaven drowsy with the harmony."

— *Love's Labour's Lost,* Shakespeare

Shane came home to kill a man.

Suzanne came home because she already had.

Prologue

When was Suzanne born? Yesterday? A decade or so ago? At the turn of the century or tomorrow? Possibly without a date at all but in some timeless, mythological crater under the watch of circling angels? The truth is, she wasn't born as it's commonly thought. She arrived in her paradoxical world as a little hatchling, an anomaly whose purpose was to flee the nest and never return, and yet she did.

Her birth name was Jenny, but in her teens, after her father lost the trial, ultimately causing her mother to leave home, and soon thereafter, when her father left this world, she chose the name, Suzanne. She adored the song by the same name, written by Leonard Cohen in the mid-Sixties and sung by Judy Collins, but more than that, she loved the hissing sound, the faux echo of the double sound of "ss-ss" when the name, Suzanne, was spoken. It reminded her of the resonances in the word, suicide. But for the first few months of her life, she was called The Little Bird, and here's why.

Born prematurely and breeched as well, she descended through her mother's womb with her tiny toes flexed and caught on the muscled wall of the uterus, delaying her arrival. Chelsea, the midwife, sensing that something was wrong, yelled for a doctor, causing Jenny's mother to jerk violently in alarm. The canal walls shook. Jenny's toes quivered and then pointed, releasing their grip. In a gush of warm and welcoming blood, she slipped upside-down and pencil-thin through the gateway of life into Chelsea's trembling hands. Jenny's arms, forced high and straight as she arrived, reminded the midwife, an avian caretaker at the local zoo, of a sparrow's wings. She'd never seen such a birth nor known that it was even possible.

Chelsea immediately realized that baby Jenny wasn't breathing. She shouted again for a doctor but knew she had no time to waste. Applying the same gentle rhythm she'd often used to bring little birds back to life when they'd fallen from a nest or flown into the screen around their cage and lay in shock, mistaken for dead, she began to stroke Jenny's chest tenderly, but with insistence. Jenny's mom came to her elbows and watched, gasping and sobbing as her baby's skin slowly turned red and then purple. Chelsea stopped stroking and dropped her ear to the baby's chest. Jenny's mom was about to scream in despair when the midwife rose with a grin and shouted: "She's alive, Mrs. de Ville! She's alive!"

Chelsea detached the placenta. "Here's your little bird," she said, handing the hatchling to her mother.

Being born upside-down was just the first irony in Suzanne's life, a forewarning that her struggle with existence had just begun.

Chapter One

The haunting memory of Jesse's murder came to Shane in torrents now. Jesse, the Black teenage boy who'd help raise Shane after his mother died, was beaten to death by a cop for showing up at a white high school baseball game.

It was the opening game of Shane's senior season, the first game played under the school's newly installed lights. Excited, Jesse had come to see Shane pitch, to find out if the secret practice sessions they'd had in the marshes had paid off. There, in the pre-season cold of winter, when the sky's grey dome helped conceal them, Jesse, saddled with determination, had tried to teach Shane to throw a baseball a hundred miles an hour. At that speed, Jesse said, the ball would make the air whistle.

Shane was on the mound, having struck out the first two batters he'd faced, when the siren wailed. He would learn that Sergeant Talley, the drunk cop, had skidded his patrol car to a stop behind the bleachers. Gun in hand, he jumped out of the car to catch Jesse watching the game from the trees behind the right-field fence. There, in less than a minute, Talley beat Shane's brother to death with the stock of his gun.

Three months later the case against Talley, prosecuted by Suzanne's father, was thrown out in court, a decision praised by the community.

Jesse's murder happened almost eight years ago, but like a record spinning on an unstoppable platter, his scream for help had replayed in Shane's head ever since. It was now 1972, just over a week before Thanksgiving.

Though numerous baseball scouts had come to his games, Shane had given up on any hope of playing professionally, and in the summer of '64, as soon as he graduated from Jefferson, he left Meridien to join the Marine Corps. He volunteered to serve two tours of duty in Vietnam.

He'd made a tragic mistake that led to Jesse's death and hoped that he could bury it in the soil of forgiveness. Instead, the guilt and shame for what he'd done, or failed to do, gathered strength in combat, in daily killing, where his disgrace vanished the moment the deed was done, only to return in his sleep. At last, his guilt jumped the jagged gap between the past and present to plant in him a resolute demand for revenge.

He mustered out of the Marines in mid-November and was returning to Meridien from Camp Pendleton for the first time since he'd enlisted. An intense storm in the Gulf grounded his plane overnight in Dallas. He spent the long delay at an airport bar. He kept promising Jesse in an increasingly slurred tone that things were going to be set right now that he was coming home.

Defying the next morning's hangover that flattened him to his bed at The Oleander, Meridien's ancient, Victorian boarding house, he stretched up toward the ballfield's argon lights flooding the scoreboard. For one magnificent moment, he felt himself take flight. The lights engulfed him. It was as if the moon had exploded. His teammates appeared as tall as trees, as powerful as gods. The sound of Ethel Merman singing "Take Me Out to the Ballgame" filled the evening air. The hand-chalked foul lines seemed to float on her voice as he soared from the mound, away from the shouting crowd, rising and falling with the wild night wind. Just as he was about to clear the scoreboard, he heard Jesse's scream, and for a moment so empty that he thought his heart had stopped, he hovered in the silent, amber night, searching for his brother. Then he plunged into an abrupt darkness. Swiftly into the darkness, a stuporous, bourbon-soaked interval somewhere between sleep and waking.

His body was shaking so hard that the bedsprings screeched. A frost-embedded wind made its way through the cracks in the window, but although he was lying in his underwear, he couldn't cover himself.

Abruptly, the lingering agony of Jesse's scream was replaced by the excited voice of Shane's small catcher, Toby, shouting the same thrilling words he'd shouted when the last batter struck out that day, "We won, Shane! We won! We won!" In moments like these, Jesse came back with a cramped and unbearable reality, as though he'd squeezed painfully through some narrow void in the past. Shane saw the joy in Jesse's large brown eyes and felt the dream's deceptive surge of hope that he might still be alive.

Although his belief in God had sunk into the mire of combat, Shane pleaded with The Almighty to let Jesse return. The begging came from the back of his throat, loud, rolling and guttural before slipping into a scratchy vibrato that pierced the murky layers of his hangover, engaging his brain to draw him out of sleep. He sensed that time was moving uncontrollably toward dawn and that life was about to turn on again. The true nightmare was in waking — when it would start all over, that stalking, gut-wrenching shame that threatened to extinguish his life at some blind and dark intersection. If it hadn't been for him, Jesse would never have come to the game.

Shane tried his damnedest to avoid waking up to that, but his eyes wouldn't obey. They caught the late afternoon sun and stared as if it had something to tell him, some cold cosmic secret that had sprung from its surface only moments ago, something that would help explain why he was years behind where he should be, years behind redemption.

He started counting backward from one hundred. As the numbers flowed past, he visualized them dropping behind his eyelids to rest next to one another as they once did on the huge wooden scoreboard. His heart plunged as if his chest had abruptly become a pit. His head snapped from the pillow. A familiar pain leaped from the wound on his neck, the ironic, if not comical wound he'd sustained in Da Nang the night before he was scheduled to leave Vietnam and return to Camp Pendleton.

Shane expected a flutter of heartbeats followed by a swooping cavity in his chest that might be his undoing, but he was wrong. His heart slowed and then instantly thudded, as if God was prodding him awake. Gasping, he rolled out of bed, slipped and stumbled into the bathroom, where his jeans lay on the floor. He took his wallet out to see if he had any money left, but when he opened it, the worn Polaroid of Jesse fell onto the floor. He picked it up. Jesse's broad smile stretched so wide that it appeared to match the bill of his baseball cap. The oversized letters threaded across the chest spelled out the word Cardinals, the major league team that Jesse's older brother, Jason, once played for. Shane forced the picture back into his wallet in the doubling down of guilt and hatred.

He'd come home to avenge Jesse and, by doing so, banish his remorse. No, not home, he corrected himself. Yes, he was born in Meridien but it wasn't his home. A town hidden from a changing world, a place long reserved for retribution, like Dante's ninth rung of the Inferno, reserved for those who'd committed treachery and were to be punished in the equivalent of their sins. Would that be him? Would his return be the beginning or the end of his life? It would be one or the other but nowhere in between, he'd promised himself.

He went to his suitcase, yanked it open, and ran his fingers through the clothes to brush the soft velvet box that held his Purple Heart. Under it, he felt the cold, prickly handle of the .45, his furtive gift from the war.

Relieved, he took the pistol out of the suitcase and checked the chamber. It was full. He pecked the barrel and slid the gun back into the suitcase. At long last, yesterday and today were one and the same. And if that paradox wasn't enough, tonight he would be venturing out to a party, the one that Medic, his beloved high school English teacher, threw each year on the twelfth of November — the day in 1945 when Medic's Marine unit was summoned home from Europe, where he and his fellow soldiers had been assigned to help free prisoners from the death camps.

Shane had called Medic from Pendleton to make sure the party was going to be held this year. The operator said that the phone number was out of commission and the person he was trying to call was no longer listed in the phone book. Afraid that something had happened to Medic, Shane immediately sent his question by telegram, and to his great relief, Medic replied, letting him know that this year's party was being held for any former students, but this year it was for his retirement, a synonym for freedom, he wrote, the reason he'd named it the Emancipation Party.

He reached into the suitcase and took out a fresh pair of dark blue Marine dress pants, a wool shirt, and his fading, earth-colored trench coat. He tried to convince himself that he was looking forward to something cheerful, and if not, at least an event blessed with whisky. But more than anything, the reason he'd made such an effort to go to the party was to find out if Medic still believed what Shane had overheard him say in the hall outside his classroom when he was approached by a fellow history teacher, the kindhearted Miss Collins. She'd asked Medic if, given his involvement in freeing prisoners from the concentration camps, there was any room in his heart for forgiving the Nazis?

Medic's answer was imprinted on the inside of Shane's skull. "Miss Collins, there are some sins that cannot be forgiven, because to do so would be to commit an even greater sin."

Chapter Two

Shane did fifty unstable push-ups to try and clear his head and then showered, shaved and dressed before heading to his rental car. Downstairs in the living room, he looked for Mrs. Abernathy, the legendary owner of The Oleander, to thank her for letting him book the room on such short notice and to apologize for arriving so late.

But except for a vintage piano and what appeared to be a maze of wheelchair impressions on the Persian rug, the room was empty, or so he thought until he glanced at the wall. Hangover floaters that resembled dark hieroglyphics were crossing his vision. He shook his head to make sure he wasn't seeing things because on the wall next to the stairs hung a longbow and a quiver filled with arrows.

"Mrs. Abernathy?" he called out. There was no answer. He raised his voice slightly. "Mrs. Abernathy?" Only the sound of silence replied.

He went outside, reminding himself to call her later and let her know that he'd probably be late again tonight. Nailed to one of the posts at the top of the porch steps was a framed photograph of a young man wearing a dated Army uniform and a cloth hat. Shane had missed seeing it the night before. Letters printed below the photograph said, "Welcome home, Abe!"

He got into the car, a tight-fitting Nash Rambler that resembled a caramel apple. He barely remembered the drive from Meridien's tiny airport and wondered how in hell he'd made it. He shook his arms as if to ward off the thought and readied himself to drive through the town's unnerving remains, made all the more intimidating by the fading sun.

The small town, isolated almost two hundred miles southeast of the Blue Ridge Mountains, sat like an island between the Atlantic and pincers of the Mal, a thick, teeming bay-like river whose waters were stained the color of dried blood by the tannin from tobacco plants rooted on its shores. Shane crossed the river's arcane bridge, made for the first automobiles in the early twentieth century and never widened, causing the road to narrow into a fine point like a gunsight focused on a distant enemy. He slowed down, as many did when they crossed the bridge, worried that they might be squeezed into oblivion. He glanced at the muddy banks on the town side of the Mal, where he'd taught Jesse to swim. The memory couldn't be avoided.

The moment they had arrived at the river that day, Jesse jumped off his bike and rushed into the surging Mal in an effort to show that the swimming lessons Shane had given him in exchange for fastball practices had paid off, but trapped in the current, Jesse suddenly disappeared beneath the surface. Shane leaped off his bike and ran to the water's edge. Jesse's muscular arms came flailing out of the water, whirling like a Mixmaster, but his feet and legs couldn't surface as the undercurrent swept him downstream. Shane's heart galloped. Jesse was moving too fast and was too far from the shore to jump in and try to catch him, so he sprinted down the riverbank, desperately trying to keep up with him.

About fifty yards from the dam, Jesse's fully toned body rose to the surface and leveled out on the water. Stroking madly, but in perfect form, he managed to cut away from the current toward the shore. He rolled over three times in the punishing flow but came to the surface each time and made it to the muddy riverbank. As he stumbled out of the water, Shane slid down the bank as if he were stealing second, came to his feet, grabbed Jesse's arm, and wrapped it around his shoulders. Together, they slogged through the mud to the top of the bank and plopped down, gasping as they struggled to sit up.

"Thank you for saving my life," Jesse rasped.

"You saved your own life, brother," Shane replied.

"Only because you taught me how to swim. God thanks you, too."

Shane left the bridge with Jesse's generous voice in his ears. He turned onto Riverside Drive, which soon intersected with the past. Main Street was lined with blocks of slate-roofed, Victorian houses, each with a wide-brimmed porch and an occasional widow's walk. Once the homes of tobacco millionaires, the houses had aged markedly and were pockmarked by curds of peeling paint. He passed the library, complete with a cupola in which a retreating Confederate Army once stashed belts and munitions. Shane had swiped a copy of To Kill a Mockingbird from the library, before the library had banned it from the schools, and given it to Jesse, who read the book and came away thinking that Atticus Finch was a god.

The original gold-leafed dome was now burnished copper, weathered by rain and rust to make it appear that it had been that way forever. Adjacent to the library was a graveyard where Meridien's sons of the Confederacy were buried. Small white lights were draped over the scattered tombstones to brighten the names of the soldiers, whose identities, for the most part, had given way to time but whose fated purpose had not.

A hearse, with rear doors flared open like angel wings, rested in the crumbling driveway of Sills's Mortuary, the Black funeral home where rumor had it they'd taken Jesse's body for the court-ordered "burial at sea" — where the bodies of those who the hateful Judge Aiken ruled to be dangerously infected with disease or sin were placed into tar-sealed plywood coffins and sent afloat on the Mal, launched into its treacherous waters with the downstream destination being Crow's Beak. There the coffins would get trapped in the mossy slime and rotting tree trunks and left to decay. Those who avoided the epithet, dangerously infected, were allowed to be buried in Blackberry Hill, where in the summer's weeks of torrid heat, the untended dry ground would often crack open and their caskets would break through the fractured earth, their bows pointing to heaven.

Shane was jarred by the sound of a distant siren and wondered if it might be Talley, maybe driving the same cop car whose trunk he'd thrown Jesse's body into and taken to Sill's? Tempted to forget about Medic's party and hunt the siren down, Shane caught himself and steadied. He'd left his gun at The Oleander, and in truth, Talley was at the top of his must-do list but not first on his to-do list.

First on the to-do list was a vow Shane had made to go by his old house where he and Jesse were practicing out back when the explosion ignited by Shane's father occurred. Second on the list was a vow to go to his mother's grave to declare his love for her and let her know that the odds were good that he'd be seeing her soon. Last on the list was a vow that could only be upheld when Talley was dead — to go to the ballfield, provided he hadn't been caught by then, and bring a double shot of good news to Jesse, whose soul would be thrilled when Shane shouted out in joy, "The bastard is dead, Jesse! The bastard's dead!"

As the siren faded, Shane took a deep breath. The countdown had begun.

Chapter Three

A bevy of cars lined the street in front of Medic's house, a strangely structured, one-story aluminum home on Mount View. It was an abnormally long and narrow house with a one-car garage whose yellow aluminum door was still dented. The house had only a single bedroom and two bathrooms but an expansive living room that took up virtually the entire square footage of the home. Shane remembered a shanty that served as a chicken coop and had always stood down the hill behind the house. He imagined it would still be there, overflowing with chickens that Medic could never bring himself to kill.

He parked at the end of the block and made his way to the house. As he started down the driveway, he heard the familiar sound of Gerry and The Pacemakers singing, "You'll Never Walk Alone," Medic's favorite song. In the winter months, whenever Medic detected that the grey skies and the cold were dispiriting the students, he would play the song in class, while encouraging them to stand and sing along, which the crowd inside his house had just now begun to do. The sound was welcoming and heightened Shane's resilience.

He stepped through the kitchen door into the chorus. The sight of mostly young visitors with their closed eyes and hands in prayer brought him to a standstill. His picture in the senior yearbook surfaced behind his glazed eyes. Dressed in a coat and tie that bunched the collar of his father's dress-shirt around his thin neck, he seemed to be a caricature of himself. His wavy chestnut hair, now disheveled, was slicked back into a rebel's ducktail. A pointed flip of hair, glued in place with Pomade, stuck out over his forehead in a widow's peak, while a wide, forced smile did its best to hide the memory of Jesse, who'd been killed three weeks before the picture was taken. Shane stared at the conundrum staring back at him. He would never be that person again.

The song ended, and in the following gap of happiness, he wiped his eyes and smiled as the sound of Norman Greenberg's "Spirit in the Sky" filled the living room to instant cheering.

"Shane McCauley! My God, I can't believe my eyes!" Medic exclaimed, prying his way through the crowd. He threw his arms around Shane, his breath heavy with the smell of rum. His short, once-dark hair had greyed and lengthened into the image of a waterfall. Set in a tapered face his narrow eyes always seemed full of empathy. He stepped back gripping Shane by the shoulders while staring at his former student in delight.

"Shane, I am thrilled, as well as shocked, that you got my telegram, and here you are alongside the ghost of a fellow Marine, once upon a time also stationed at Pendleton. Thank goodness, you made it back from the war. My God, I don't think we've seen each other since spring of your senior year. When was that, a century ago?"

"Just about," Shane replied, stirred by the joy in his teacher's voice.

"When you joined the Marines, everyone else was being drafted. It surprised all of us. We thought you were on your way to the big leagues." Medic paused and tightened his grip on Shane's shoulders. "I certainly understand your wanting to get away from Meridien, and I admire you for doing so. In this town, very little's changed, and I'm afraid it never will." Medic squinted, leaned toward Shane, and lowered his voice. "I've tried to leave, numerous times, but hoping to witness at least some progress with equality always held me back. But I'm off on a journey tomorrow, a journey I've never taken because until now I feared returning, maybe a bit like you coming back after all this time. The past can get its hooks in you, can't it?"

"Where are you going?"

"To Auschwitz."

"Auschwitz?" Shane said, startled.

"To be with the souls of the children I left behind. They've stayed with me forever, but I've never been able to board the plane. Of all people, I'm sure you understand. I booked a place in Oswiecim, a small town whose name, translated, is Auschwitz. Please, don't forget me."

The words registered as a farewell forever, causing Shane to fear that he might not have another chance to ask his long-awaited question. "Medic, there's no way I could ever forget you, especially the day after class when you and Miss Collins were standing out in the hall, and I heard her ask if you'd ever forgiven the Nazis for their sins and you told her that ..."

"There are some sins that can never be forgiven, for to do so would be to commit a far greater sin. It's as true today as it was then," Medic replied. "Shane, I believe I see approval in your eyes."

Shane felt he'd waited eight years for this moment. "Thank God for you, Medic."

Medic's eyes smiled and dampened. "May we meet in heaven or in the other place, if we're wrong," he said and glanced over his shoulder at the full room. "I'd better finish giving everyone my thanks for coming. Please, make yourself at home. Oh, Shane, just so you're aware, and possibly to avoid any shock or embarrassment, I should tell you that George de Ville's daughter sent me a note saying she was coming tonight. She left college a couple of weeks early for the holidays. You might remember her as Jenny, but when she went off to college, for some reason, she took on the name Suzanne. I don't know if you ever knew her. Back in the day, she was always a little quirky, sometimes hard to follow, but artistically, she was as talented as they come."

"Mr. de Ville's daughter? I never met her."

"I've heard that coincidence is God's way of showing He cares. Okay, the booze is calling! Stay as long as you like and help yourself."

As Medic disappeared into the crowd, Shane scanned the room but recognized no one. Everyone seemed so much younger. When he started toward the hearth, he noticed that Medic had taken down the inscription he'd cut out of Balsa and nailed over the fireplace, but the impression was still there. Taken from the ghastly death sentence that spanned the gates of Auschwitz, Arbeit Macht Frei, "Work makes you free," he'd converted the hideous lie into Liebe Macht Frei, replacing the German word for "work" with the German word for "love." He'd written his version on the blackboard time and time again. Once, a student asked him if he'd ever been in love, and he replied that yes, he had been and was still, but that it wasn't with the living.

The memory escorted Shane from the hearth back to the bar. He told himself to go easy on the booze, lest he start asking about Talley and sounding an alert.

He took a swallow before looking down at the reflection of what appeared to be the elder twin of the person he'd seen in the yearbook. His face seemed drawn as if he'd lost too much weight. The skin below his eyes was puffy and purple. His wavy hair, which turned the color of mahogany and carried a gun-barrel luster in the sunset, still possessed a shine. He twisted his head to check the wound below his chin. The stitches were gone but the scar made it look like they were still there. He grimaced at the memory of the doctor leaning over the stretcher to lace the wound without an anesthetic, for thanks to the enemy, he'd run out. It hurt like hell, but the military tank where the doctor normally practiced his trade had been blown to bits.

Drink in hand, he weaved about the room, saying hellos to anyone he caught looking at him and briefly shaking hands with a few, while unable to recognize a soul, until he stumbled upon Toby, his high school catcher, so short that he was allowed to stay on his knees behind home plate instead of squatting. Toby had helped him to the locker room that day when the game ended.

After Shane struck out the last batter and his teammates ran off the field yelling in exhilaration at the unexpected win, he'd stood on the mound, disoriented and immobile, watching as his mind replayed the sight of Talley throwing Jesse into the trunk of his car like a bag of trash and driving off with the wheels whining but the siren silent. Toby ran out to Shane, took him by the arm, and led him into the locker room, all the while reminding him that they'd won the game, the game they weren't supposed to win because the Martinsville Tigers had been the conference winners three years in a row — the game Jesse never got to see, the game where for the first time Shane's fastball reached a hundred miles an hour, creating the dubious whistle that Shane prayed Jesse still heard.

Toby always won the spelling bees and could seldom find anyone to challenge him because he never lost. Shane imagined that Toby looked like Bilbo Baggins, for he had round cheeks, long brown hair that curled around his ears, and a smile that seemed to perch on a branch somewhere between naivete and cunning. And yet he was neither. Exceptionally modest, he took no credit for his intellect. He seldom said a word.

Behind Toby loomed Ever Reed, the enormous, speckled-faced, redhead football player and the second biggest asshole Shane had ever known. Once, Ever kicked the crutches out from under Stevie Goldman's armpit because one day when Stevie was trying his best to get to his crowded class on time, he accidentally jabbed Ever's foot with his crutch.

Ever shoved Toby out of the way and stuck a bottle of Blue Ribbon toward Shane. Shane reluctantly reached for it, but Ever jerked the bottle away, aped a smile, downed the beer and burped like a tuba. "Hey, major leaguer, rumor has it you joined the Marines and went off to 'Nam. If there's any truth to it, I'd have to admit that I envy you."

Shane ignored the comment and glanced at Toby. "It's great to see you, Toby. What are you doing now?"

Toby extended a small hand. "I followed Medic's example and became a high school English teacher. I moved down to Asheville."

"Why Asheville?"

"Because that's where my favorite author, Thomas Wolfe, grew up. His house is still there. Just to drive by it makes me feel that I'm back in his time. Ever's down there, too," he said, gesturing at the giant beside him. "He works in the Mill. He lost his driver's license the other day because of too much Blue Ribbon. So I drove him up tonight. I haven't missed one of these parties since I was in Medic's class, and from what I understand, I guess this is going to be the last one, unfortunately."

Ever interrupted, pointing his empty bottle at Shane. "If you don't mind, let me ask you something. How many Cong did you kill over there?"

Shane tensed. "Just curious, were you, Ever, in the service?" he asked, fully aware that the play on words went sailing past the jerk.

"You bet, I was."

Toby rolled his eyes and looked up at Ever. "No, you weren't."

"I've told you before, Toby. I went to war in my goddamn head." Unexpectedly, Ever's eyes turned sheepish. He had trouble looking at Shane and his lips began to tremble. "They wouldn't let me sign-up because I was allergic to wool, but, believe me, I wanted to go. I went to four draft centers but none of them would let me in. I mean, it was in my head every day and still is. So, I was there in my own way." He glanced at Shane. "Now that we got that straight, would you be so kind, big-leaguer, as to give me an answer to my question?"

"Death be not proud, Ever," Toby said, quoting the opening line of Donne's famous poem, which Medic had recited whenever any of his students asked how many Nazis he'd killed.

"What the fuck does that have to do with anything, Toby?" Ever demanded. He waved his hand at Toby and then pointed at Shane. "I want this bullshitter to tell me some stories about the war he claims he was in, so I can tell if he's lying, like he did at that Black boy's trial."

Shane felt tempted to throw the bastard into a Marine chokehold and squeeze the life out of him, but a voice in the back of his head shouted for him to walk away or lose all chance at retribution.

"That's enough, Ever, we've gotta be going now," Toby snapped, grabbing Ever's arm and urging him into the crowd. Looking over his shoulder at Shane, Toby rolled his eyes. "I'm so sorry," he said under his breath.

Shane worked his way back to the bar, topped off his glass and went to take a time-out by the fireplace. Tell that fucking jerk stories about the war, stories about death, as if they were myths or fairytales available for enjoyment? Tell him what it was like to kill another human being and wake up in fear and shame every hour of the night, wondering how much time you had left before an enemy leaped out of the dark and bayoneted you? What about having your closest friend since boot camp, Private Payne, blown to pieces by a Claymore? Holding him as blood kept flowing from where his leg had been as the suffering unexpectedly left his contorted face. Wading in a pool of hatred while watching Payne's eyelids flicker and the moonlight tremble in his eyes as he whispered, "It's okay, Sergeant, it don't hurt no more. I'm going home now, where there ain't no worries."

Home, where there ain't no worries. If only, Shane thought. Squeezing his eyes shut, he took a gulp of bourbon and made his way to the hearth, letting Medic's long sought-after comment steady him. He would not commit the greater sin of forgiveness.

Chapter Four

Suzanne resisted leaving for the party as long as she could bear it. When the sunset turned into its second phase, nautical blue, she was taking a shower and felt her father's presence hovering outside the curtain. About to freak out, she swiped it open to emptiness. It was as though, by sleight of hand, she'd made him disappear. A terrible thought struck her. She had.

She toweled off in a frenzy, grabbed her mother's black, velvet, V-neck dress from a nearly empty closet, a pair of her sandals for riding the Tiger — the ancient motorcycle her father had named after its roar and bequeathed to her — and a pair of high heels to change into for the party. After throwing on her clothes and having no time to rectify how disheveled she might be, she snatched her hair dryer from the shelf by the sink. In one motion she grabbed her father's leather motorcycle jacket and dashed into the living room only to stumble on a pile of her canvasses. Managing to stay on her feet, she ran out the double doors to the driveway and jumped onto the Tiger.

Speeding to the party, she tried to outrace her nerves. Once there, she wedged the Tiger between the cars in Medic's driveway and dropped the kickstand by the kitchen door. Enlivened when she heard the music, she flipped off her sandals and entered the room, rushing in barefoot with her dryer in one hand, the high heels tucked into the curve above her hip, and her stormy dark hair still wet on her neck. She hurried to the bar, poured a splash of bourbon, took a deep breath, and rushed toward the bathroom, conjuring up the image of an incredibly sculptured dancer who'd come to the party straight from a circus.

With the empty glass in hand, she returned as another person. Flecks of gold glitter sparkled on her high cheeks. She'd tamed her hair so that it fell to her shoulders in soft rolling waves. Uneasy because she'd overlooked her bra, she pressed her fingers against her breasts as if telling them to stay in place, took a deep breath, and scanned the throng of bouncing heads to search for Medic. She glanced at the fireplace and, for a moment extracted from time, thought she recognized the person looking at her. She shivered as a vague flush tinted her face.

But the guy sitting there seemed too much an adult to be the youngster whose yearbook her father had kept and whose senior picture she vaguely remembered. She was tempted to go over and ask his name when, without warning, Medic came up to her, grasped her face, kissed her on both cheeks, and herded her into the crowd.

Confirming Suzanne's suspicion that he'd already had a few too many, Medic started introducing her as Van Gogh's niece. Embarrassed on two fronts — the glorified association and the fact that Van Gogh had no niece — she asked him to please stop. Wrinkling his forehead, as if he had no idea why she would ask such a thing, he started introducing her as Monet's granddaughter. Only better on one front, Suzanne thought, because Monet did have a granddaughter. After a swarm of silly smiles and embarrassing attempts on her part to override the absurd introductions, she slipped away, only to find Lois Spangler, a former classmate, staring at her in astonishment.

Lois Spangler, the shapely and gorgeous president of Suzanne's senior class, had insisted on wearing a two-piece bathing suit for her graduation picture. She'd taken the idea from her favorite movie, the dated Bikini Beach, and had been given permission from the school's principal, her father's golf buddy.

Worse, from Suzanne's point of view, Lois's father had been the victorious defense attorney in the murder case against Talley, and in the community's prideful celebration of the verdict, Lois, at her mother's insistence, had taken on the challenge to try and turn everyone in her class against Suzanne, while Lois's mother had targeted the community at large. Both of them had been successful. Suzanne had been cast out from being shunned by her classmates. No one to hike with her in the forest or go with her to the beach or to the movies. Her parents had the doors to all social gatherings closed to them, even the neighborly Sunday afternoon whisky fests.

Dressed stylishly as she and her friends always had, Lois wore a tight-fitting, low-cut, green silk dress. Her charming face was somewhat hidden in a voluminous shaggy hairstyle. As she stared at Suzanne, the astonishment in her eyes was replaced with a reproachful smile. Her lips quivered as if her nerves were attempting to send Suzanne a message.

Bitterness swept through Suzanne. She hurried to the bar and refilled her glass. When she put the bottle down, she glanced over her shoulder to see Lois approaching. Suzanne's heart beat faster and faster the closer she got. She took a quick gulp of whisky and started to move away from the bar when Lois showed up beside her.

"My God, what in the world are you doing back in Meridien, Suzanne? It must be so difficult, given all that you went through."

"It's the fifth anniversary of my father's death," Suzanne replied in a flat tone. "Excuse me, but I have to go."

"I'm truly sorry, Suzanne. Your dad passed from severe arthritis, as I remember."

Suzanne's eyes narrowed. "No, my father passed from losing the trial. Enjoy the party," she said, hoping she'd delivered a stiletto.

"Please, Suzanne, just give me a minute. I want to tell you something… something I've never been able to come to…" Lois hesitated. Her eyelids fluttered. "Something I've never been able to come to grips with. It's haunted me since the day your mother left, and when your father died, it got worse, much worse."

Her voice carried a sense of urgency that seemed to show the weight of the concealment she'd been living with. Against every scornful emotion available to Suzanne, she replied only in frustration. "What is it, Lois?"

"It's what I did to turn our classmates against you. All the parents joined my mother and went against your family. That should have been more than enough, but oh, no, I took it upon myself to make sure our friends at school did the same. I was wrong to do that, so very wrong. The two of us were good friends. You tried to teach me how to paint but I had no talent whatsoever, yet you tolerated me and kept trying. Remember when your mother would host the bridge club and you and I would play dominoes while they drank and gossiped, not to mention the times we went to the beach together and took off our tops?" she paused. "I turned into a self-righteous bitch. I'm so, so sorry."

Stunned, Suzanne brought the glass to her lips, wondering if Lois was playing a joke of some kind. If she lashed out would Lois start laughing and wave to her friends to signal that the joke had worked? "Why are you telling me this now, Lois?"

"I thought that over time it would go away, but it only got worse and, until now, I never had the chance… never had the chance to ask you if there would be any possible way you could find it in your heart to forgive me?"

Her question both touched and assaulted Suzanne. The music faded as Lois's face grew smaller and smaller. The space between them sank into an embarrassing silence, and her answer became more difficult, the dilemma more troubled. Suzanne knew all too well the curse of the unforgiven. She and Lois were together in a familiar world.

"We were young, Lois, barely in our teens, almost too young to know right from wrong. I'm sure that if you had it to do over again, you wouldn't."

"But can you forgive me?"

Suzanne felt the silence tighten around her as she tried to separate her mixed emotions. At the unwavering fork in the road, she replied, "I already have."

Lois broke through her shock and started to throw her arms around Suzanne, but Suzanne stepped back.

"Now, I have a question for you, Lois."

"I am so grateful. Ask me anything you want. Please."

"Why did your father defend Talley?"

Lois's glazed eyes narrowed. "Suzanne, as I'm sure you know, the boy went after officer Talley with a hoe, broke his cheek-bone and wasn't going to stop. Talley didn't have any choice. He had to defend himself. Fans down at the end of the stands saw it happen." Lois hesitated. Her eyes strayed. She drew in her bottom lip as if to prevent her from going on, and then her mouth opened. "The question on everyone's mind was this, why did your father volunteer to prosecute an innocent man? He had to have known the truth, as I'm sure your mother did. I mean, how long after the trial did it take her to divorce him, a week?"

Suzanne's heart thumped like someone's who'd been pulled over for speeding. She had to admit that the truth about the trial lay on the edge of the local diatribes, including her mother's. That much she had to concede, but Lois's adamancy that her father had willingly chosen to prosecute an innocent man infuriated her. She emptied her glass in a swallow, told Lois that she needed to use the bathroom and walked away. She was tempted to leave the party but went into Medic's bedroom and sat down on the bed, wondering how her mother's version of the trial could possibly be true?

Elaine had shared her detailed account with wrath, swearing to Suzanne that the community had excluded their family because the lawyer she was married to was a "reverse bigot," the worst kind of hypocrite, one who prosecutes a worthy, innocent man for treachery, a crime that began the moment her father went before Judge Aiken and demanded that he be allowed to take on the case.

The day her mother left home she tried her best to drag Suzanne out the door with her, but Suzanne refused and called her a witch for treating her father so horribly. Her mother lashed out to tell her that Judas had invaded her soul. Before Elaine took off with suitcase in hand, she confided to Suzanne that she'd left her father emotionally weeks before she was ready to leave, when it became clear that her friends had excluded the family from the community and had no intention of taking them back.

Elaine became another person — far from the loving mother she'd always been — and left Suzanne and her father in more ways than just leaving home. When Suzanne happened to be in the presence of her father, her mother never joined the two of them, never even sat with them in the same room. She wouldn't join them for a meal and no longer went with Suzanne to Luna Lake to watch her perform her self-taught double backflip from the Lake's highest diving board.

Elaine even threatened her father, warning him that she'd better start sleeping somewhere else because if she stayed home, one morning he'd wake up dead.

Notwithstanding the threat, but maybe because of it, Suzanne had always questioned her mother's account of the trial, even though her father had refused to share his. She knew that he would have never prosecuted an innocent man, but whenever she asked him about the trial, he would cite his legal obligation to accept the defeat, keep the shame to himself, and move on as best he could. She looked up the term, legal obligation, but could find nothing that supported his position. Yet, she never pressured him because she felt that he'd endured enough. He'd remained forever faithful, even though it meant letting her mother blame him relentlessly. Suzanne had always wondered if he'd chosen to let the truth of the case die with his death?

When she emerged from the bedroom, her knees were weak. She had to sit down. Lois had rejoined her group of friends and they'd moved to the far side of the room. Suzanne squinted at the fellow on the hearth she'd noticed earlier. His beleaguered aura was accentuated by a strange scar on his neck that suggested that he'd most likely had experiences that most men hadn't, or ever would, and yet, he was strangely familiar. What would she say or do if he was Shane McCauley? Would she be able to summon up the strength to ask him about the trial? Would he even answer, and if he did, would he tell the truth? But then again, how would she know it was the truth any more than what her mother had said, or her former classmate?

What would it depend on? His tone, the look in his eyes, a brief pause when he tripped over a word while attempting to sort through the memory? If he immediately got up and left her sitting there, that would be the indisputable tell. But there would be no answers to sift through if she didn't try and perhaps none if she did. How many times had she heard her father tread on the old baseball analogy, if you don't swing at the third strike, there's no chance of hitting the ball.

She went for a fresh glass of whisky hoping, it would calm her nerves.

Chapter Five

As she approached Shane in her high heels, he couldn't believe that she was the same windblown person he'd seen racing into the room minutes ago. Then, she'd been Bonnie Parker, Clyde's gun moll, raw and disheveled, but now there was something vastly different about her. Even her shoulder-covering, low-cut dress appeared to blend into a vague and incongruous deflection. At first he thought the booze was acting up but realized that it had to do with something apart from the whisky and her restored beauty, something hidden and inexplicable, someone emerging from another time. The black velvet clung to her hips as she eased through the crush of people toward him.

She looked briefly into his eyes and quickly beyond, as if wondering who would be the first to say something. She nervously licked her lips with the tip of her tongue.

"Excuse me, I'm so sorry for bothering you," she said, trying to seem light-hearted, "but would you mind if I ask you a question?"

"Ask away."

She hesitated. "This is going to sound really stupid, but by any chance… by any remote chance, would you happen to be Shane McCauley?"

"I would, and you are?"

She let her reply out slowly. "I'm Susanne de Ville, George de Ville's daughter. Back in the day, people knew me as Jenny."

Shane drew back in astonishment. "Medic mentioned that you were coming but I never…

"May I join you for a minute?"

Shane shifted to the side to make room. "Please, have a seat."

She put her drink on the hearth, sat down next to him and slipped off her heels. Her head swung lazily to the side and she tossed her hair, as though trying to seem relaxed. Her dried and brushed hair was now wavy and embedded with blonde rivulets that flowed from her cheeks to her shoulders. Shane could smell the freshness of winter in her hair and watched as she leaned back on her hands and stretched out her legs.

"How in the world did you know it was me?" he asked. "I don't believe we ever met. We were what, three, four years apart in school?"

"More than that, in a way," she replied. "That's when the freshmen classrooms were being built at Jefferson and the incoming class, mine, had to spend an extra year in junior high."

"Yes, I remember."

Wondering what to say next, Suzanne recalled her father's advice about how to proceed when a case seemed overwhelming — take a deep breath, ideally without anyone noticing, and from there, proceed one step at a time.

She took the deep breath, hoping that it bypassed Shane. "My father loved baseball," she said. "He played in college until he graduated and went to law school. He went to a lot of your ballgames, but he was in court that horrible day, the day Jesse — I could never remember his last name — was killed. When he prosecuted Talley and knew that you'd be called on to testify, he stayed away from the ballpark, worried that he'd distract you if he showed up. But he watched from his car and timed your pitches with a stopwatch."

Shane smiled. "Always an inspiration, your dad. Before it all happened, he'd come early so that he could watch the warmups. During the games he would sit at different places in the stands, always refusing Coach Wilson's invitation to sit with us in the dugout. Once, he told me that he preferred to be among the crowd so he could cheer when the fans cheered, jump to his feet when they jumped to theirs, and rely on the opinion of others about a close call on a particular play. That always surprised me. I've thought about him a lot. Is he still practicing?"

Her eyes widened. "You didn't know? He passed away almost five years ago, from complications with severe rheumatoid arthritis, which started after the trial. He was so ashamed of losing. He never got over it and I've always thought that it caused his arthritis. He refused to see a doctor because he said that the pain was his to endure. He believed that he deserved it because he lost. It got even worse when my mother left us."

"I had no idea," Shane said, jarred. "I'm so sorry. I don't think I've ever met anyone so kind and with so much integrity as your dad."

An abrupt stillness blindsided Suzanne as her father's demand that she not call him 'Dad' resurfaced. "Shane, would you mind if we went over by the window, behind the dinner table? It's probably a little quieter. There's something I'd like to ask you."

They slipped away from the crowd and made their way into the small dining area at the far end of the living room window. The moonlight offered a broad, shadowed view of the valley below. Medic never went to the window when winter's gray clouds settled into the gorge because he said it reminded him of the smoke that rose from the chimneys at Auschwitz and carried the ghostly images of the children he'd helped free.

Whenever he shared the thought with his class, his eyes would glaze over as he visualized the bodies of the children, their skeletons visible under their skin as though their bones were about to poke through. He always looked for the children first. He was drawn to their bewilderment and dubious faces as they wondered who this person wearing an unfamiliar uniform and speaking a strange language could be, and what was he about to do to them? Seldom, though it did happen, an emaciated youngster would smile at him and he would tenderly touch the child's cheeks, afraid of hugging its fragile body.

Suzanne stood facing the window, searching the shadows in the valley. The chicken shanty was a dark silhouette. She turned away from the window struggling to look Shane in the eyes. She told herself to keep her mouth shut, that she wasn't entitled to drag him back into the past, a torture she put herself through regularly, but she couldn't help herself.

"Shane, you're probably going to leave and go straight back to the party, so let me apologize ahead of time for my question. After all, I barely know you."

"No, no, it's fine."

She delayed the question by taking a sip of bourbon, which before she said anything became several sips. When the burn faded from her throat, she raised a hand as if to apologize. "If you don't want to talk about it, I certainly understand, but except for my mother's version, I've never really known anything about the trial. My father seldom said a word, which he justified by telling me that he had a legal obligation not to talk about it, not with anyone, not even his family. I had no idea what he was talking about and what my mother had to say about the trial confused me even more. I've never known where the truth lay."

"Suzanne, you do know that your mother wasn't at the trial? Judge Aiken didn't allow anyone into the courtroom but the jurors and those testifying. Jesse's parents weren't even let in. Regardless of your father saying that he couldn't talk about it with anyone, I'm sure he must have shared what took place with your mother. And I'm sure he told her the truth."

Suzanne felt a hint of embarrassment. "Maybe that's why she left us."

"Because of the truth?"

"No, because of the lies."

"What lies?"

"The lies she said he made up in order to convict Talley."

"The lies? What did she say?" Shane asked, stunned.

Suzanne wondered if this was what it felt like to be called to the witness stand. She went back to the window, only moved closer to the glass this time. Her eyes reflected a deep pool of restlessness, an ocean of reluctance. Her breath clouded the glass. "Bear with me, please," she said.

After a long silence, she stepped away from the window. Her eyes searched Shane's and she cleared her throat. "Here's what my mother told me the day she left us. She was at the front door, holding her suitcase, waiting for the taxi to show up to take her to the train station. She blurted out that my father had sacrificed their marriage to prosecute a cop for beating a Black boy to death for no reason other than his color. It was a lie, she said, because Talley was acting in self-defense."

"In self-defense?" Shane's voice was threaded with sarcasm.

"She said that when Talley ordered Jesse to leave the ballpark, Jesse picked up a hoe and swung it at him. Talley pulled out his gun and told him to back off, but Jesse swung the hoe again and connected. Tally started hemorrhaging and blood spurted out of his ear. That's when he smacked Jesse in the head with his gun, slamming him again and again until he fell into a pool of his own blood. Talley cuffed him and being the good person he was, as my mother described him, he dragged Jesse over to his car, dumped him into the trunk and took him to the hospital where Jesse died. Mother said Talley was a folk hero."

"Stop right there, Suzanne. Your mother's hand-me-down version of what took place is as far from the truth as Talley will be from heaven when his day comes."

Suzanne let her breath out slowly. "Even so, my father drew up the divorce papers in her favor, giving her almost all the money he'd saved. He offered her the house but she refused. Later, when she left and he became ill, he willed it to me. After he passed away, I tried to sell it, but no one in Meridien would buy it because it was tainted by association — you know about that absurd belief, I'm sure. Even if it was torn down, the property would never be built on. She wouldn't even take the Pontiac he gave her in hopes that she'd stay.

"He tried to kiss her goodbye when she was headed to the door but she shoved him away. I was standing there, watching them. I didn't know what to think because I didn't know what to believe. She wanted to give me a farewell kiss but I turned away. She looked at me with alarm in her eyes and said, 'Judas has invaded your soul,' and ran out the door. We never heard from her again. Since then I've always felt that the truth was trapped somewhere between her version and my father's silence."

Shane was tempted to say how fortunate Suzanne was that her mother had left, but he held back.

Suzanne felt that what she was about to ask was unbearably selfish. Her almond eyes slid across Shane's face and over his shoulder. Her heart began to race, but her conscience stayed on track. "Shane, would it just be too much to tell me what happened in court that day? Was my father lying by keeping quiet?"

Chapter Six

Her tone of voice and her confusion struck Shane as an unmistakable plea for help. It seemed to alter time, instantly bringing the past forward and joining it to the moment at hand. Her eyes glistened with anxiousness. At long last, someone in Meridien wanted to know the truth. The now distant music sent vibrations though his chest.

He'd been through the trial a thousand times, even in Vietnam during those strange moments of seeing his way home across the imaginary bridges, even then the day in court frequently returned as if he'd recorded it. He remembered every question, every answer, every nuance, and most of all the incredible look of shock on her father's face as he stood staring at the judge in total disbelief when the verdict was rendered.

As he headed down memory's aisle to sit next to her father, he experienced the same sense of loneliness and fear as when he entered the courtroom that day and realized how empty it was. No one was there but the Judge, his clerk and jurors, Suzanne's father, Talley, Spangler and Carlisle, the Black mortician at Sill's. Jesse's parents weren't allowed to attend. The prohibitive decision about who could and who couldn't attend had been made by Judge Aiken, a proud, self-declared 'godly' racist. He'd been the circuit court Judge for over thirty years during which he'd made every possible effort to prevent the spread of desegregation in the schools, the churches, the cemeteries, the movie theaters, the rest rooms and even the drinking fountain at Ballou Park where once Jesse was caught drinking water and jerked out of the Park.

As her father's first witness, he called Carlisle to the stand. With years of experience as a mortician, Carlisle testified that when Talley showed up at Sill's with Jesse's body, in addition to Jesse's broken jaw, there were multiple bruises on his face and neck and that his chest was a mix of purple and amber. Carlisle conceded that it was hard to see the bruises because they started under the skin and were slow to make their way through, but that he'd been able to find them with his magnifying glass. He'd seen no bruises or cuts or scars on Talley's jaws or cheekbones.

Mr. Spangler objected and asked the judge to dismiss Carlisle's testimony for it was well-known that bruises could not be seen on a Black person's flesh. As far as Talley's cheekbones were concerned, Spangler forcefully stated that Carlisle was lying, that Talley, with the tremendous respect he had for Black people, had mustered all the strength left within him to overcome his injuries and take Jesse to the morgue.

Spangler reminded the jurors that the court had written records of the sworn testimony of two lone fans sitting in the right field bleachers. They'd sworn that they'd seen Jesse smack Talley in the face with a hoe and that Talley had rallied with the only hope he had left, the stock of his gun.

Carlisle started to refute Spangler, but Aiken interrupted to agree with the attorney and ordered Carlisle to step down, leave the courtroom, and never think about becoming a doctor.

Suzanne's father protested vehemently but Aiken overruled him with a banging of his hammer. Aiken went on to say that the defense attorney had unquestionably refuted the mortician's testimony about Jesse's alleged bruises with the science of common sense. Then, in his deep Rhett Butler brogue, Aiken asked her father if he had any other witnesses. He answered that he did and called Shane to the witness stand.

At that point in the memory, the trial returned more sharply than ever with the dialogue crossing Shane's eyes like a moving script.

"Suzanne, I couldn't keep it inside. Before your father could ask me anything, I told the court straightaway that Carlisle had told the truth and that anyone saying otherwise was lying. Aiken shook a finger at me and warned me that another comment like that could land me in juvenile jail. Your father apologized on my behalf and approached me. I knew what was coming."

"Shane McCauley, were you on the pitcher's mound the day Jesse Willip was beaten to death by officer Talley?"

"Yes, sir, I was."

"Did you see the officer strike Jesse Willip with the stock of his gun?"

"No, sir, but I heard a scream and had reason to think that it might be Jesse, so I took off for the fence. When I got there, he was crumbled up in a pool of his own blood. Talley grabbed him, dragged him to his car, threw him into the trunk and took off. I was dumbfounded. I couldn't move. I stood there like a coward, staring at Jesse's blood."

"Did you see a hoe or any evidence to suggest that there was one, either in Talley's possession or anywhere on the ground where, in his rush to flee the scene of his crime, perhaps he'd left it?"

"No, sir. Why would anyone bring a goddamn hoe to a baseball game?"

Aiken stiffened and yelled at me. "Watch your language, young man! This is a public hearing, but God's in the jury booth."

"Not giving a damn what might happen to me, I asked him why, if it was a public hearing, weren't Jesse's parents allowed in the courtroom. Aiken raised his gavel only to have it freeze in the air. The jurors stared at one another. The room was quiet for so long, I thought maybe we were on the edge of an explosion. Your father apologized on my behalf and winked me, suggesting that maybe the jurors had been inflicted with a pinch of doubt. Aiken let the gavel down slowly and told your father to continue but that he was going down a path that was about to end.

Your father responded right away. "Your Honor, please let me remind the jury that in Mr. Talley's defense, the hoe itself hasn't been presented as evidence, and it is necessary to show proof beyond a reasonable doubt that there was a hoe."

Spangler sprang to his feet. "Your Honor, the hoe was undoubtedly used in an effort to harm, if not murder, Officer Talley. Two witnesses have testified to that. One of my staffers did his best to find the weapon the next morning and he was told that it had been found and trashed. May I remind the court that there doesn't have to be any physical evidence to show proof. The proof is in the honesty of the witnesses who saw the altercation."

"You are correct, Mr. Spangler, Aiken said. "Master McCauley you are hereby excused from the witness stand."

"Suzanne, chills ran through my body. I was about to yell at Aiken, call him a fucking monster when your father shouted, 'Your Honor! That is lunacy!'"

Aiken's mouth dropped open. "Mr. de Ville, this trial is over, and another word from you, so too will be your career. Both you and your mendacious young counterpart remain on your feet. Will the defendant and his attorney please rise. Based on the evidence at hand, I find the defendant, Officer Barnes Talley, innocent of the charges brought against him."

Talley waved his hand. "Your honor, there's something I'd like to say…"

"Officer, you needn't say another word," Aiken interrupted. "The lack of evidence before this court is plentiful." He turned to the jury. "Mr. Foreperson, if I could have your agreement, I would like to declare this trial over."

"You have my full agreement, your Honor."

"The jurors started to leave and your father kept arguing, pointing out that two dozen Black men had volunteered to serve on the jury and none were chosen, and yet white spectators, who supposedly had been at the game, were heard from in solitude and granted immunity for supporting the defense."

"Mr. de Ville, this trial is over!" Aiken declared.

"Your father offered a rebuttal that stunned everyone, including the jurors who froze in their tracks when he told them that Jesse's grandfather had served as a pilot in World War II. They'd let him into the service as an air cadet in the Army's only Black squadron, The Tuskegee Airmen. He'd help bomb the hell out of Germany but was shot down and never awarded the Gold Medal because those of color were only considered for the honor years later.

"Aiken told your dad that if he continued on, he'd recommend that the State Bar Association consider his disbarment. And that's how it ended," Shane said, remembering the doors thudding shut as he and Suzanne's father walked out of the courtroom.

Chapter Seven

Suzanne's ears shut down but her mind created its own thunder. She found herself crawling out of the abandoned gap of doubt between her father and mother. She looked at the shadow of the chicken coop and beyond into the Valley. Shane's reflection returned to the window and joined hers.

"Shane, you said that my father didn't do anything wrong."

"Trust me, Suzanne. It wasn't that he just didn't do anything wrong. He did everything right. He told no lies whatsoever, not one. Suzanne, your father was admonished for telling the truth."

She heard the exasperation, honesty and strength in Shane's voice. Her father had done everything right? Everything? A word that ricocheted off distant stars to return with the impact of a lightning bolt. A word too big, far too big, to let anyone wrap its meaning around anything, until now. Suzanne tilted her head to the side as if she were listening to an accompanying spirit. Everything.

A surprising sense of calm crept over her. The feeling reminded her of being on the veranda waiting for the moon to emerge from the clouds. It happened every time she painted or tried to sculpt, when she knew her eyes were seeing something she couldn't see but was about to come to the canvas, first from wherever and then from her heart and at last from her fingers.

She flinched as Medic suddenly leaned between them.

"With tears of relief in both your eyes, I would have trouble telling the recipient from the sender," he said.

Suzanne glanced at Shane and smiled.

"Your searching eyes give me license to ask a question," Medic said. "In the story of Heloise and Abelard, do either of you recall, when, in the first letters between them, Abelard confessed that he'd written a detailed and honest letter to an unknown monk, revealing in depth all he'd done wrong by having an affair with Heloise?"

As if competing in class, Suzanne and Shane immediately raised their hands. “The letter of consolation!” they exclaimed, as though they’d been waiting forever to tell someone.

“Yes!” Medic asserted. “Imagine that, two former students who actually learned something from me! Do either of you remember what the letter was about?”

Suzanne took the lead. “It was a letter that described someone’s misfortunes so vividly that the recipient of the letter would… would…”

“You’re on the right track, young lady. So that the recipient would…?”

“…would feel better about his or her own misfortunes!” she blurted out.

“Perfect!” Medic said, “The prize is waiting at the bar.”

Suzanne wondered if Shane’s exposure to the trial was his consolation letter to her. At long last, with doubt now ensnared by the trap of belief, she was convinced that her father was innocent of the allegation that he’d knowingly prosecuted a guiltless man. He’d done everything right. He’d pursued the truth, and yet, those who’d defeated him hadn’t

Shane looked down at the chicken coop. “Wait a minute. Medic, just curious, where are the chickens?”

“I freed them.”

Chapter Eight

Suzanne couldn't remember when she'd ever felt such relief. Medic turned the music down to the level of the guests' voices, which had ebbed into a slur. Suzanne thanked Shane with tears before accompanying him to the bar where they gazed at one another and clinked glasses.

Shane, lightheaded from his trip in time, was not only relieved but grateful to have shared his memory of the trial.

The revelation not only allowed but heartened each of them to move from the courthouse through the years between then and now. Shane asked Suzanne where she went to college and why she'd come home. She told him about her time at the artistic Pratt Institute in Brooklyn, and that she'd dropped out because she needed rest from the endless boredom of the required core courses that had no relationship to art, and afterwards, when she'd left, about her days at the Brooklyn Museum, where she'd tried to get one of her paintings hung on its walls to overcome the guilt of leaving school, but to no avail, having been told by the curator that her paintings were too abstract, too intangible and lacked clarity of purpose. "They went far beyond the wont of our attendees," the woman said.

Suzanne took her talent to the West Side of Manhattan, the only part of the City she could afford, and soon found herself selling daily sketches of passers-by for a dollar a piece, barely enough to cover her meals and her nights at the notorious Chelsea Hotel. She said that she loved the creativity of the hotel's drunken dope-heads and was sad to leave. "It was bizarre," she said, "but, in a way, I loved it."

Shane harkened back to what Medic had said about artistic people, that they were often considered to be round-the-bend, but in many cases it was the source of their creativity. Medic had taught that many talented people such as Dali, Coleridge, and Salinger simply walk away sober, drunk, hooked or clean, to the edge of their own cliffs where they see and feel what no others can. Sometimes they go too far and their gift is lost in a life taken early, but even then, perhaps especially then, Medic believed that we can learn from them.

"Then, why did you leave Brooklyn?" Shane asked.

Suzanne sighed. Shane had been upfront with her, so she felt obliged to answer as honestly as she could, which was just a thin layer above the truth. "It's the fifth anniversary of my father's death. I came back to show my love and make amends."

"Amends?"

She hesitated. "On the one hand, for loving him so much and on the other, for causing him so much pain."

"I don't understand."

"Neither do I," she said, dipping her head and glancing at the fissure under Shane's chin. She touched it gently with a finger and he flinched. "You were injured in combat?"

"Not exactly. The story's a little weird. Actually more than a little."

"I love weird."

Shane smiled and took a long sip. "The night before we were scheduled to leave Vietnam, we went to this bar in Saigon for more than a few drinks. At one point there was a loud ruckus and before I could tell what was going on, this stripper sliced me with a bottle opener. She'd mistaken me for somebody who owed her money. They rushed me to the Evacuation Hospital, where they had to an emergency tracheotomy. When they brought me out of out of the anesthesia, I thought I'd died because I couldn't speak, couldn't make a sound, and across the operating room through what appeared to be this swirling hailstorm, I thought I saw a man in a bee suit playing golf on the surface of the moon. I didn't realize it was TV footage of Neil Armstrong walking on the goddamn thing."

"What did you do?"

"I tried to scream, of course."

Suzanne couldn't help herself. She laughed so hard that it sucked Shane in, wondering why the memory had never seemed funny before. It had always seemed so tragically ironic, but her laughter let him see it for what it was, ridiculous.

When she asked why he'd returned to Meridien, he, too, had to search for an answer that would seem credible. He couldn't let himself be sidetracked by her allure, for his time in Meridien was going to be short and maybe his stay on earth as well.

"I've been away so long and like you, Suzanne, I wanted to come back to visit the house I grew up in, as well as my mother's grave. She died of cancer in the summer of my sophomore year when I was sixteen. And if I can summon the courage, I'm going to pay a long overdue visit to the ballfield. I'd like to visit your father's grave as well. Was he buried in Highland Cemetery?"

Again, Suzanne searched for a credible lie. "He was cremated at a mortuary in Reidsville."

"Why Reidsville?"

One lie always seemed to lead to another. She had to think it through. "Aiken refused to let Sill's cremate him, because Carlisle had worked there. He told the owner that he'd shut him down if he dared."

"Jesus Christ," Shane sighed.

"My father wanted his ashes scattered in the ocean, but I couldn't bring myself to reach into the urn. So I did what I hope was the next best thing. I sealed the urn and buried it at sea, and there he rests." She wavered. "Shane, I don't know how to thank you for tonight."

"Nor I, you, Heloise."

She smiled. "And both of us, for letting one another have an opportunity at consolation. Oh, Shane would you be so kind as to do me one more undeserved favor?"

"Maybe."

"Would you walk me out to my motorcycle? I might need some help getting it up the driveway through the cars."

"Your motorcycle?"

"It was my father's. He left it to me, along with the house."

"Are you sure you want to ride a motorcycle? We've both had a little too much. Let me give you a ride home."

"No, no. I'm fine, or fine enough."

On the way out, Suzanne noticed that Lois and her flock were sitting on the floor by the window. The group's laughter was garbled. Suzanne brushed past them to thank Medic, not only for having the party but for all he'd taught them over the years. She smiled when he repeated how proud he was of her talent and her going to Pratt and of Shane for serving the country.

Just before parting, he told Shane that if he'd ever had a son, he could only have wished that the boy would have been as upright and brave as Shane. Shane was weak in the knees when they shook hands goodbye.

Suzanne put on her leather jacket and retrieved the hairdryer. Shane held her elbow as they left the kitchen for the driveway. He'd forgotten to phone Mrs. Abernathy but it was too late to call now. He'd apologize for disrupting her life tomorrow.

The motorcycle was a shadow between the remaining cars. Suzanne put the dryer and her heels into the saddlebag and slipped on the sandals.

She wasn't sure what happened next, nor was Shane. When she turned around to say goodnight, she found his lips barely a breath from hers. The only thing between them was the warm, bronze aroma of bourbon. They stood wading in the phantom pool of a kiss, staring at one another like a couple of anesthetized patients. She couldn't seal the kiss, though every impulse told her that she wanted to. She wondered if her reluctance was irony, love's favorite playing card, or was it because of her fear that if she gave in, it would be yet another betrayal of her father. To betray him again, after what she'd done, would put her a step ahead of Judas, the unforgiven apostle who seemed to accompany her everywhere.

She knew what not to do in order to detour around the moment, but she did it anyway. She asked Shane if he would come visit her tomorrow, in the late afternoon but before sunset. She kept the reason for the time of day to herself.

Shane looked past her, avoiding her eyes. "I'll try," he replied, wanting to leave some space for what couldn't be foretold. Suppose circumstance broke in his favor and late in the day he was on the run, or in jail or maybe dead? Sooner or later, she'd find out what he'd done, and most likely be thrilled, maybe to the point of implicating herself as his accomplice.

"By the way, do you know how to get to my house?" Suzanne asked.

"I do, thanks to your father."

"My father?"

"Yes, your father." And he told her why.

Her father had given him a ride home the day the verdict was rendered. He'd slowed the car to a crawl as they passed her house. "That's where we live," he said. Clinging to the steering wheel, he shook his head in sorrow and apologized to Shane for losing the case. He swore that eventually justice would be done, that Talley would pay and a celebration would be held.

Shane looked at Suzanne's quivering lips. "With any luck, I'll see you tomorrow," he said.

Her lips stilled and her eyes widened. She was both excited and afraid.

Chapter Nine

Shane barely slept. After a late breakfast hamburger at the Come and Go, he drove off to visit his old house, unnerved and having second thoughts about stopping at Suzanne's later in the day. But he couldn't shake the memory of the two of them standing in Medic's driveway, staring at one another, as if trapped in a chilling movie frozen in mid-frame, suspending them aghast and alone in an inexplicable world that held them together and at the same time kept them apart. He'd never been caught in such a moment and wondered if Suzanne had.

As he drove to the house, the streets and stores didn't seem that familiar and made him wonder if his home had been demolished. Even so, the lot was probably still vacant, considering one of Meridien's many mythological suspicions that were so widespread and believed, even to the point of being upheld in court by Aiken. Suzanne had alluded to it at Medic's when she mentioned the "suspected evil" that the community felt resided in her house. It went this way — if a tragedy takes place inside a home or if an egregious sin is committed by those who live there and the home is left vacant, the spirit of Death takes up residence, rent-free, and pleads for neighbors and passersby to stop by and pay a visit so that the spirit can earmark them for persecution.

The myth was rumored to have found credence in Oak Ridge, a home just outside Meridien, where in the 1800's its owner, a Confederate spy, was trapped by the Yanks and shot to death in the living room, immediately installing a renegade of frightening spirits determined to lay claim to the property. When the War ended, the house was mysteriously burned to the ground. According to legend, the spirits settled into the ashes, shaping the debris into grave-like mounds rumored to house the lives of the spy's children and grandchildren, allowing the spirits to remain forever in an unrestored playground for the dead.

Shane ended his recollection of the myth with a sigh when he found himself passing an all-too-familiar, small brick building across the street from Hester's Coal Yard where, in his early teens, a young girl in a stroller had been yanked away from her parents by the vicious winds of hurricane Enola. But, by the grace of God, in the beliefs of the town, she was delivered safely in her stroller onto a path between two piles of charcoal. Her mortified parents found her smiling and happily licking the soot off her fingers.

The small, box-shaped brick building on the other side of the street, The Cure-All Pharmacy, had been his father's drug store. Since its beginning the store had fed the family with dollar bills that his dad took daily from the cash-register. The funds also paid for the never-ending flow of chemicals used in his frantic research to produce a cure for Shane's mother's cancer. The pharmacy had been shuttered, not by death, but by his father's desertion and was never reopened, given the damage Enola brought to this part of town.

A fence of iron bars crisscrossed the front window of the store, making it look like a jail, but they couldn't keep Shane's memory from entering. His mind's eye pictured the three aisles and what they'd held — bottles of Bayer Aspirin and six-packs of Coca-Colas, boxed donuts and cans of Sterno, used mainly by the moonshiners to prepare their mash. The cathedral-shaped cash register on the check-out counter hid the cashier from the customer and cast a huge shadow over the bins of cash when the register was opened. Behind the counter in the mixing room above the cabinet drawers where the yellow-jacket capsules were stored, had been the baffling message his father had inked on the wall. "Death, you will die!"

When Shane reached the sawmill he slowed. The roof of the mill had caved in, the mountains of sawdust were gone. The long dust blowers that had fed the mountains hung swaying in mid-air by their guide wires. When Shane heard them creaking, his memory took flight and he pulled over.

He envisioned the looming mountain of sawdust that he and Jesse struggled to climb the day they plodded up the mound with the flattened pieces of cardboard they'd snitched from the pharmacy's trash bin. On top, while getting covered by sawdust from the metal blowpipe, they took a minute to turn away from the wind and catch their breath. When recovered, they laid chest-down on the cardboard and were about to take off when an owl hooted from inside the mill. The sound carried through the blowpipe like a foghorn. They glanced at one another, slid onto their piece of cardboard and took off as if someone had blown a starting whistle. They raced down the hill side by side until they hit a dip in the sawdust and banged into one another. Toppled off their sleds, they bounced to the bottom of the hill when the hoot came again.

"Let's hoot it back," Jesse said. Together they responded with a loud overwrought version of a hoot, prompting the owl to do the same. They and the owl traded hoots until the competition became a hilarious, howling refrain so hearty that they didn't head downhill until they were rasping. It was over. The owl had won.

Shane's laugh faded when he turned onto Veteran Street. It was as though the line of identical clapboard houses had been shifted around and reset in a strange and unfamiliar location. The once barren hills behind the houses had become a forest of pines and bare evergreens. The postwar houses, built for veterans, were smaller than he remembered. Like homes for elves, they possessed pinnacle roofs that covered the attics whose ceilings were punctured with sharp nails that bound the shingles to the wood. The houses had six small rooms and a tub the size of a sarcophagus. Set close to the street, most of the homes possessed cracked cement porches hemmed in with latticework now covered with thick, leafless vines curling snakelike up the facades onto the rooftops.

Relieved that his house was still standing, Shane pulled over and sat staring at the front door. While he was growing up, his mother, Elena, opened the door daily to let in the fresh air before going to her knees in prayer. When her condition got worse, Shane would help her to the door and open it, then kneel beside her and try to understand what she was saying to God. It took several tries but the pieces came together. She pled again and again, reminding The Almighty that she was too young to die and asking Him to please consider granting her extra time to raise her son. It appeared that God passed the responsibility for keeping her alive to Shane's father who relentlessly attempted to obey the command.

Shane got out of the car and went around to the backyard, an area besieged with good intention, where all hell had broken loose during his father's determined effort to save Elena's life.

She'd developed intestinal cancer that had spread throughout her body before it was diagnosed. Devastated at the discovery, Kenneth, Shane's father, devoted himself to easing her pain and trying to find a cure for the disease. He sat by her side while she lay in bed and read to her. He fed her, took her temperature incessantly and prayed with her before she went to sleep. He kissed her forehead and blew her a kiss every time he left the bedroom, always leaving the door open in case she called out for him.

He researched everything he could find about abolishing her disease. He ordered studies from the medical school at the University of Virginia, where he'd received his degree in pharmacy, from Duke University and Wake Forest. He concluded that the worshipped leader of psychedelic drugs, Timothy Leary, had the most to offer with lysergic acid, better known as LSD. It made perfectly good sense. After all, Leary had invented the drug for those who wanted to live in a pain-free world adrift in its hallucinations.

Kenneth had heard what many said was only a rumor — though he'd chosen to believe in full — that Bryon Wilson, creator of his favorite rock group, The Beach Boys, had found tremendous creativity and insight by moving into the psychedelic world. It allowed Wilson to hear and understand in music what he'd never been able to. Shane's dad took it as a sign that he was on the right track and played the group's music incessantly as he worked to find a cure.

He turned the little kitchen in the rear corner of the house it into a laboratory filled with vials, needles, test tubes, Bunsen burners, two microscopes, towels, rubber gloves, stands, racks, and notebooks.

Sampling each of his mixtures, he assembled a pill with a blend of crushed LSD powder and methamphetamines. He tried the pill on Elena, and it worked, but only for an hour or so. After a few days, the cancer whittled the pill's effectiveness down to a few minutes.

As her condition worsened, he tried his utmost to add various drugs to strengthen the concoction, not only to stifle her pain but in hopes of eliminating the cancer altogether. He tested them on himself. By the time Elena passed away, he was hooked on the drugs; his mind invaded by poetic calls from the spirits and flowing cartouches that offered him temporary distraction from her death.

She was placed into a shiny, mahogany casket and buried in Highland Cemetery. Kenneth had a tombstone made, spelling out her full name, Elizabeth Elena McCauley, but there was no date of death because he refused to accept the fact that her death was permanent. He filled his notebooks with equations, each ending with equal signs that equated the numbers with the word resurrection.

One day, afloat on drugs, he told Shane that given the progress he was making in the lab, without question she would reappear.

Kenneth was as kind to Shane as he had been to Elena. He always brought him dinner and gave him money for lunch and the movies, encouraging him to see double features on Saturdays and Sundays. He hired Jesse, who worked as his delivery boy at the pharmacy, and paid him double to bring Shane home every day after practice and stay with him while he went to pray over Elena's grave.

Kenneth's life spiraled from admirable insanity into madness. He furiously sampled the pills and became unable to walk a straight line. Jesse had to drive him to the cemetery, sometimes twice a day while Shane was in school.

His father was on an irreversible path to destruction. It sprang into the open late one summer day when he and Jesse were out back playing catch. Suddenly, Kenneth stumbled out of the kitchen, forgetting that he'd left his most recent concoction baking in the oven. He looked at the boys, miffed, as though he wasn't sure what they were doing there. He started to return to the kitchen, but when he reached the stoop, the potion exploded.

The screen and back doors were blown off their hinges and he was knocked to the ground. Before Jesse and Shane could reach him, he scrambled to his feet and ran off into the sunset, shouting that he'd found the cure for death and that Elena was on the way home.

The neighbors heard the frenetic shouting and called the police who found him on the porch of a house under construction in the next block. Yelling in exhilaration, with his arms outstretched to replicate the Crucifixion, he told the cops about his finding and they took him away in handcuffs. The following morning, under a doctor's orders, he was sent to Western State Hospital in Stanton where shock treatment, neutering and lobotomy were the options of the day for those labeled as insane.

When it was determined that shock treatment provided no help, he was scheduled to be neutered. But Milena, a kind migrant nurse from Bulgaria, with a name that blended harmoniously with Elena's, had nursed him through the shock treatments and was by his side every day. Because of her name Kenneth could not separate her from Elena. Time and time again he blessed her for returning and said he was in love with her and would be forever. Drawn to his sweetness, the moment she found out that he'd been assigned to undergo the horrifying procedure, she dressed him in a doctor's white garb and snuck him out of the hospital.

A month later he made a long-distance call to Shane to let him know that he'd married Milena and to explain why they were leaving the country with no intention of returning. The authorities would not let him back and would jail him if he tried to return. In a choking voice, he confessed that abandoning Shane was a sin to the umpteenth power but that he had no choice and hoped that his son would forgive him.

Two weeks later a letter arrived from Kenneth. "Your mother sent me a message to tell me that she owed it to God to stay with Him and not come home, but that she loved us. I loved your mom more than I can say and in time I hope to love Milena as much, for she carries your mother's name. They even look alike. There are times when I wonder if Milena is your mother's reincarnation."

Using the address on Kenneth's envelope, Shane send a letter to his father but never heard from him again. He always carried the letter that he did receive with him and read it countless times, until it was lost in the mud in Vietnam. It raised his spirits to know that his dad loved the woman named Milena so much. It allowed him to feel that his father's new wife was Shane's mother at heart.

A year later, having been granted orphan and emancipated minor status by the Lower Court, Shane was allowed to live in the house. Soon after, he received a letter from Milena, saying that his dad had passed away from drug use.

When the memory weakened, Shane found himself sitting on the back stoop by the kitchen, staring at the remains of the yard where he and Jesse had been playing catch the day the potion exploded. Surprised that a ceiling of grey clouds had settled overhead, he wondered how long he'd been sitting there. He had to move on, so with a racing heart, he drove away without looking back.

When he entered Highland Cemetery, a million fireflies were flickering in strands of gold and silver. Fireflies normally came out in the summer and why they arrived in Highland Cemetery every year as Thanksgiving was approaching no one knew. Shane's father once told him that the flies gathered there to help lift the spirits of all who entered in the weight of winter.

By the time he found his way around the endlessly curved road that led to his mother's grave, fog was crawling over the ground and the fireflies were creating a shallow aurora of twinkling lights. His mother's grave wasn't far from the curb. He pulled over and opened the door. The faint smell of flowers in a nearby vase reminded him of the roses his dad had often brought to the grave.

Shane remembered the funeral, leaning over the edge of the casket to kiss his mom's forehead, how cold she'd seemed, how thin her neck and fingers were and how pale the green color of her favorite dress was. She'd worn it every Wednesday night when she invited the neighbors to watch the weekly fights on television and get loaded on Pabst Blue Ribbon, the town-folks' favorite brew. He remembered her smile when she tucked him into bed every night and whispered the child's prayer, "Now I lay me down to sleep..." He would repeat the prayer until he reached the sentence that she repeated to herself the day she passed away, "If I should die before I wake, I pray the Lord my soul to take."

Backing away from the grave, he blew her kisses, as his father always had, and forced a smile. "I'll see you soon, momma," he said

Shane sat in the Rambler scanning the graveyard. The tombstones were small, blurry obelisks. Several paths angled through the sites to a small chapel on the far edge of the cemetery. It reminded him of a crypt. There was a bell on top of the chapel that the family members of those who'd just passed away were entitled to ring after the burial. His father was given the opportunity but refused, telling Shane that he'd only ring the bell when Elena returned.

Shane glanced at his watch. If he was going to Suzanne's, he'd better move on. Two of the things on his to-do list were done, so he told himself that he had a little free time. He wiped his eyes and started the car. At last, the years since Jesse's death had shrunk into moments, with only a split-second left before his to-do list would be fulfilled.

Chapter Ten

Throughout the day, Suzanne struggled with the moment in the driveway. In an effort to stay with the memory while at the same time preventing it from taking over, she went to work on a painting that spanned the living room wall. As the day passed, she all but finished. Another high-gloss coating was needed but she had to wait for the paint to dry, so she pulled off her smock and went out onto the veranda to have a sip of bourbon, wondering if Shane had been too drunk to remember that he'd agreed to stop by.

Until now, her involvement with men had never brought her father to mind, not even when she left Pratt and settled in at the Chelsea. There, her attachments to the opposite sex weren't pegged to her heart but to her ability to pay rent, letting her enjoy the expensive hideaway with tiny servings of opium and a lot of booze. But more than paying the rent, she'd hoped that if, by chance, she fell in love with someone, it would allow her to rip apart her father's leash that bound her to the anniversary of his death. She knew better, but that was then. Last night was now.

The withering sunlight blanketed the wild white sage that, even in winter, sprouted from the rocks that walled the shore of the beach below her house. In the distance, lightning danced over the rolling spine of bluffs known as the Barrier Islands. Clutching the bottle, she watched as great clouds began to creep into the sky, sending long shadows across the shoreline and darkening the remains of the old pier, destroyed by Enola, from which she and her father had set sail. The dark ocean would be turning vicious by sunset, chasing away any hope of sighting a dolphin or even a sailboat but doing nothing to obscure her father's presence.

She'd been home about a week when his spirit emerged from a painting she'd just made of him and hung on her bedroom wall. Telling herself that she was having a nightmare, she held onto her scream, but when his image started toward her, the scream erupted. Before it ended, she was out of bed and on the veranda where her father's boat, The Lilly, became her bedtime hideaway.

The sighting prompted her to see a psychiatrist, who, before agreeing to meet with her, required that she take a series of psychological tests that were so weird and inane that she saw no reason to keep her upcoming appointment, but she'd paid thirty bucks and felt obligated.

The gray and depressing light clung to the palisades along the cliff whose multicolored stone walls encased the Shore of Heracles, so named by her Father whom she could no longer call "dad" because as his pain worsened, he became intensely religious and insisted that borrowing God's appellation of Father would bring him closer to The Almighty. The closer he came, the greater the chance that the Lord would approve of his effort to move to the head of the sufferers' line.

Three months or so before her father died, he'd begun to lose his mind due to the endless assault of arthritis and shame but forever the attorney, he argued his case ceaselessly before the Almighty. Whenever Suzanne heard him in the bedroom, on his knees pleading for God to let him die, she'd go to him and try to calm him down and get him into his bed, but he never obeyed. One night he told her why. He said that he'd made a call to Reverend Bradley and the preacher told him that he wasn't experiencing the necessary amount of pain for God to allow him to die. Bradley explained why, telling her father that he stood at the rear of a long line of sufferers and could not move ahead unless his pain became greater than theirs.

During the last weeks of his life, he disconnected from reality and sought guidance only from the Bible and The Odyssey, both of which Stavros, his long-time friend and founder of the local Greek restaurant, helped him struggle through. Her father would crawl into the living room every morning to watch Bradley's televised sermons. He told Suzanne about the visions of Christ that accompanied him to the high school baseball games — which he was no longer able to attend — where victory went to the team with the greatest number of pure souls.

But most gut-wrenching was his imaginary visit to the terrifyingly high trestle on the south side of Meridien. There God appeared and spoke to him, asking him to be patient, to abide the pain and wait his turn in line until granted the opportunity to move forward and enter the Gates of Heaven. He spent hours praying to God to allow him to die, but God turned a deaf ear, at first.

Suzanne had no idea how he'd ever managed to make his way up the shaky attic ladder into the mouse-ridden loft. Even though Bradley warned him that by committing suicide he was going against the will of God, he managed to convince himself that in the split second between life and death the severe pain of what he was about to do would warrant instant forgiveness and allow him to leap to the head of the sufferers' line and enter the Kingdom.

With his fingers cramped into claws, he'd looped a rope over the rafter above him and somehow managed to tie a slipknot, turning the rope into a noose. He wrapped a flour sack around his neck to ensure access to the brief moment when pain and forgiveness would come together. Then he snugged the rope around the sack and leaped into the void.

Suzanne was in her bedroom painting the picture of him when she heard a thudding sound, quickly followed by a weak effort, like a child's cry, to make a noise that would serve as undeniable evidence of his pain. She jumped out of bed and ran down the hall to find him swaying back and forth in the creepy, yet calm momentum of strangling to death. He'd known all along that she would be the one to find him. With her mother gone, there was no one else.

Damn him.

The smell of bourbon was leaching from his striped pajamas.

Damn him!

She'd been his caretaker for almost five years, refusing to go off to college or even leave the house during the day, unless she had to get his medicines and groceries. She cooked for him and drove him to his doctors and to see Reverend Bradley and to Stavros's Restaurant where he and Stavros became sincere friends and her father first learned about the Odyssey. As he approached the end, she would take him into the shower and dry him off. And to think he would do this to her.

Goddamn him!

She'd wanted to pound his lurching body, but instead she ran into the kitchen for the butcher knife and rushed back into the hall begging God to do something. She vaulted up the ladder beside him. His eyes were bulging out of their sockets. A harsh, accusatory stare streamed from them, demanding that she explain why she happened to be beside him. She had no right to intervene, no right whatsoever, because in that jarring second when the noose grabbed his neck, she must have known that at long last God had given him permission to die.

As she hacked at the rope, he drifted back and forth against her. She told him that she loved him. Steeped in their past together it was in her eyes and written on her face, but he sneered at her. She watched transfixed as little red flecks broke out all over his face, tiny crosses exploding into crimson ciphers the size of ticks. The bare skin of his temples reflected the hall light, and for a moment she thought she saw her twin image reflected in the sheen.

She sliced through the rope and he dropped to the floor. For a moment, he stood there, as if about to stride off to his bedroom, and then crumbled into a heap.

She jumped off the ladder and shook him ruthlessly. His eyes were glazed with fluid but it did nothing to mask the anger beaming from them. Quickly, she shoved the heels of her hands against his chest as hard as she could. It was all she knew to do, a lesson passed along from Chelsea, her mother's midwife.

Suzanne's mother told her numerous times about her breeched birth. Skeptical, Suzanne took it upon herself to hear it from Chelsea, so she went to the hospital when she was a freshman and asked if it had happened as her mother described. To her astonishment, Chelsea told her that the tale was true.

Shoving at her father's ribs with determination, Suzanne asked him again and again why he'd done such a thing — even though she knew the answer lay in his fantasy about the sufferers' line. She bit her lip but couldn't feel a thing, except for a fuzzy, drifting sensation as though she were no longer attached to anything or anyone, not even herself. Suddenly, he gasped and opened his eyes, as shocked at her reappearance as she was at his.

She thought his neck had to be broken and that it was only a matter of seconds before he passed away. But as she would learn, occasionally a few of those who choose to hang themselves don't experience a broken neck but die from a lack of blood to the brain, and assuming the blood flow does not resume, it often takes a few minutes before they're gone, unless the heart restarts.

"Where am I?" His voice came out around his thickened tongue muffled and forsaken like a homeless person praying in the night. His heart began to throb.

"In the hall, on the floor," she sobbed. "You just tried to kill yourself. Be still." She carefully removed the noose and unwrapped the sack from his purple neck.

"The pain, I can't… go on… I have to move…" he rasped.

"I know, I know, to the front of the sufferers' line. I know all about that, father."

"No, you don't," he said, "or you wouldn't have saved me."

"I saved you because I love you."

"Hush, daughter. "You didn't keep me from dying. You kept my pain alive." His voice seemed to stick in his throat, but he growled like a mad dog to force the words out. "You will have no access to my love until… until you join me on the other side and we kneel together before The Almighty."

It made no sense, no sense whatsoever. She told him to be quiet. With the help of a scatter rug, she dragged him into his bedroom and jerked the blankets from the bed to cover him. She slipped a pillow under his head. Her heart was beating so fast she thought it was about to leap out of her chest. "I'm going for help," she said.

He grimaced but managed to raise his voice. "No, no, no!"

She ran into the living room and grabbed the phone to call for an ambulance. "Operator, operator, my father…" She stopped in mid-sentence. His words came back to her.

"You kept my pain alive."

Sobbing, she hung up and started to run back to his bedroom when she noticed that the television was on. She wasn't at all surprised to find it tuned to the Channel of the Apostles where the word of God was broadcast twelve hours a day, seven days a week. Evangelist Caleb Bradley, the preacher at Southhall Baptist, was rambling on about the joys of eternity, while smoke from his cigar filled the screen.

Suzanne snapped off the TV and hurried back to her father's bedroom. "Whisky," he demanded when she entered the room.

She reached into the closet where he stored his liquor and seized a half-empty bottle of Jim Beam, his favorite bourbon. Seeing that his hands had knotted, she opened the bottle and tipped it to his mouth. He slurped at the whisky like a hungry puppy. As he swallowed she noticed that his throat seemed to be responding normally. It brought a modicum of relief that she hadn't called for an ambulance. His lips closed and the whisky started to dribble down his chin. He released a deep breath and began to snore.

She placed an ear on his chest. His heart was thudding. "I love you more than anything in this world," she whispered, repeating, "I love you," until his heart slowed. "Thank you, God," she said and headed down the hall.

She picked up the noose and the flour sack, climbed the ladder until she could smell the attic's mildew and heaved them into the darkness. She climbed down, snapped the ladder into place, slammed the Dutch doors behind her and went out onto the veranda. Breathless, but relieved to have gotten rid of the creepy remnants, she took a deep breath.

If only she could find a way to obliterate the memory. If only, she thought — regret's favorite phrase.

Chapter Eleven

She left the veranda for the living room, hoping she could put the memory to bed and finish the painting before Shane arrived, assuming he was going to. But when she opened the Dutch doors and stepped into the hallway, her hand-painted door panes cast a forewarning image of a spear that pointed up the wall toward the crimped attic door. Closed and crossed by shadows, it reminded her of the entrance to a mausoleum she'd seen in the Green-Wood Cemetery in Brooklyn, where people were inspired to visit and sleep with their buried fathers.

She tried her best to shove her urge aside but didn't have the strength. She reached for the chain and slowly lowered the crippled ladder. Cold aging air rushed down from the attic as if it had been waiting forever to get out. She thought she could still smell the cigarette smoke trapped in her father's pajamas and held her breath as she started to climb the ladder. Looking up into the emptiness, it seemed as though she was staring into a grave turned upside-down.

She imagined the joists on either side of the stairwell as railings used to lower a casket. Her legs began to shake so hard the ladder screeched against the floor. Why was she doing this? Was it because of what the invitation at Green-Wood or was it something more foreboding? Had she inherited the death-wish gene of from her father, or was it that what he demanded she do to redeem herself had taken precedence over her life?

She climbed until she was waist-high in the attic's version of sunlight, dimly filtered by the lone pilot window on the far side of the loft. The insulation smelled like mold. The flour cloth lay bundled next to the chimney. The long end of her father's chopped rope was curled on the rock-wool between the joists. She reached for the rope. It felt hard, scratchy and rough-skinned. She had no idea how to make a noose, but she did remember that the loop around her father's neck was held in place with a round, three-fingered knot.

She wrestled with the rope, trying to figure out how to tie the knot. She formed a loop but when she started to bind it into a noose, the rope snapped apart. "Goddamnit," she muttered and stepped up on the joists along the opening with the rope in hand. Straddling the opening she looked down into the strangely luring image of an empty grave. She watched transfixed as the blue and gold tones of weakening sunlight turned the bottom of the pit into the color of the ocean. It must have looked the same to her father, but his death was far more than the pull of some momentary twist of color in his imagination.

She remained wavering on the squeaking joists, tethered to her traitorous conscience that left her in a labyrinth of fear and shame. "I'm sorry I betrayed you," she said. "I love you."

Caught in the whirling stasis of fear and shame, she began to fumble with the remains of the rope.

Chapter Twelve

Shane checked to make sure he'd locked the glove compartment where he'd stored the .45. He climbed out of the Rambler and stood on the curb across the ravine from Suzanne's house. It looked out of place, from another time, so different than the way it did the day of the verdict when her father had given him a ride home from the court. The red bricks were encrusted with age and the shades were drawn in all but one window. The faded yellow trim was peeling, the gutters choked with branches and twigs. The tines of the TV antenna, which had most likely been twisted by Enola, rested on the beleaguered roof.

Mr. de Ville's old Pontiac was parked in the graveled driveway. A barely visible trailer hitch jutted out from under the rear fender. What appeared to be bird shit and grime covered the hood and front windows. The words "White Trash," which had been scratched on the driver's door in the community's celebration of his defeat in court, had turned to rust but were still visible. The car's hood ornament was a zinc replica of a flying goddess, wings flowing behind her strong-minded face seemingly determined to find her destination. The motorcycle rested against the front fender as if attempting to console the car.

The rope bridge leading over the gorge to the narrow front yard swayed, causing the planks on the walkway to clatter. Shane gripped the damp ropes that served as railings and moved ahead cautiously sliding one foot forward at a time on the moss-covered planks. The wind picked up and the bridge began to move to and fro. He squeezed the ropes and started to go back but his grit wouldn't allow it. When made it to the other side, he stepped onto the mushy ground with his head ringing like a belfry.

Through a pane of glass in the front door, he peeked into the living room. Sunset, refusing to be held prisoner by the gathering clouds, had turned the bare cedar floor into a fiery rink. He pushed the doorbell but it didn't ring. He knocked but there was no answer. Hesitantly, he cracked the door open.

"Suzanne?"

She gasped and nearly lost her balance on the joists. Moments ago she would have been thrilled that he'd come, but now she felt only disgrace. It was as if she'd tried to drown herself and been abruptly yanked from the sea.

Shane's voice resurfaced, calling her name. She dropped the remnants of the rope on the insulation and backed off the joists to step onto the ladder. She climbed down to find him squinting through the front door. As if her heart knew better than her conscience, a pang of happiness swept through her. She yanked the door open and stepped back, hoping her eyes would ask him in.

Unable to break away from her stare, Shane stepped inside, closing the door behind him. Suzanne seemed to be looking through his eyes, searching for what he would say next, but when took a step toward her, her eyes became apprehensive, though her lips took on an eerie smile. Shane shivered. It seemed colder in the house than outside, yet Suzanne was wearing only a pair of cut-off denims and a paint-smudged sweatshirt which despite its bilk could not hide the symmetry of her breasts

"Thank you, Shane… no, bless you, for coming," she said, embarrassed that only moments ago he'd taken her off the edge of a cliff.

"You asked me to try and get here before sunset," he said.

He'd offered her the perfect explanation and she expanded on it instantly. "Not only for the setting sun, but for some bourbon, and this!" Relieved and threateningly excited, she pointed to the painting on the wall over the mantle.

Turned amber by the sunset, a constellation of stars hovered above a vast, silky layer of sand that reminded Shane of the sparkling sand in Da Nang's Non Nuoc Beach at night, where he and his platoon had gone to the bar and he'd had his throat sliced. The painting's heavens were shaded in a blue darkness so mystic that what he took to be the sea appeared to conceal someone trapped high in the firmament and another in the glitter of the sand.

"It needs gloss," she said and snatched two spray cans from the bookshelf. Rushing across the room while spraying the painting, she created a sheen that coaxed the stars to glisten.

Shane watched as the angelic figure of a woman surfaced in the sky. Below her emerged the faint spectral of a young girl wrapped in a white gown carrying a cross. As Suzanne waved the spray back and forth, the stars gathered in the aura like speckled granite. A moment later the figures seemed to have been part of the painting all along.

"Do you know who they are?" Suzanne asked.

"Not at all."

She pointed to the female figure floating in the sky. "She's Achelois, the moon goddess who inspires the creation of art and literature so they can wash away our pain. Below her flows the burdened soul of Joan of Arc carrying her cross..." Suzanne paused. "...across the river Styx, which, according to my father is the tributary from our past on which our hopes and aspirations will float like refuge unless we turn to Achelois for help. And even then..."

"Even then, what?"

She turned to him. Her eyes appeared to show her soul. Her brow creased and her lips seemed to curve upward but not in a smile. "Shane, have you ever done anything in your life that still haunts you, that refuses to let go, that ties you to a stake like a hungry dog?"

He hesitated as Toby shouted in his head, "We won, Shane! We won!" For a moment he wondered if the wall goddess had brought Toby's voice back in a mistaken effort to ease his pain. If only Jesse had been able to hear those words. If only he could shout loud enough for him to hear them now. The answer to Suzanne's question wasn't hers to know.

"Suzanne, how in the world did you do that, paint a painting on top of a painting while you ran across the room?" he asked.

"The truth is, I didn't paint anything. Achelois has been there all along. She just needed help getting out. It's called fantasy art. It's based on what you feel, not what you see. Where passion exists, art has no boundaries." Suzanne's lips glisten in the floor's tawny reflection. She cocked her head and smiled. "It's a whore's mouth," she said, setting the spray cans back on the bookshelf.

Shane hadn't known her long enough, nor well enough, to realize that what she considered to be humor could break out at the most unexpected times, in the most unexpected ways. Before he could return the smile, she started laughing — an eerie, ringing laugh that revealed something about her that he felt he'd heard at Medic's but couldn't pin down. It was as though she'd just played an uproarious joke on herself.

At first, he thought the rumble of thunder might be coming from the painting and stepped back. It came again, but it was real.

"Don't you love the time just before it rains?" she said. "Let's go out on the patio and hope the lightning strikes over the islands."

He followed her out onto the veranda. The clouds veiled the sunset, silhouetting the islands. She leaned onto the warped wood railing.

While the sun's fading hues gradually slipped into the ocean, Shane recited a line that Medic often quoted in class when referencing Salinger's character, Leah. "She wasn't doing a thing that I could see, except standing there leaning on the balcony railing, holding the universe together."

"Leah, from A Girl I Knew," Suzanne replied, her eyes fixed on the sea, her heart grateful for the thunder.

"Unreal," Shane said, amazed that she remembered.

"Isn't everything?"

His eyes were drawn to a canvass-covered rowboat latched to a rickety trailer that was parked under a chestnut tree next to the veranda. The words, The Lilly, were painted on the stern. Suddenly, a breathtaking gust of wind set off a bevy of windchimes strung through the tree's branches. The chaotic squawking rose sharply before tapering into a soft, harmonic tinkle.

"Gave me the chills," Shane said.

"I hung the chimes out here to serve as an alert, in hopes of keeping my father's ghost at bay. I sleep in The Lilly now."

"You're joking?" Shane said and waited for a smile but instead she rested her elbows on the railing's ledge and kept looking at the sky.

"I wish I were. I took his ashes out to sea in The Lilly," she said. "Achelois brought a wind to help spread them as far as possible, but I couldn't bring myself to open the urn." She motioned with a tilt of her head. "Come closer. Have a look at Crystal Cove or as renamed by my father, the Shore of Heracles." She pointed towards the rocks at the far end of the beach. "That's the Cave of Heracles and nearby, the remains of the old pier. Just a few planks left, courtesy of Enola. It's where I launched The Lilly the day we — I mean, just me — and my father's ashes went to sea." She turned toward the shore. "See that cobbled road running down from the parking lot? It's closed now because there's nothing left to set sail from."

"Did you sail a lot?"

"Not so much. I swam all the time. My friends and…" she paused. "I'd go to the beach every day, to let the water wash my ankles and hug my waist as I waded in. I loved it when I was about to duck under, hoping to catch the incoming tide and having it splash against my forehead. I loved it best in the winter, especially during what my father called the harvest moon, when the tide rises and recedes almost simultaneously. You don't know if you're going to be washed ashore or wind up in France. It's like Japanese art where there's only impermanence. The Japanese loved to paint the sea because they believed that waves were the perfect example of how things never stay as they appear."

Bewildered, Shane watched the cobalt waves pound the shoreline. Clouds were gathering from all points on the compass, as though the wind had become a swirling circle released from the sky in a funnel. The clouds sent long shadows across the sand where a flock of seagulls huddled, heads tucked into their wings. Only when the thunder rumbled so loud that he expected the house to move did Suzanne come off her elbows. The sun's rays were fading, slowly pulling the islands away. A streak of lightning burst above them, creating an array of silver and gold icons that lingered when the bolt disappeared.

Suzanne glanced at Shane with an I-told-you-so smile.

To his surprise, she slid her hand over his, but just as he tried to interlace his fingers with hers, she pulled away and in one simultaneous move, grabbed onto the railing and hoisted herself onto the ledge. As she straightened, her legs began to wobble. Startled, Shane jumped behind her and grabbed her ankles. Her legs shook harder.

"What are you doing?" he said, alarmed.

"Putting my soul to the test," she replied between quickening breaths "Not to worry. I was born a little bird, so if the wind blows me off, I'll flap my wings and float to shore."

The wind blew fiercer and his grip tightened. The muscles in her calves spasmed. "Get down!" he yelled.

Lightning struck again, more sharply this time, as if disagreeing mightily with whatever was in Suzanne's head. To his relief, Shane felt her ankles soften.

"You can let go now," she said.

He wasn't about to. When she crouched to grip the ledge he released her ankles and immediately grabbed her waist. She stretched a leg down toward the veranda.

"It's okay, Shane," she said as her foot touched the floor.

When both feet landed, he let go. "Suzanne, what the hell were you doing?"

She hesitated. "The night before my father died, he crawled out here. I caught him reaching for the ledge, but his hands gave way before I could catch him and he crumbled onto the patio. I wrapped my arms around him to try and sit him upright, when he looked at me with a reminder in his eyes. I'll never forget what he said, 'Smile, my darling daughter. You will have your…'"

"Your what?"

It stirred the embers. She'd crossed the line and had to retreat. Feeling Judas at her side, she thought that whatever lie she was about to tell would in due time replace the guilt and agony she'd carried since that horrible day. A lie might even set her free to fall in love with someone, especially if she could con her father by pledging that she would never utter the words "I love you" to another man.

She waited for the lie to reveal itself. When the revelation came to her, a tinge of fear made an unwelcomed presence, but an edited version of what had just happened unrolled.

"Shane, let me tell you something that you didn't ask for."

"You don't have to do that, Suzanne."

"It might help explain things."

It was more than he'd bargained for, and then it dawned on him that maybe it was Suzanne's version of a consolation letter. "Sure, then go ahead. Tell me."

"On Saturday, a week after he passed away, I was putting on his motorcycle jacket and inside one of the pockets I found the keys to the Pontiac and the Tiger, as well as a note he'd left me. His hand writing resembled something from an ancient manuscript. I translated the words as best I could and filled in the blanks with guesses. But I was able to make sense of it, at least I think I did." She faltered, not so much for the drama, but for the truth that she was about to weave through her story.

"It's okay. You don't have to say anymore," Shane said.

She put a finger to her lips. "Yes I do," she said. "He wrote how much he loved me and how grateful he was that I'd put off going to college to take care of him. Yet, in saving his life, he said that I'd put him through seven horrible days filled with increasingly unbearable pain. 'Time has come to depart this world,' he wrote, and also, that he wanted me to make sure he was cremated at Sill's, in honor of Jesse, where the same Carlisle who testified on Jesse's behalf would place a bottle of Jim Beam in his arms as he lay on the cremation casket and God would welcome him with open arms.

"I did what he asked. When it was over, Carlisle gave me the urn, along with a bottle of Jim Beam and the message my father had given him, asking me to scatter his ashes at sea and reminding me that he would wait for me on the banks of the River Styx where I, his 'darling daughter,' would have a chance for redemption. He wasn't being sarcastic. He was just quoting from the Greek myths about death that Stavros had shared with him.

"The next morning, I hitched The Lilly to the Pontiac and drove down to the pier where I launched his beloved Lilly and rowed his ashes out to sea. When I stopped rowing the sun was almost down. I couldn't bring myself to open the urn, so I let it sink into the water and, after a long crying spell, made it back to shore. That night I held a commemorative service in my bedroom where I'd painted a picture of him with twin images of his daughter in his eyes."

"But enough for now," she said. "Let's get away from this delirium and go where there's even more."

"And where would that be?"

"Shane, this is going to sound like another bizarre request, but tomorrow would you go with me to the trestle?"

"The trestle out by the Narrows? In this cold? Good God, it's what, a mile high?" he said, thrown by the abrupt shift from her touching story.

"But the view from up there must be so beautiful this time of year, though that's not the reason. Let me be honest with you, which sometimes is hard for me because when my mind jumps into overdrive, I have very little control over how it separates what is from what isn't. The two blend, making it impossible for me to tell one from the other. So, sometimes I say whatever comes to mind and never stop to ask myself if it's true or not because I have no way of knowing."

"You're losing me, Suzanne, and besides, I've got a lot… I'm sorry, why do you want to go to the trestle?"

"My father put it this way, 'Out on the trestle, you are but a breath away from the face of God.' Hold on a second. Shane, I can tell that your eyes are about to roll. Let me explain. I haven't been able to keep the promise I made to him that I would go to the trestle after he passed away, where he claimed he'd seen the face of God. I promised him that I'd go and thank The Almighty on his behalf for allowing him to skip forward in the sufferers' line at the very last second between life and death. It's weighed on me ever since, but I'm afraid to go alone. It's a dangerous place, as I'm sure you know, and a terrible favor to ask, but with you at my side, maybe I could not only keep my promise but survive."

"What's the sufferers' line, Suzanne?"

She took a breath, knowing she had to answer. "It's where we line up when we're in tremendous pain and in need of God's permission to end our own lives."

Shane opened his mouth but, for a moment, made no sound. Finally, he said, "I'm sorry, Suzanne. I've got a lot on my plate tomorrow."

She wanted to break through the barrier in the driveway, plant her lips on his, and beg him to stay the night, but she couldn't bring herself to move. Instead, she cupped his hand between hers and apologized for what she was about to say, that the party had more than exhausted her and that she had to get some sleep, when in fact she wanted him to stay in order to see how long, if at all, his presence would keep her father at bay. She neglected both options and implored him to go with her to the trestle.

Thunder growled and, seconds later, lightning tap-danced over the islands. Shane tried to drag his response away from the temptation to go with her to the dreaded trestle, but the pressure of her hand on his increased, making the dilemma all the more difficult.

"I'll have to get back early," he said.

She smiled. "I hope to as well."

Chapter Thirteen

He drove to Suzanne's the next morning with her father's comment, "Out on the trestle, you are but a breath away from the face of God," streaming across his mind as if on the windshield, now dappled with rapidly disappearing snowflakes. He turned up the speed of the wipers. The flakes streaked momentarily, blurring the glass, and her comment vanished. He tried to convince himself that by having visited his house and his mother's grave, he'd earned a day off before tracking down Talley.

He'd never been to the notorious trestle nor had he ever been tempted. The year before he started high school it had been closed to the public when a group of teenagers hiked to the rails after their homecoming celebration. The oft-told story had it that the celebrants were drunk, a fight broke out, and one of them was blown off the trestle into the valley below. Though the death was considered by the railroad to be a rumor, the men who worked the tracks were forced to wear weights around their legs to keep them grounded.

The sight of Suzanne in her driveway wiping the Tiger to a shine increased his anxiety, and yet his fascination with her impelled him across the rope bridge. When he'd made it over, she gave him more than a glad smile. Her eyes harbored all kinds of surprise and eagerness. The struggling sun poked through the hint of snow in the grey clouds, dappling her black leather jacket and reflecting off the shoulder buttons in sharp, silver darts. Her tight, self-colored elastic pants outlined the curve of her calves. She tossed her hair, then tucked it into the collar of her jacket.

"Is that the jacket that belonged to your father?" Shane asked.

"Yes, he willed it to me, so it belongs to both of us now. I had it re-stitched and braided, so it would fit better. I wore it to class every day in the winter." She zipped the collar tight under her chin, turning her face into an effigy.

"Sure you want to go up to the trestle in this weather?"

"Makes it less likely we'll get caught," she said. "Besides, there are some promises that must be kept, even though they were made to those who're no longer here."

The urgency in her voice stretched far beyond the poignancy of her comment.

Remembering the veranda, a swell of worry washed over her.

She gave him a curious look. "Don't worry, we'll outrun the snow. Now, he who is about to disappear into the great unknown, climb on behind me. In the Wild West, they called it riding two-up or double saddle. If the one with the reins gets shot, there's somebody to take over and not lose a stride. You're that someone." Her muscular calf flexed as she stepped onto the footrest and swung her leg over the seat.

Sculpted even more by the pants, her perfect bottom came into play.

She caught Shane's stare in the Tiger's rearview mirror. "Once, I was told by a poet at the Chelsea, who was high on who-knows-what, that I had the best-looking ass on the East and the West Side. It appears you might agree, but beware, for as I told the gentleman, the price you have to pay for it is crippling. Now, Shane, put a boot on the foot peg, kick it down, sling a leg over the seat and hoist your ass on board."

He'd never been on a motorcycle. When he squeezed onto the narrow jump seat, his jeans gripped his scrotum. "Ouch!"

Suzanne chuckled. She'd heard it more than once, when her father rode behind her teaching her to drive the Tiger. "When I start the engine and sit down, hold onto my hips and remember, when I shift from side to side on the curves, move with them. Don't tense, don't squeeze — as much as you might like to. Don't let me feel your fear."

"How about the snow?"

"How about it? They're just speckles. Nothing to worry about."

Before he could respond, she rose up out of the seat and came down forcefully on the starter. The roar of the engine clogged his ears. She twisted the throttle and the bike rumbled and shook. He clutched her hips.

As they ramped onto Route 28, her back was planed to the road which, though only glossy, was wet enough for a deadly slip of the tires. Suzanne's elbows stuck up like chicken wings. Shane imagined that she was grinning. When they entered the Narrows, a chicane of rapidly flowing turns, the walls of the cliffs seemed to pinch the two-lane road in half, allowing no margin of error.

Shane clung to her hips as they flew into one turn after another, zigzagging as if they were trying to dodge death itself. When they came to the looping last curve, the Tiger tilted so close to the road that he was sure the tires were going to slide out from under them. He tried to yell for her to slow down, but his cheeks were flapping like mourning doves. When they emerged from the Narrows, the wind was squeezing tears out of his eyes, blurring everything but the flash of a towering, warped billboard announcing the arrival of the Harvest Fair. As if they'd just crossed some imaginary finish line, they coasted to the side of the road and stopped. With the engine still running, Suzanne planted her feet on the ground, stood up straddling the gas tank and clapped in victory.

"What did you think about snaking those curves?" she said, elated.

"I thought we were done for," Shane said, panting to catch his breath.

She laughed and pointed to a steep, cindered road about a quarter of a mile away that disappeared into the upper woods. "That's the maintenance road that leads to the trestle."

High above the wooded area, stretching across a huge divide, the trestle looked like a smeared sketch of the bridge leading to her house.

The exhilaration of the ride was beginning to creep into Shane's veins. It now seemed far more like a ride at the fair than a ride to the morgue. "Hit it!" he shouted. She chuckled, sat back down, and charged forward. At the beginning of the steep cinder grade, Shane realized that his hands had never left her hips.

The creepy trestle seemed to be floating without stanchions in a nest of swirling fog. "Looks like something straight out of the movie Psycho," Suzanne yelled back at him.

She hit the gas and the Tiger seemed to shriek in appreciation. They soared up the maintenance road, spitting loose gravel onto the shoulders. They swerved around a tree limb that had fallen across the road and caught some shoulder, spitting dark clumps of mud into the branches of a low-hanging willow. Dead leaves were sucked into the Tiger's draft and whirled into the air. They were moving so fast the slope seemed to flatten. As they approached the crest of the hill, she crawled to a stop so they could get off and guide the Tiger around a thick chain strung across the road to block access to the trestle. A warning sign hanging from the chain made it more than clear that no one was welcome. Don't dare go another foot! It demanded. Once around the chain, they climbed back on and rumbled up the hill with the tires slipping and sliding in the gravel.

At the top, there were no signs of life. A concrete oval shed cut into the side of the hill reminded Shane of a cave in Vietnam where injured soldiers imagined that beasts from another world were kept. The arched shed was packed to the roof with logs that would be transformed into railroad ties.

"Those logs are just waiting for a chance to get laid," Susanne joked and Shane laughed.

The brown-brick service office was closed. There were no cars or trucks, only a two-man, hand-car on the U-shaped spur that guided the rails across the trestle. On the far side of the lot, two bent pieces of railroad track lay across a pile of rotting ties. The image was a familiar one. They were called Sherman neckties. During the Civil War, the Union general's forces had heated them to a bendable level and wrapped them around trees, making them unusable for the Confederates. The bowed rails, still in the countryside, had become a traditional source of hatred for those still angered by the outcome of the war.

Shane helped Suzanne roll the Tiger to the spot where the spur shoehorned into the tracks. A rush of wind came up from the distant valley below, warning him to follow her when she stepped away from the spur onto the trestle.

Suzanne looked out toward the bay. Instantly, she felt herself back on the ledge of the veranda. Her face was sallow, her eyes filled with disbelief as though she'd seen something horrible in the chasm. She glanced at Shane, worried that he might grab her and jerk her off the trestle. She'd called the train station to get the schedule and knew the train was due soon.

"Stay put, Shane!" she shouted, moving farther out on the ties. The wind swelled again, surrounding her with a feeling of isolation. Was she being pulled away from him by her father's ghostly hands? "Did you feel that?" she called out, wondering if her voice had been muzzled.

"Yes! The wind's getting stronger!" Shane shouted.

"No, not the wind, the loneliness," she replied, seeming miffed that he hadn't known the answer. She wanted him closer but knew she had to withstand the temptation. "It claws at you," she yelled, "but resist it at your peril, because each time you think you've broken its spell, it returns even deeper." She planted her feet, each on a separate tie, twisted toward Shane and cupped her hands around her mouth. "When at last you find someone you feel you can pour your soul out to, you stop in shock at the words you utter."

"What's that? I can't hear you well."

"Sylvia Plath," she replied

They stood their tenuous ground. Suzanne glanced across the trestle. The silver rails and the spikes in the crossties glimmered amid the slowly disappearing snowflakes. Even the creosote that bound the cracks together gleamed. The stanchions creaked as if they were trying to warn Suzanne to stay put. Fog, the color and thickness of egg batter, began to roll down from the bluffs and mask the ties, turning them into a surreal painting. The trio of wooden fire barrels along the tracks faded. Suzanne unzipped her jacket to the waist. She sensed Shane approaching.

"Where do you think you're going?" she shouted.

"With you."

A breathless tremor rolled over her. "No! I told you, this is for me to do alone. You're only here to bear witness. Now, go back."

"Bear witness to what, for God's sake?"

"It is for His sake and my father's as well. Stay put, Shane. Please."

A chill spread across his chest as she continued out. His heart sank when her jacket surged up around her. She teetered and went into a crouch, grabbing the rails to duck-walk forward. Half-way out she drew even with the last visible safety barrel. Shane's balance left him. He got down on his knees. The wind was so strong he had to lie crab-like on the ties and clutch the rails to make headway.

Suzanne straightened, grabbed the top of the barrel and clung to the steel rim. Just when Shane thought she was about to jump inside, she let go, flung her arms out from her sides and sidled to the next tie. She braced for a moment and turned slowly toward the gorge.

A sharp, piercing noise like a mass of tinfoil crumbled in his ear. "The train!" he yelled. The locomotive's gleaming headlight was spread wide by the fog. Susanne gave no indication that she heard him or the train. She looked straight ahead toward the bay and rose up on her toes.

Shane's terrified eyes led her soon-to be-decimated body into the abyss. "Get in the barrel!" he screamed.

She leaned into the fog like a clipped-wing raven. The mist swallowed her whole. The loadstone struck Shane: she'd committed suicide. It was why she'd come in the first place. She said she'd brought him to bear witness. Why? For what? To help find her goddamn body?

The train's whistle blared, sending shock waves through the trestle. Shane lunged for the closest barrel and toppled inside, squirming to hug his knees to his chest and squeeze into a ball. When the monstrous engine burst onto the trestle, the barrel shook as if it were coming apart. It was worse than being trapped in a foxhole. Just when he thought his skull was about to cave in, the train cleared the trestle, leaving everything so still and silent that he wondered if he'd been shaken to death. His arms were wrapped so tightly around his knees that he had trouble uncoiling. Gradually, his fingers separated and he pulled himself onto his wobbling knees and hesitated not wanting to come out of the barrel into what he feared to be the loneliness she'd mentioned.

When he saw her standing in the middle of the trestle, he froze, as if it was an apparition she'd sketched in that fraction of time between life and death. Her jacket was twisted around her shoulders. She kept opening and closing her mouth. Her perplexed eyes found him and became expressionless. Shane was sure that she had no idea who he was.

The memory of the fireflies at the cemetery flashed behind his eyes. His heart trembled. He felt his weight sinking into the barrel, helpless at the belated hands of fear. He was familiar with the phenomenon. He'd been lost several times in Vietnam. When a gunfight ended, and soaked in mortified relief, he and his men would sink into a flooded paddy or onto a swampy ridge. But any sense of relief avoided him until Suzanne leaned over the edge of the barrel.

"Here, take my hand," he said.

"I already have," she chuckled.

With his hand clasped between hers, he managed to seize the rim of the barrel and struggle to his feet. Her hands went to the top of his arm helping his rubbery legs sway out of the barrel onto the ties, and together they inched breathlessly to the spur.

"Here, let's sit down," she said.

"What the hell were you doing out there?"

Her eyes tightened in embarrassment. She shook her head.

"I told you, Shane. I had to keep a promise I made to my father. He was brought out here by Stavros, his last friend on earth." Suzanne paused. "Stavros brought him here when his pain became unbearable. I know this sounds weird as can be, but he came specifically to see the face of God and ask the Almighty for permission to die. The day before he passed away, he made me promise to come here on his behalf and thank God for allowing him to end his life. I swore that I would but until now, until I met you and felt I had some protection, I've never been able to."

"He wanted you to give thanks for letting him die?"

"For letting him live, as he saw it."

"But you leaned over the edge, like out on the veranda… and I thought you, as I did then…"

"Were tempting fate? No, Shane, I bent over the rail to make sure I could see the Almighty's face. It was tough to find Him in the fog, but I had to take the chance. Out on the veranda, I was hoping He might do me a favor and spare me the trip out here, but apparently, He was too busy."

"Did you, just now? Did you find Him?" Shane asked, on the verge of cringing at his sarcastic tone.

"Yes, but He wasn't at all what I expected. He appeared with the breath of an ox and one enormous, demented eye that featured a hurricane the size of Enola." Suzanne's eyes widened and laughter tumbled out of her mouth. Gradually, she collected herself, wondering why Shane hadn't joined her in the laugh.

He tried his best to swat away her bizarre comment, but like a pissed-off bumblebee, it kept circling around, buzzing, threatening until it stung him. Suzanne was insane.

"Shane, what I just said, I was just kidding. The truth is, I did see the face of God. It was the face of a kind and welcoming parent, a true father who cared bountifully for his daughter, no matter the questionable things she'd done in her life. The message came through. Life's a gift and must be viewed as such, and those who deem it so shall be rewarded. Is that a more convincing version?"

Shane wasn't sure. What about Jesse, he wondered. No one believed any stronger than Jesse that life was a gift, and yet, from him, the gift had been taken. And Talley? Why, with such a disregard for human life, was he allowed to stay on this earth? Neither made any sense whatsoever.

Suzanne moved closer. Her searching eyes were seemingly in conflict with her assurance about what she'd seen and heard on the trestle. Her breath warmed the cold air between them. Shane framed her face with his hands. Her lips opened. He closed his eyes fully expecting that they were about to overcome the barricade they'd encountered in the driveway.

She knew his every thought and desire because she felt them just as strongly as he did. And yet, she couldn't give in to them. Instead, she forced herself to admit to another of the enigmas that so often tossed her like a ragdoll. The greater her attraction to Shane, the harder it was to let him know. She pulled his hands away and drew back.

"Look at us standing here like we had time to waste," she said. "I wish, but the clock is running now." She caught herself again, relieved that the perfect explanation for her worrisome reply had arrived just in time. "The roads will be getting slick soon if they aren't already. We shouldn't wait any longer. Oh, almost forgot. If you haven't declared me totally insane by now, is there any chance you'd have a drink with me tonight at Blinder's?"

"Blinder's? I've never heard of it."

"It's where Roadies used to be, up on Hampton Hill. Before you came back, I went to the ABC Store for some whisky and the guy told me that Blinder's was a very different bar, but different in a good way, so I went and I'll tell you, it's different alright, but in a wonderful way. One of the waitresses, See-Through of all names, is completely blind and the owner himself is visually impaired. Apparently, because of his troubled sight, he redesigned the restaurant so that she could have a job regardless of her troubled sight. If you'd like to join me, I'll meet you there at sunset, as soon as I'm done with the painting. The sky needs more stars."

Fate swiftly compressed the rest of the day into the next, with no moments available in between. Tomorrow he'd likely be gone. He took a deep breath and forced his mind to relent. "Okay, okay. Would you like me to pick you up?"

The tug of war with her father's eyes was in play. "Thank you, Shane, but I should go alone, in case I have to leave early."

"I'll leave whenever you like."

"No, you can't."

He didn't want her to explain. He'd had enough. "Okay, whatever. I'll see you at sunset. Time for some rest. I'm exhausted," he said

"Who wouldn't be for putting up with me? Hop on and I'll take you to your car," she said in a cheery voice.

Chapter Fourteen

Though glad for the chance to get some rest, Shane drove back to The Oleander bewildered, consumed with thoughts of Suzanne despite all that happened on the veranda and on the trestle, or maybe because of it. Yes, she certainly came across as unhinged but strangely, it seemed that's what made him want to be with her, possibly to get the most out of his life for the last time. But paradoxically, he had to allow for the possibility that he, too, was going nuts because after what he'd witnessed on the trestle, he'd have to be insane to believe he wasn't.

It was as if she was following him to the Oleander, or maybe he was following her. Impossible to tell. She appeared at every stoplight. He sat with a car behind him blowing the horn while she crossed Virginia Avenue, paying no attention to the traffic. Stabbing at the brake, his foot nicked the gas pedal and his head snapped back. Magnified by the surprise, a blinding light, smaller but sharper than the locomotive's, was bearing down on him. He mashed the brake and immediately threw up his hands to block the glare as a motorcycle streaked into the intersection.

Handlebars, pipes, and fenders erupted in red and orange flares. The machine skidded wildly. In a sudden swerve, the driver got the bike under control and flew out of the intersection, the tail-light vanishing like a blown-out match.

Stalled in the stillness, Shane thanked whoever might be listening that it hadn't been Suzanne. For a moment he couldn't remember where he was. His legs were trembling as he put a foot gently on the gas and eased over the crossroads toward what he recognized as the old Rialto Theater where Blacks had been allowed to see movies but only if they sat in the upper balcony, far from the movie screen. They had no access to the restrooms or the candy stand, so they had to sneak snacks inside and pee into empty soda bottles.

He and Jesse had gone to the Rialto to see the James Bond movie, From Russia With Love. They had to buy tickets at separate entrances, Shane's at the front of the theater and Jesse's at the outdoor ticket box located at the rear by an iron stairway that led to the top of the theater just above the balcony. For whites only, an inside stairwell connected the orchestra with the balcony. Shane bought a large box of popcorn and a large Coke, snuck up the stairwell to the top of the theater with his jacket wrapped over his head and found Jesse. The two of them crunched the popcorn and hid the thrill of following Bond through his adventures until the show was over. They, like the hero himself, had escaped the villains unharmed.

It appeared that the theater had been closed for a while. Dirty Harry was strewn across the broken marquee. It looked as if the letters had been struggling to hang there since the day they'd gone there. In a familiar framed poster that had been showcased at the theater forever, a fading James Dean still smiled, coat over his shoulder and a cigarette hanging lightly on his vague, eerie smile.

For a moment, Shane wondered if he was starting to hallucinate. It happened often in the jungle where fear created delusions. Spots of darkness and light became huge insects, a tree's shadow became the enemy, moonlit streams were paths that led to death. Or was it that Suzanne's craziness was contagious? He saw her again on the trestle standing on her toes, her eyes to the sky, her arms stretched wide as if she were about to mount a cloud and ride off into the sunset.

She stayed in his mind as he made his way through town, skirting absently past the Post Office and the Recruitment office where he'd enlisted. A block later he passed the library, already decorated with holiday ribbons and Long's Sporting Goods where he and Jesse once went to buy Jesse a catcher's mitt and were turned away. Turned away until Mister Long closed the shop later that day.

They'd waited behind the store and as the sunset began to shadow the building they jimmied open the back door, snatched the mitt and ran off, trading the glove back and forth and laughing. Jesse laughed even harder days later when they passed the store on their bicycles and saw the sign Mr. Long had pasted on the window. It read, "No Blackkks!" spelled with the Clan's initials and the numeral one inserted as an exclamation point. "Whites can't spell worth a shit!" Jesse shouted as they sped away.

Shane was surprised to find himself at The Oleander. The peeling, two-story clapboard seemed to take up space the same way an abandoned trunk takes up time. It was far off the private road, situated at the end of a long path of willow trees known in the community as Hook's Alley. Set in the dark nook, the trellised walkway with its numerous birdbaths leading to the wide-brimmed porch resembled a huge keyhole.

The widow's walk with its tongue-like plank jutted out from the eaves on the top floor. Willow branches dangled over the porch like lashings around the masthead of an ancient ship. A deep moat of wild oleanders pulled the house even more into the past.

The Oleander was named by its owner Eunice Abernathy, another of Meridien's legends. Shane had never met her, but when he lived in Meridien he'd heard the stories about her, as everyone had. No one saw much of her because she didn't venture far from her porch. Instead, she paid wayward boys a dollar to do her grocery shopping and a nickel a blouse to wash her dirty laundry.

Eunice Abernathy, an elderly smoking maiden who lived in a wheelchair where she'd waited thirty years for Abe, her allegedly AWOL husband to return from his tour of duty while serving in France during the World War. Abe, who was killed in the Battle of the Bulge, was accepted as dead by everyone but Eunice. His obituary had appeared in the local Register but Eunice accused the writer of being a liar and held onto her conviction that Abe was still alive. She wrote sad, angry poems about him, which she'd convinced Mayor Grow to place on display in the Meridien Library as an undeniable version of true love. Each poem ended with an ironic, dear plea for Abe to come home.

Rumor had it that one day at sunrise he was spotted in a tent in the Smokies living the life of an outlaw wannabe. Since then, every day at sunrise Eunice would go out on the porch in her wheelchair to wait for Abe. Intent on bringing him to justice for his desertion, she hired a poor truck driver to take her to the Confederate graveyard several times where she searched for Abe with the homemade bow and arrow that now hung on the living room wall above a piano with a few missing keys.

Shane took the .45 out of the glove compartment and slipped it into his coat pocket. He made his way through the Alley to find Eunice sitting on the porch in her wheelchair, smoking a cigar and shivering.

"You're freezing," Shane said. "Let me help you inside."

"When you live in Hell, you can't freeze," she said. "How many years did you play ball with Mel Ott?"

Eunice was staring at him with an expression so odd that he couldn't tell if she was smiling or frowning. Smoke from the cigar ringed her grey hair in a fuzzy halo. His eyes couldn't help skipping from the cigar down to the wheelchair's shiny footrests. He tried not to stare but couldn't take his eyes off her spindly legs wrapped tight by sheer stockings, reminding him of Medic's description of the skeleton-like children in the concentration camps.

Shane felt sorry for her and thought that the better course was to play along with her kind, aged memory rather than correct her. "I played with Mel for about three years," he said.

She inhaled and let the smoke out. "I saw both of you on television, the night they turned on the lights at the Polo Grounds. It was a special night. Ethel Merman sang, "Take Me Out to the Ball Game." When she finished, fireworks went off over the scoreboard and you took the mound to throw a no-hitter. As I recall you drove in five runs that day and waved to me. I'll never forget. I only wish Abe had been there to see it, before they moved the stadium to… to California, as I recall."

"That was quite a day. Thank you for the memory, Mrs. Abernathy, but I need to get some rest now."

She took the cigar out of her mouth. "Would you like a puff?"

"No, ma'am, but thank you."

"You have a ballgame in the morning?"

Shane sighed through a smile. "It's in the afternoon."

"Well, get a good night's sleep, and let me know what channel you're on. I've got a television, you know. And if you're up early, I'll be on the porch. Remember, I wait for Abe every day starting at sunrise."

"I'll sure let you know," he said, reaching for the front door. Since he'd come back, he'd refrained from even mentioning Talley to anyone, but it came to him that Eunice's frail memory would probably be decent protection against anyone finding out why he'd returned. "Mrs. Abernathy, by any chance do you know a policeman here in town with the last name Talley, officer Talley. He's in the local…"

"Shhhh," she whispered, putting two fingers to her lips. Is there anybody coming up the Nook?"

"Not as far as I can tell."

She remained silent for so long Shane assumed she'd forgotten his question. He was about to wish her goodnight when she pointed at him and shook her finger. "Talley… dear officer Talley, the scourge of Meridien, though I might be the only one in a group of one who calls him so. To the joy of many in this town that no-good white man killed a young Black boy. It was some time ago, but Talley sits in my head like a rat in a dark crevasse."

Surprised that she'd come into the present so suddenly, Shane thought she was probably done until she put her fingers to her lips again. "Look yonder. Anyone in the alley?"

Shane glanced into the darkness. "No, ma'am. Not that I can see."

"I was at this new ballpark with fresh lights, I think on a plot of land granted by the Catholic Church. I was sitting there trying to follow the pitches, but they went too fast for me to see them. I thought for a while it was a Halloween trick or maybe I was at a game that wasn't really happening, if you get my drift. Well, I turned to this person sitting beside me to ask if he'd straighten things out for me, but as soon as I opened my mouth, I heard the boy scream. I heard it with my honest ears and so did everyone else but it didn't matter a whit to anybody else."

She took a long puff on the cigar, but Shane didn't wade in because he could tell she wasn't done.

"Days later when I was told what everybody said happened, I had a hard time believing it. It was very suspicious because I've lived in this town too long not to be. So, I took a bus down to the police department, along with my bow and arrow, to hunt down that piece of Satan and find out the truth. I filled the quiver with a bunch of arrows just in case one wouldn't be enough. They stopped me at the door and held me there laughing before they wedged me into the backseat of a cop's car and brought me back here. They said they'd forgive me this one time because I was elderly as a tree in the forest but they said if I ever showed up again, they'd put me in a cell without a cot."

"So, Talley's still here?"

Her eyes widened as she stared into the keyhole through the trees. "As far as I know, he's not. I'm told he left town not long after he killed that boy. Maybe the burden of his ways came down on him, like someday it'll come down on Abe, if he refuses to show up before I'm gone."

It took Shane a moment to remind himself of the poor woman's mind but his heart began to race. "Do you know where he went? Forgive me, I mean, Talley, not Abe?"

"Nobody knows for sure, including him most likely. Rumor has it that he became a drunk and went to the A-Cave."

"The A-Cave?"

"A natural cave behind one of the highest waterfalls in the Smokies. They call it the A-Cave because alcoholics and dope addicts go there when they've given up on life and are determined to die for their sins. If they can't be turned around in a given period of time, they're allowed to die in the arms of their caretaker, someone who cares about them and takes them on while respecting their wish to leave this earth. Most who go there die there, it's said. They take the bodies to Sliding Rock and for the last moment, slide them down the rocky slope so they can bounce into Heaven's arms, or so they claim. That's what they believe happened to Talley, and who knows, maybe to Abe as well."

"You did say that Talley, the cop, became a drunk and went off to this A-Cave to die?"

"A cop he never was, Mel, and never will be because now he's downstairs with the Devil, stoking the fires."

Her trips between then and now astonished Shane but made him wonder. "Are you sure about all this, Mrs. Abernathy?"

"I wouldn't have told you otherwise."

"But didn't you say it was a rumor?"

"Something people in a town like this called a rumor, you can count on being the truth. If you don't believe me, try asking down at the court, not the police station. No reason to go where the cops hide because they'll never tell you the truth. It'd be too embarrassing to admit that one of their kind, the worst of their kind, became a drunk and ran away to die. They ought to know down at the court and even if they lie about it, you'll be safe there."

Shane's heart was hammering his chest. "Thank you, Mrs. Abernathy. I'll let you know what I find out. Sleep well."

"Mel, please call me, Eunice."

"I'm sorry. Good night, Eunice."

Shane hurried into the living room where he had trouble finding the staircase because the drawn velvet curtains shut out the remaining daylight and trapped the darkness. He wanted to believe Eunice and yet he didn't want to believe her because if Talley was dead, he'd never be able to let go of his hatred and his need for revenge. He'd fed on them forever. If Talley was dead by any means other than at his doing, would there ever be any chance of forgiving himself for letting Jesse come to the game? He stumbled into his room wanting desperately to shout, "The bastard's still alive!" But he held back. Somehow he held back.

The room was tiny. The roofline dropped sharply down to the wainscoting, pinching his mattress into the slant. There was a small dresser with a buccaneer mirror flecked with gold mica and an old photograph of Mel Ott that he hadn't paid any attention too, until now. Mel was smiling beneath his Yankee cap, as if he, too, had heard the news that Talley had died and now was overjoyed.

Shane showered quickly and climbed into bed. With doubt surging in his mind, he fell asleep at last. As the day passed, he catapulted through his dreams. He caught sight of Suzanne sitting in the bleachers. Falling, rising and falling again with the changing wind, he soared toward her, but just as he was about to sweep her from the stands, Jesse's face flashed before him. For a moment so empty that he thought his heart had stopped, he jumped out of bed and rushed around the room sliding his hands frantically over the walls trying to find a light switch. A ghostly glow appeared in the window and he heard Medic ask in his Shakespearian drawl if Shane could see the dagger before his eyes, the handle toward his hand? Shane saw the image of his .45 on the table by Mel and clutched at the impression, but had it not.

He couldn't delay a moment longer. He threw on some clothes, stuck the gun in his jacket and rushed downstairs. Eunice was still on the porch.

"Are you late for the game?" she asked.

"I'm taking your suggestion and going by the court."

"By the court?"

"Yes, remember, a little while ago we were talking about Talley, and you suggested that I should check down at the courthouse to see what they say happened to him."

Her eyes widened. "You saw the bow and arrow and the quiver on the wall, yes?"

"Yes."

"Take them with you, in case he's there."

"Don't you worry, Eunice. I've got protection in my coat pocket."

Chapter Fifteen

With the dominance of the courthouse boosted by a dozen Doric columns at the top of at least a hundred cement steps, the courthouse reminded Shane of a painting of the Parthenon that Medic brought to class in the Spring of his senior year while studying Greek literature; Medic considered the playwrights to be the eternal masters of tragedy. He pointed out that the playwrights believed it was actually from tragedy that life abounded. It made little sense to anyone in the class, especially Shane, because Jesse had been killed the week before.

He locked the car and tapped his coat pocket to make sure the gun was there. He started to rush up the steps, caught himself and slowed down to take them one at a time. He had to control himself. He was in a hurry but there was no need to be. He didn't want to find proof that Talley was dead but in a far-flung way he didn't want to discover that the bastard was alive.

The building's heavy bronze doors were masked with gold paint. Beside the doors, Confederate Flags flapped their wings from the tips of two outreaching copper spikes. It was as though he was seeing the courthouse for the first time. On the day of Talley's trial he'd paid no attention to the building or the flags or even the haughty fifty-foot statue of Jefferson Davis, the eternally praised president of the Confederacy, who stood expressionless on his sculptured podium, hand on hip, his right foot raised and pointed as if he were wearing high heels. An obituary etched on a white maple plaque didn't declare him dead and pressed for everyone to eternalize him by keeping him in their prayers. Of course there was no inscribed plaque or statue in honor of Martin Luther King, who'd come to nearby Danville in the early Sixties only to be ridden out of town by the town's mayor, who'd rallied the police in order to "protect the town's heritage."

When Shane entered the building, the clacking of his boots echoed in the huge foyer. He remembered Suzanne's father warning him not to say anything in the hallway, for fear that the spooky echo might carry every word into the defense attorney's ears. A huge chandelier hung overhead, spreading an aura of gold light on group of Confederate soldiers, saluting in a painting on the wall. A framed Dixie flag hung on the wall beside them.

"Sir, may I help you?" A woman's voice rebounded softly off the walls before fading away.

To Shane's surprise, a young Black woman was sitting behind a worktable with a thick granite countertop. Her face was beautifully efficient, a face that relished files, lists, neatness and order in all its forms. A pair of enormous, silver-rimmed glasses widened her eyes, reminding him of Jesse's huge eyes, which according to Jesse's father were a gift from God, so that Jesse could see into a white man's soul and know his intentions.

"Sir, may I help you?" the woman repeated.

"Sorry," Shane said, "I was somewhere else for a moment. Yes, I have a question, but I'm not sure I've come to the right place or even what the right place is."

"Let's give it a try. I'm Brianna, by the way."

"Brianna, I'm Shane. You're very young and probably don't have any recollection of this, but by any chance would you happen to remember, several years ago, a young Black boy being killed by a cop out at Jefferson High School, by the baseball field?"

Her eyes widened with a sudden anxiousness. "Are you a reporter or an attorney?" Her words were carefully spaced.

"I'm neither."

"A cop, maybe?"

"Certainly not."

"Just curious," she said. "Why are you interested?"

Shane hesitated. In court the answer he was about to give would have had gotten him into a world of trouble. He cleared his throat. "Because the boy was my brother."

"Your brother?" she said in disbelief.

"Not by birth but… well, my father was a pharmacist and Jesse worked for him delivering prescriptions. And when my mother passed away, he asked Jesse if he'd take care of me when I came home from school every day. We became close friends and wound-up calling each other, brother."

Brianna glanced down the hallway, then leaned forward on her elbows. A look on her face jetted between worry and the desire to say something. The words rushed out. "I remember that day like it was yesterday," she said in a chilling, ominous tone. "After school I used to work down on Craighead, selling jars of homemade honey to rich white people who were scared of bees. When I got home that day, my mother was sitting in the kitchen with my dad, crying her eyes out. She'd taught Jesse in Sunday school and had gone to his baptism, or tried to. It was raining hard that Sunday and she hit a curb and blew out a tire on the way. She jumped out of the car and ran as fast as she could to get to the church on time, but when she got there the service was over, and she never forgave herself." Brianna took a quick look down the hallway and whispered, "The cops fined her fifty dollars for leaving her car unattended. Please come a little closer. I have to keep my voice down."

Dazed, Shane moved to the edge of the desk.

"Every night when I was a little girl she put me to bed, always tucking the covers tight under my chin before we prayed together, but the night Jesse was killed, her voice gave out midway through the prayer. Tears started dripping from her eyes onto my face, and she struggled to tell me what she'd heard from Boris Learner, a friend of hers, who worked at Jefferson, scrubbing floors and cleaning toilets. Have you ever heard his name mentioned?"

"No, never."

"Well, that day, when he was done with work, he was heading to the bus stop when he heard this blood-curdling scream. He took off in the direction of the ballfield and got there just in time to see a cop, a cop named Talley, slam Jesse into the trunk of his car and drive off."

As if she'd experienced every turn in the story, Brianna's eyes took on a look of absence. A long silence endured before she flinched as though she'd forgotten Shane was there. "Why did you come here?" she asked.

"To find out if Talley was ever brought to justice," Shane said, straying slightly from the truth. "I've been away ever since it happened and just wanted to know if justice was ever served."

Brianna's voice lowered to a whisper. "To put it kindly, they say that Talley brought justice to himself. Apparently, he became a drunk and the Department let him go. Fired is a better word, something I never would've thought could happen in this backwards town. They say that the day he killed Jesse whisky was as much to blame as his hatred for Black people. The story goes that after a while he went off to live in the Smokies, where his drinking got worse, and one day he committed suicide by throwing himself down a waterfall. So, in a way I guess you could say that justice was served but in a way it wasn't, and quite honestly, I don't expect it ever will be because when people kill themselves, they sometimes deprive others of life." She eased back into her chair.

"Nothing could be truer," Shane said, thinking of Suzanne.

The conflicting emotions he'd struggled with since hearing the story from Eunice vied for his attention, leaving him with nowhere to go. Realizing that Brianna would be expecting some expression of relief from him, he tried to mask his desire to tell her the truth about why he'd returned, but he checked the impulse. He'd not gotten the answer he wanted, but an answer he had to accept. What Brianna said corroborated what Mrs. Abernathy told him. It was all too bizarre to be anything but the truth.

He thanked Brianna in the spaces between his erratically beating heart and headed for the door. While it didn't seem that a lot had changed in Meridien, the fact that this woman had a job in the white man's world and that the Police Department had stepped up and fired Talley, gave him a confused sense of hope that maybe, just maybe, the town was beginning to creep in the right direction.

The moment he saw the Rambler, he threw his fists into the air and shouted, "The bastard's dead!" It attracted a smile from two suited white men that he took for attorneys on their way to the court. Jesse's murderer was dead! He couldn't wait to tell Suzanne but as he'd pledged and put on his list, first he had to share his excitement with Jesse, and what better place to do so than the place that haunted his dreams, a place more draining than the cemetery, the ballfield.

Chapter Sixteen

Though he would gain no forgiveness for what he'd failed to do, Shane hoped the message would resonate in Jesse's soul with excitement. The bastard who ended his brother's life on earth was dead!

Shane wound his way through the tinsel-laden holiday streets. When he arrived at the ballfield, he pulled off the road flabbergasted at what he saw. The field was barren, the mound so flat that the pitching rubber stood out like an abandoned cement block. Mounds of dirt were piled on a tractor-furrowed outfield. The thickly wired backstop lay broken and twisted in a bundle of confusion. The outhouse down the left field line sat with its door open, abandoned like a bunker from some forgotten beachhead. The centerfield light pole, shaped like a cross, was the past's only hand-me-down still in place, but the scoreboard over which it once hovered had collapsed. The outfield fence, bent like a wave, barely made its way from one foul line to the other. The bleachers were caving in. The screens across the announcer's booth were ripped open and the speakers attached to the corners of the booth were thrashed and drooping. On the face of the booth the word Enola was written in huge letters. The pines where Jesse had hidden were the same, no larger, no smaller, as though frozen in time. In a rush of cold wind his eyes started to water.

He looked at the familiar red brick buildings, the gym, the auditorium, the principal's office and remembered the time he'd spent in each, especially the principal's office where in his sophomore year he'd been called from class to explain to Mr. Blankenship, the vice-principal, why he'd been late to school three days in a row. "Because my mother has cancer and I have to feed her every morning so my father can go to work," he'd replied.

Shane remembered how the principal's eyes narrowed just before he relented and told Shane that he was excused. There would be no after-school punishment, as long as he made it to baseball practice every day.

His eyes returned to the field, hoping that he'd witnessed some crazed inversion of time and that the field would still be there in all its beauty, but no. It was as it had been a moment ago, empty, bleak, the woods still, time immobile, all forever trapped in the trees behind the right field fence.

Hesitant, he made his way down the foul line to the battered fence and stepped over a group of splintered slats piled on the ground. Fearing but hoping that he'd find some trace of Jesse, even a bloodstain or a velvet flower or a purple weed that had sprung from the nourishment of his blood. But instead, there were only thinly scratched lines in the dirt, crossed and grated, resembling the scratches on Mrs. Abernathy's porch and rug.

He stared at the marks and gradually they reassembled. When fully decrypted, he realized that they weren't scratches but distorted, abstract letters, dug with a shaky hand, spelling out the name, Jesse.

Someone had remembered. Maybe one of Jesse's parents or his older brother or possibly Brianna or her mother. It made no difference, at least someone had. Shane knelt, traced the letters with a finger and whispered, "Talley's dead, Jesse." It dawned on him that Jesse had never known his murderer's name. "Talley was the name of the cop who killed you, and he killed himself."

He wanted to shout out his joy again, but his shame for letting Jesse come to the game washed away the flimsy cover that Talley's fate provided. The verdict in the trial was a catastrophe for the de Ville family, and who would be more relieved, if not forever grateful, to learn about the bastard's fate than Suzanne?

Chapter Seventeen

That evening Shane drove to Blinder's in a state of eager anticipation. Talley's death was a disarming discovery that would be a hidden treasure for Suzanne and an endless rabbit hole for him, but when all was said and done, he had to put himself aside and let her know that her father had, in a way, won his case at last. His prediction that justice would be served had come to fruition.

The parking lot was packed, but he found an opening at the edge of the lot, facing the bay. The sun was slipping over the horizon. Its fading shafts lay on the ocean seemingly aloof from any concern about what he'd learned from Brianna. In a swath of color, the mist was thickening. Slowly, in a flowing metamorphosis, the channel's glassy water began to smoke out and a patchwork of pink and blue homes along the waterfront faded to gray. An ironic neon sign appeared over the entrance to the tavern. Lit in spacious layers of red, green and yellow, cordially inviting passersby to:

Stop for a round of Hope and Goodwill
on the way to
the Sanctuary of your home.

Shane hurried inside to look for Suzanne, but the room was so jammed that the couples on the dance floor appeared sewn to one another and he couldn't find her. Beer bottles clinked and hammered the bar. Several shouts of "Over here!" came from the tables squeezed along the wall. Above the bar the long minute hand of a huge clock lunged forward to six o'clock. Above the clock, what sounded like a miniature foghorn blared its warning six times, reminding Shane of the day he and Jesse went to the sawmill, and more patrons packed the floor. The warm air was filled with cigarette smoke, the stench of the men's sweat and women's perfume.

Even though Suzanne had told him about the waitress, he watched in wonder as a young woman dressed in a red apron and a ring of small but bright lights banded to her head, carefully followed a path routed by yellow ropes that veered off at thin posts sporting large wooden numbers. The dancing patrons were on guard as well, moving courteously away from the posts as she made her way through the labyrinth.

Shane was scanning the room hoping for an empty table when Suzanne surfaced above the crowd, standing on a table top on the far side of the room.

She'd been waiting for over an hour and had used the time to put a dent in a bottle of bourbon. She shouted for him and waved so frantically that despite her high heels, she started dancing. She wore a brightly sequined, hippy blouse and a sixties miniskirt that didn't seem out of place or dated because she'd blotched it with colors of purple, blue, green and gold. Despite the distance and her frenzy, their eyes fastened on one another. Momentarily, Shane disappeared into the crowd, suddenly emerged to lift her off the table and ushered her into a spare slot on the edge of the dance floor.

As they spun around, the happiness between them was tangible. Steppenwolf took everyone to the edge of frenzy with the rock hit, "Born to Be Wild." As the singer's voice ripped throughout the room and began to crescendo, Suzanne spun into the crowd, leaving Shane alone to dance with himself for a second and then hurry to catch up with her. A few beats later, like someone in a magic show, she re-emerged spinning from nowhere to stop by the Wurlitzer precisely on the last note of the song.

She pivoted toward the jukebox as the needle's arm lifted from the forty-five. She found her song and inserted a dime. Suspended somewhere between ecstatic and tearful, she watched as the record lowered onto the turntable. When Judy Collins's rendition of Suzanne began, Suzanne's cheekbones emerged in the Victrola's window. The orange glow from the machine's light shaded the smooth hollows of her face while lighting the tiny gold stars that hung from her ears. Her lips moved, and as if she were a child trying to utter an unfamiliar word, she hesitated and whispered her name and Shane's. The S sounds in their names weren't perfectly aligned but they were close enough.

Reaching through her reflection into yesterday, when they were on the trestle, she leaned into the mist. The room began to tilt. She flipped off her heels and planted her feet, doing her best to straighten as the lyrics rose.

When Shane rushed over to ask if everything was okay, she faced him with inquiring eyes, as though she had no idea who he was. She wanted to tell him to keep his distance, to tell him once again, hoping he could translate her message, that she'd only asked him to accompany her to the trestle to bear witness — no more than that. And then surprising both herself and Shane, she threw her arms around his neck.

"I've got something I want to tell you," he said.

"Please wait until the song's over."

Pleasantly pushed away from what he wanted her to know, he ran his fingers down the ridge of her spine to the taut slope of her rear. Her arms tightened around him. She wasn't concerned in the least because a crowded dance floor wasn't the place to take things any further, but she shivered and it spread like an infection. Quivering, she rose to her toes and drew him closer.

"Hang onto the music and onto me," she said, breathing on his neck and smiling as she remembered the story of his wound. They barely moved as she lifted her pelvis and pressed against him. She could feel his hardness. As the song played, her lips touched his ear and she whispered, "Do you know what the song's saying?"

"I think so. I get the words."

Her eyes rose to his. "Not the words," she said, leaning back to gaze into his eyes. "But between the words, when in that split second the moment ends, making way for another, in that flash of silence that sucks you in to tell you that it knows something you don't. It's your heart taking you on a journey with an imagined destination, like the sensation a little bird has when it leaves the nest."

"I'm not following," he said, again wondering how she came up with such things.

"Shhhh. Let the song settle around us."

When the needle lifted, she slipped into her heels and they shuffled back to the table. She was dizzy and her eyes blurry. It reminded her of being in The Lilly, she and her father dangerously far from shore in the rapidly changing ebb and flow of the waves riled by the harvest moon.

Breathing easier, they worked their way to the table. A piece of folded cardboard bearing the word, "Reserved", was in the middle of the table along with a pint of Jim Beam and two glasses, one containing a spoonful of whisky that she'd failed to finish. She turned the card over and pointed to her scripted handwriting on the corner of the card. The words were small and hard to decipher, written inside a penciled sketch of a whisky bottle whose maker's name had been omitted by rays of a fading moon she'd drawn above it.

"Watch," she said, raising the sketch so that the overhead light cast auburn shades on the words, bringing them to life. "A Beam of light for you in appreciation for going with me to the trestle!"

"Ho-ho, I get it," Shane said.

"Our wonderful waitress, See-Through, asked us to go easy on the booze, so that we could come together in a world apart but with a path that leads straight back to us. I don't know what led her to say such a thing, but how about a pour and then tell me what you wanted me to know."

He held off to take a swallow.

"Well?" she injected into his silence. "Are you going to tell me or do you need another shot?"

"Suzanne, you're not going to believe this, but…" He stopped, trying not to shout.

"But what, Shane?"

At last, his nerves joined with fervor and his heart erupted, "Talley is dead!"

"He's dead, is that what you said?"

"That's what I said. The son-of-a-bitch is dead!"

"How do you know?"

"Mrs. Abernathy told me last night, but sometimes she gets things confused, so I went down to the courthouse this afternoon to make sure. I started by asking this young Jamaican woman who works there, if she'd ever heard about a Black boy being beaten to death at the Jefferson ballfield, and her eyes lit up. She said that she remembered it like it was yesterday. I asked her if she knew what happened to the cop who killed him and she verified what Mrs. Abernathy…"

"Did somebody kill him?" Suzanne's voice interrupted with hope.

"If only I'd been that somebody," Shane said. "As it turned out, Talley was the somebody. Apparently, he killed himself. He was stone drunk down at this weird place in the Smokies and took it upon himself to slide down the rocks at one of the waterfalls, and that was the end of him."

Suzanne sprang out of her seat, hoisted her glass again and cried out, "Daddy, did you hear that! Sorry, I meant, Father, did you hear that!"

Shouting erupted, filling the room. The dancing came to an abrupt halt. Shane tensed, afraid everyone was responding to her toast and would want to know what in God's name she was referring to, but that wasn't it. At the end of the bar, shockingly, a fellow, maybe in his twenties, was frantically smacking the flippers of a pinball machine and cheering himself on as he scrambled to rack up enough points to hit the jackpot. The green and yellow lights on the machine blinked crazily, bouncing enthusiastically off the glass top, turning his pale face a freakish blue.

He was wearing dark, wrap-around sunglasses like those Shane had seen in photographs of Elvis. He even bore a slight resemblance to the icon. Curly dark hair trailed over his ears in an unkempt and heavy thatch. He wore a scuffed black jacket with sleeves rolled up to his elbows exposing a tattooed series of bronze-colored, coiled pipes like those bootleggers used to make homemade whisky. Emblazoned on the back of the jacket was a small pair of iridescent, praying hands. Below them, a saying read, "God helps those who help others."

Each time the machine rang up a series of bonus points en route to the jackpot, he shouted a nasal, "Hallelujah!"

The machine's bells suddenly screamed in unison. Coins spit out of slots on the side of the machine as if the contraption had had a gutful. Nickels and quarters spilled all over the floor. The player dropped to the floor, cheering and scurrying about under the machine to grab every coin. A dog woofed excitedly and jumped into the fray. When the coins stopped flowing and the bells began to fade, the guy climbed out from under the machine and came to his feet, grinning large.

The sack he'd made out of the tails of his jacket was sagging with coins. He hugged his winnings so they wouldn't fall out, bent over to kiss the golden retriever and grabbed the dog's yellow leash. The seeing-eye dog led him to the bar while the patrons applauded.

A thin, wiry waitress approached their table wearing goose feathers in her orange hair. A sharp red light beamed from the band wrapped around her forehead.

"Well, hello, Suzanne and welcome once again," she said. "Jacob, the bartender, told me you were here."

"Shane, meet See-Through, the wonderful waitress I told you about. See-Through what in the world just happened?"

"Rummy Ascot, at least that's what he calls himself, hit the jackpot. He's almost as blind as I am. I feel so good for him. Can I get you folks anything to eat?" She glanced at the bottle. "Or a little more to drink?"

"He's blind?" Suzanne asked, ignoring See-Through's question.

"Yes, he is. He was drunk and running homemade whisky one night when the truck he was driving ran off a bridge. To hear him tell it, the second he hit the water, he was 'blinded by Heaven's light' but only after he met Roland did he realize that the purpose God had in store for him all along was to devote his life to helping others, before himself. Roland heard Rummy's story and redid the alcove, which back then was being used for storage. He put in the pinball machine and set it to trigger more wins than chance alone would've granted. I'm sure you know about the gang called Whitewash, another name for the Klu Klux Klan. Well, Rummy was a member, until he met Roland."

Suzanne sat down and reached for the bottle. "Roland's the owner?"

"Yes. After the accident Rummy backed out of Whitewash because of Roland and paid a price. One night, those scum-bags beat the goodness out of Rummy over by the Masonic Lodge and dumped him outside Hotel Burton with the homeless gathered by the doorway. On occasion, Roland stops by the hotel to pray with the poor and leave them some change. When he showed up that night, Rummy was face down on the sidewalk and barely breathing. He managed to tell Roland what happened, and those among the hobos who could, helped get him into Roland's pick-up. He brought Rummy over here and put him up in the storage room where he blessed and fed him until he recovered."

"Is Roland here?" Suzanne asked.

"He went to get some supplies. We're short on mustard and ketchup and a few other things, but he'll be back in a while. He has to drive slow because not only is he partially blind but he drinks a bit, well, more than a bit, yet he says we never have to worry about him because he's got God on his side, for sure. Now, what can I get you two? Suzanne?"

"How about another pint for now? After all, it's a night to celebrate!"

"What's the cause, a birthday?"

"Emancipation Day, and we'll leave it at that," Suzanne said, smiling at Shane. "How 'bout a pizza?"

"Great," Shane said returning the smile. "Be back in a minute everyone. The restroom calls."

"Better hurry," See-Through said. "On break it gets plenty crowded."

As Shane disappeared into the crowd, See-Through put her hands on the table and leaned towards Suzanne. "Is he the fellow you mentioned the other night, the one your voice suggests you're drawn to?"

The honest answer skated on Suzanne's lips. More than anything she wanted to tell the truth and answer, yes, but she couldn't bring herself to because it would have been a misleading, though ironically truthful lie. She realized that the thought made no sense, that it was a foolhardy contradiction. But, when contradictions collide, she was taken to wonder if the result could be a discovery far deeper than the paradox itself. She wished she knew the answer. Dear God, she wished she did. Her hands began to shake, causing the glass to rattle on the table.

"Suzanne, you okay?" See-Through's voice floated on still air. There was no music, no chatter, only sound as fragile as a whisper and as forlorn as the tinkling of the chimes on the veranda.

"Just fine," Suzanne whispered. "And how about you, See-Through? Do you have a boyfriend?"

"I used to, but he's my husband now. I met him at the bar one night, not long after I went to work here."

"How long have you been married?"

"About two years. I don't have a ring, at least not one you can see. But for sure there's a ring around my heart. His name is Wren, like the bird. He's a traveling shoe salesman for Craddock and Terry and he's very handsome, by the way."

"How can you…?" The question was barely out of Suzanne's mouth when she felt her face flush and clinched her teeth. She wanted to stuff the words down her throat until she coughed up an apology, "Oh my God, I'm so sorry."

"I've been hoping forever that someone would ask me that, but no one ever has," See-Through responded with enthusiasm. "For folks like us love can't be what the other person looks like, but how we imagine them to be inside."

Suzanne felt her heart pulse. "But how do you know that it's love, true love, and not just the excitement of the first few days?"

"Because as time passes and true love emerges, we realize that love is about some of the good qualities we have deep inside ourselves but have no access to. In essence, we fall in love with the person we aren't completely, but want to be. And all the while we must find not only the courage to admit it, but the strength to stay with it, and if we do, the access to our hidden selves opens."

The grandfather clock clicked off the last seconds leading up to six. When it reached the hour, it clanged like a church bell and See-Through straightened. "Now, let's get to some real bar talk and not that of the prophets. I'm off for your pizza and whisky. I'm sure you've learned never to ask me another question."

Suzanne forced a soft laugh through her astonishment. She watched as See-Through made her way along the labyrinth of paths. What she'd said brought to mind the unyielding moment in Medic's driveway when she and Shane stood staring at one another. Had the two of them remained quiet and still while attempting to see inside themselves and one another in an effort to identify the qualities that they'd always cherished, but had no access to? Or was that too much to ask, or even to suspect? But with Talley gone, had the barricade between them fallen? Would their bond now somehow diminish the unremitting demand in her father's eyes?

She finished her glass with a deep swallow.

Chapter Eighteen

Suzanne came out of her confusion to applaud when she saw Shane making his way back to the table.

"Sorry it took so long, but the restroom's for both men and women, so there was quite a line," he said.

"Leave it to a woman to keep things in-line. Otherwise, men would be lost," Suzanne said, welcoming him with a chuckle. "Glad you're back. Shane, I can't believe it. Talley is dead! The murdering son-of-a-bitch is dead!"

Shane raised his glass. "Yes!"

"When did it happen?"

"I'm not sure, maybe two or three years ago," Shane said

"If only my father had known."

"Maybe he does," Shane said.

"Then, he should've told me."

Before they had a chance to thank God again and invite Him to clink glasses, See-Through's bright red beam cut through the path it created. She set a thick-crusted pizza on the table. "I know the timing's probably not right but if you want, I can share Roland's story with you while you start your dinner. He lets us take the time-out to tell it but only after our guests have been served."

Suzanne and Shane glanced at each other and nodded.

"Go right ahead," Shane said, filling both glasses. "Meanwhile, if it's not too impolite, I'm going to start on the pizza. But first, let me pay you before I forget," he said, reaching for his wallet.

"No, no. You're paying me by listening. Roland not only encourages us to share his story, but he feels that it has to be shared, and if I do, he'll pay me an extra fifty cents."

"Let's hear it," Shane said.

"I'll be quick." She took a deep breath. "He was a poor and distraught drunkard living down in Greensboro years ago, when he was ousted by his church for preaching his own version of the gospel, which flew in the face of the church's version. During the Sunday service, he'd sit outside in his pick-up truck, drinking and trying to come up with his own sermon for the day. When church was about to let out, he'd go up on the steps to greet the parishioners leaving the church and would start preaching to them. If they shoved past him, he'd yell at them and accuse them of turning their backs on God."

"What did he preach?" Suzanne asked.

"The sixty-four-dollar question. When you ask him, he says that he has a hard time remembering because of the state he was constantly in, but hopes that it was about finding the good in life that God gives us. 'Be proud of who you are and grateful for what you have because big or small, we can't take His gifts with us when we go,' is how he puts it to anybody sitting at the bar who happens to be down in the dumps and complaining about their lives. And I mean anybody, even members of Whitewash, before they left town."

"Excuse me, See-Through," Shane said. "Whitewash left town?"

"Pretty recently, to settle down in Malville. It's said that they needed more recruits, more hatefuls if you will, and had to have a bigger town to draw from." See-Through took a deep breath. "I'm sorry to ask, but could I take a sip of your whisky before going on, that is if I'm not boring you to death?"

"You're certainly not boring anyone. Help yourself," Suzanne said, reaching out to place See-Through's hand on the bottle.

See-Through grinned and sipped. "The touch of a hand. A little encouragement goes a long way. Here goes. Back when the church ousted him, Roland left town for the Smokies, to this strange healing place called the A-Cave."

Shane straightened. "Did you say, A-Cave?"

"I know it sounds weird, but yes. Apparently, it's a cave up behind what they call the Healing Waterfall where alcoholics and addicts who've given up on life go to recover, or if it be their will, where they go to leave this earth. The choice is theirs."

Shane and Suzanne glanced at one another with the same question. "Did Roland ever mention meeting a person in the A-Cave by the name of Talley? Years ago he was a cop in Meridien," Shane asked.

"I've never heard him mention that name. We can save the rest of the story for later, if you like."

"No, no. Tell us now," Suzanne said.

See-Through hesitated for a moment and then rushed to tell the story. She began with Roland being found on his deathbed in the A-Cave by a partially blind, young Amish woman, Owah, a self-proclaimed mystic.

In her mid-twenties, she'd become repulsed by the restrictive values of the Amish, especially the forbiddance of marriage to anyone outside the religion, less they be excommunicated. Owah would have nothing to do with it because she fiercely believed that love was a matter of choice, as were all decisions in life.

One day in this rickety buckboard wagon she'd been assigned to repair, she found a deck of Tarot cards and while shuffling through them became enchanted with their mystical beauty. She'd heard about a soothsayer who lived nearby in a shed on the road to Lancaster. Hoping that if she could learn the meaning of the cards and how to play the game, it might serve as a helpful distraction from her daily life. But through the seer's teachings she learned that Tarot served a much greater purpose than just distraction. It served to give a sense of new direction to a person's life.

She began playing the cards endlessly in the loft of the Amish barn. Her revulsion for the religion became rebellion, and she left the settlement determined to become her own person. She ventured off to Las Vegas to become a card dealer. In her mind it was the ultimate reprisal. She called the decision her 'intended accident,' when we do things we know are wrong but just can't help ourselves and do them anyway.

One night she woke up in an alley of trash cans. She'd been beaten by a gambler who'd made a huge bet at her table and blamed her for dealing him the losing card. From then on, her purpose in life became dealing hope and good fortune to others, even if it meant helping those who were determined to die in order to fulfill their purpose. But she held onto an exception. She would do her best to help save those whose intention to die wasn't what it should be because they had far more to live for, more to give. She knew because as a mystic she felt that she could see below the surface, into the transparency of their souls where she believed truth resides, enabling her to go against their wish to leave this life and resurrect them beforehand.

"Helping those who are determined to die." The words replayed in Suzanne's mind. She'd helped her father, and at the same time, she'd committed an act of treason. She remembered Medic quoting T.S. Eliot when the class had finished, Murder in the Cathedral. 'The last act is the greatest treason. To do the right deed for the wrong reason.' She tightened her grip on the glass.

"Owah heard about the A-Cave and went there to follow her true mission, to help the down-and-outs, those who'd been unfairly or fairly blamed for their mistakes, to become worthy of forgiveness in the next life, or help them return to this one while accepting their sins, trusting that if they could revisit the past, they would never do the same thing again."

See-Through glanced toward the clock. "I'm sorry, but what time is it?"

"Six-twenty-five," Suzanne said, barely able to

"I have to get back to work, so here goes. At the A-Cave, Owah came to believe that Roland had turned a huge leaf, meaning that instead of dying he wanted to spend the rest of his life helping others, though not without his whisky. And to fully test the strength of his convictions, she took him to the rock slide and whisked him down the flume to see if he'd fight to survive. The pounding half-blinded him, broke his nose, split his cheek bone and left a scar across his face that looked like a snake, and not only did he survive but became determined to put his needs aside to help others. In time, he got word about an unknown luncheon stop called Roadies that was going out of business. As it turned out, the owner agreed to trade the shop to Roland in exchange for a part of the profits. After Roland met Rummy and converted him to mend his ways, he changed the name to Blinder's. The rest is what it is."

The music started and See-Through let out a deep breath. "Before I go, give a look toward the clock. Is there a big burly man sitting at a table right below it?"

Shane stood up to see over the dance floor. "Yes, there's this huge guy hunched over a table."

"He made it back from his errands. Great," See-Through said. "Is he playing chess?"

"Chess? He's so bent over it's hard to tell," Shane said.

"He likes to stay close to the board because he says it lets him smell his breath, and when the smell gets too thick, he stops drinking for the night. He plays solo most of the time but sometimes, when things are slow, he lets me join him."

"Did he learn to play chess down in that cave?" Suzanne asked.

"No, I taught him."

Shane and Suzanne looked at each other with "what?" in their eyes.

See-Through responded to their silence with enthusiasm, disclosing how she'd grown up in a foster-care home just outside Burkeville where she'd learned both Braille and chess at the popular Eye Protection Center. Worried that his bad eye was getting worse, one day Roland went to the Center for help. As soon as he walked in the door, he saw See-Through in the reception area playing chess by herself, while staring into space as her fingers roamed the board searching for the next move.

Roland asked her if she would teach him to play. She told him that she'd be happy to, but if he wanted to play well, it would take about six months of training, assuming they played every other day at a minimum. To avoid driving endlessly to Burkeville and with the idea of goodness having been restored in his heart, he offered her a job as a waitress and went about to rearrange the tables and make paths for her in the bar while paying her rent.

"Feel free to go over and ask him about the policeman you mentioned. He'll welcome you, but if he's playing chess, let him finish before you say anything. It's always interesting to see if Roland beats Roland, or the other way around, as he puts it. Shout for me, if you need anything."

"Will do," Suzanne said, watching See-Through follow her headlight as it cleared the path.

Shane stood up. "I'll be back in a minute."

"Hold on," Suzanne said, "I know what you're doing but why do you need another confirmation, especially after what the lady at the courthouse told you?"

"Who was it Medic quoted who said, 'Doubt can only be removed by action?'"

"Goethe."

"Jesus, Suzanne. If I had one percent of your memory, I could remember my last name."

She smiled and as Johnny Cash's "Ring of Fire" gathered steam, she raised her glass to Shane. "Go forth, MacDuff," she said.

Chapter Nineteen

Shane nudged through the crowd as the welcoming neon sign wilted into a swirl of lime vapor. Blocked for a moment by two couples crossing in front of him to get to the floor, time began to hang ridiculously on the hope that in a few minutes he would never again have the slightest doubt that Talley was dead, thereby sealing the truth as firmly as the iron bars laid across the front of his father's drug store. And yet, what to make of the unlikely coincidence that Roland and Talley were in the A-Cave at the same time?

Roland's stout arms rested on the table, surrounding the chess board. On the opposite side of the table, stood four empty beer bottles and a fifth of vodka. Felt-green shirt-cuffs hung open around his wrists. His chair had an enlarged seat and a backing wide enough for two people. Shane edged his way to the opposite side of the table. Roland's furrowed forehead was partially hidden behind a black mask covering his left eye, turning him into a pirate. A bulging cheek bone below the eye lifted the snake-like scar on the side of his face. He appeared lost in the game, or as See-through had warned, in his booze. His stubby fingers thumped the table as Johnny Cash's voice continued to reverberate through the room.

"You play chess?" Roland asked. He snorted in irritation, keeping his head down as Shane's shadow covered the board.

"I didn't mean to interrupt your game," Shane said. "I'll come back when you're done."

As Roland's head rose, the flesh on the battered side of his face tightened, narrowing his lips and turning his mouth into a grimace.

"Sit down but hold off for a second. I have to make a move." He reached to castle the dark queen and turned the board around to move a white pawn forward while knocking a bishop onto the floor.

Shane picked up the piece and handed it to him.

"Thank you, young man. It happens a lot. I'm part blind from what's called an intended accident."

Owah's wording resonated. "An intended accident?" Shane said.

A brief smile helped Roland's mouth flatten out. "Doing what I knew was wrong. So that I might graduate," he said.

"From where?"

"Life's highest level, it's very end. You know where that is?"

Before Shane could stumble over an answer, Roland came to his aid. "You haven't lived long enough to know. But someday when you least expect it, it'll come to you. Enough for now." He said as he turned the board around again and moved a black knight into its peg in an open space.

"I saw you talking with See-Through. Did she tell you the story of my perils?"

"In detail," Shane said, "Starting with this place in the Smokies called the A-Cave."

Roland's eyes narrowed. "Ah, did she send you over here believing that you needed help with dope of booze or staying alive? You do seem affected. It's in your voice."

"No, sir. I just wanted to know if…"

"If the A-Cave's a good place to go and figure it out? I'll tell you straightaway, it is. Do you know how to get there?"

"I don't really need to know. I'm not planning to go there. I just came over to ask if when you were there, you ever met a certain person… a person See-Through said went there to die, a police officer, named Talley. He was once a cop in Meridien. He killed a Black boy by the name of Jesse Willip, a close friend of mine…" Shane paused. "So close that I thought of him as… as…"

"Your brother."

Time stopped. For a moment Shane felt disoriented and then realized he was staring at Roland through incredulous but searching eyes. He bore no resemblance to Talley, none whatsoever. His weight, his bulging face, his so-called desire to help others, by none of these measures could the person on the other side of the table be Talley. But no one else, other than Aiken or Spangler or Suzanne's father, could have completed the sentence, unless it had been leaked from the courtroom.

Roland shifted back and forth in his chair. On the verge of tipping over, he settled down and took a swig of vodka. His wet lips trembled. "I knew the bastard you're referring to. No question about it, he came to the A-Cave to die, but a very special person, a seer named Owah saved him." Roland's voice was weakening and he shuddered as if a high fever was spreading throughout his body. "She shuffled a deck of cards and spread them over him… and then… introduced the man called, Talley, to himself."

There was a tremor in Roland's voice. What Suzanne had said about a song's meaning being not in the words but in the silence between them struck Shane. "Was that you, Roland?"

Roland grabbed at his chest. Spit bubbled over his lips. He twisted in the chair, banged at the table until his legs came out from under and leaned over, coughing between his knees.

See-Through appeared with a glass of seltzer water. "Here, Roland."

Roland pushed against his knees and struggled to his feet. "Be back in a minute. Gotta get some fresh air." He stumbled away from the table toward the entrance.

"Don't you go driving anymore," she warned.

As Roland lumbered toward the entrance, Shane shoved out of his chair. Suzanne rushed over to ask See-Through if she knew what was going on. The waitress told her not to worry, that Roland most likely had had a lot to drink and Shane was probably trying to keep him from driving.

When they stepped out onto the porch, Shane grabbed Roland's shoulder. He turned toward Shane with both fear and sadness in his eyes. Blood rushed into Shane's head. He was aware of his own weight, a mounting density and shrinking locus, as if he were caving in upon himself. His muscles drew tighter and tighter until they threatened to pull away from his bones. Everything was compressing quickly into smaller and smaller spaces until he felt as compact as the core of a baseball. For one sharp moment he felt the heaviness of Jesse's body being thrown into the trunk of Talley's car. Just when he thought his skull was going to explode, he stuck his finger in Roland's face.

"You're the son-of-a-bitch, aren't you?"

Roland's confused eyes searched Shane's for some sign that he had no idea what he was talking about.

"Jesse Willip, remember him, the Black boy. You beat him to death, didn't you?"

The light from the welcoming sign boosted the alarm in Roland's eyes.

"In case you don't recognize me, officer Talley, I happened to be the boy who testified against you at the trial."

Roland's face was quivering like a child's who thought it had seen a ghost. "I have to go now."

"You're going alright, straight to Hell!" Shane exclaimed as his years of pent-up rage burst out. Why hadn't he jumped the fence that day with a bat in his hand, knocked Talley's fucking head over the scoreboard and paraded around the bases as if he'd hit a grand slam? His voice erupted louder than before, "Damn your soul!"

He sank his fist into Roland's stomach. Before a groan could escape his mouth, Shane jerked his fist out of Roland's gut and landed a hook against his cheek, then instantly uppercut his chin with the heel of his hand. Blood spurted out of Roland's mouth. He dropped onto the porch and curled up as tightly as his huge body would allow. With the toe of his boot Shane delivered a kidney punch. Squealing and snorting like a pig, Roland tried to crawl off the porch. He collapsed and grabbed at his back, but his hand couldn't reach around the waves of fat. His painful, silent scream was lost in the breath that rushed out of him.

Shane had learned how to fight and kill in the Marines and none of his skills were to be wasted here. He didn't give a damn if he was shot on the spot or put in the electric chair, as long as he killed the bastard. He straddled Roland's back and seized his throat in a chokehold. Shane was aware of how long a victim could breathe given the amount of pressure applied, and as his grip tightened he knew Roland only had a few seconds left. He heard him trying to gasp and squeezed tighter.

"You not only killed him but you saw to it that his body was sent down the Mal so all your Whitewash friends could laugh. "You motherfucker!" Shane gripped harder, waiting for that last submissive breath.

"No, no. Please, God..." Talley rasped.

"God doesn't listen to murderers!" Shane grilled into Talley's ear, waiting for his body to go limp.

Suzanne exploded through the entrance and threw herself against Shane. She toppled across his shoulders, yet recovered in a heartbeat to throw her arms around him.

"Stop, Shane! Let him go! Don't trade your life for his! I won't be able… to… love you."

Her enflamed voice lashed his ear. Despite the blaring music, the sound of the word love pierced his anger. He'd never heard her say the word, though he'd felt it in her breath in the driveway and in its memory a dozen times since. Astounded, he lost his focus and glanced at her. Alarm beamed from her eyes, and his grip on Talley loosened slightly.

"Is he dead?" she asked, her voice still frantic.

Shane eased the chokehold and rolled Roland onto his back.

Tremulous and struggling to breathe, Roland murmured, "I'm sorry, I'm sorry."

Mouths agape, Shane and Suzanne looked at one another, asking, as if in some contrived way fate had outdone itself and faked the words for its own enjoyment.

Talley's chest rose and fell in short bursts. "He's in… Blackberry Hill, never in the Mal," he stammered. "I buried him at the top, so Jesus… wouldn't have any trouble finding him."

Shane grabbed Talley by the collar and jerked his head off the floor. "Don't you dare make a joke out of what you did."

"I'm not… making a joke," he said in a voice of deep sorrow. "I bought the plot next to his… for when I join him."

Sweat was streaming down Shane's forehead. "You lying son-of-a-bitch, you did what?"

"The night after I took him to Sill's, I took him to the graveyard and buried him. Please, please believe me."

"In Blackberry Hill?" Shane said in disbelief, "Where the graves are so shallow the coffins come out of the ground? Is that the place you mean?"

"His plot is deep, twice six feet, I dug it deep so that could never happen," he said as his voice recovered. "His grave's marked with a tall cross I made when I came back from the Smokies, made it with part of an old telephone pole the power company had brought down."

"Bullshit!"

"He's telling the truth, Shane," Suzanne said.

"How would you know?"

"Because…" She held her breath and forced it out. "Because he has the same look in his eyes as my father when, when he was denied… Roland must stay on this earth until he's earned it."

"You're not making sense, Suzanne. Earned what?"

"The right to die."

It made no sense whatsoever. If ever anyone had the right to go straight to the head of the sufferers' line, it was Talley.

Tears collected in Talley's bloodshot eye. He tried to sit up but couldn't make it to his elbows. "I was drunk and sleeping in my car the day they routed me to the ballfield. I've never been able to get it out of mind." He rolled his head back and forth on the porch. "The sound of the boy's cheekbones cracking keeps me awake at night, sometimes all night. To this day it's hard to say his name. My shame won't allow it."

Shane squeezed his neck. "Jesse! His name is Jesse Willip. Say it, goddamn you!"

Talley's chin lifted toward the roof. "Jesse," he whispered. "Jesse Willip." A smile came to his lips. "I was wrong, so wrong. I tried to stand up and tell them in court that the boy didn't attack me with a hoe. He didn't attack me in any way, and those so-called witnesses who said that he did lied out of hatred for Black folks, but Aiken wouldn't let me say anything. I've spent my life paying for it, but there's no forgiving me, not by anyone, including God, and there shouldn't be."

"Let's get him back inside," Suzanne said.

Reluctantly, Shane helped her bring him to his feet and, with an arm around his shoulder, they walked them inside and sat him at his table. The bartender rushed over with a towel. "What happened, Roland?"

"Nothing happened to him," Talley answered, separating his soul from Roland's. "He watched when I fell over the railing. Too much whisky. Thank God for these two. Otherwise I might've gotten run over." Squinting to see through the veil of cigarette smoke, Suzanne took Shane's hand. "It's time to go."

They glanced at each other, agreeing that there was no more to say, no more left silent that should be said or even could be. The moment lay on its sword. They left, cutting a path of silence through the noise.

Shane walked Suzanne to the Tiger. Just before she climbed on, the fleeting look between them became a stare. She was lost inside the mystery. She wondered where Shane had found the strength to let Talley go? From within or had he done so because of her? Was he as strong as she'd taken him to be or weaker than she would have ever imagined?

"There's more to this, isn't there Shane, more than just Talley? I can feel it. I can see it in your eyes," she said.

Shane took out his wallet and removed Jesse's picture.

She stared at the photograph. "Shane, in your heart is where he should be and where he should stay," she said, sorting through the thought that had just come to her. "But, he no longer has to be in your conscience. You've got to try and summon the courage to let him out. I know Jesse loves you and wants the two of you to love one another without anything in between, no shame, no hatred, no grief. Love without a conscience, pure love."

Shane had no answer. Jesse followed him everywhere. Could he ever forgive himself for letting him come to the game? And even if he could, would he? It would be hard, if not harder than letting Talley live. He searched the sky in frustration. "I don't know what you mean," he said.

"I know you're going to stick this under your completely certifiable label for me, that being insanity, but would you possibly meet me tomorrow afternoon at the ice plant?"

"The ice plant? What?"

"If you come, I'll try to help explain. Until then, I'll spend every minute of the night and day thinking of you."

"Suzanne, what's wrong with you?"

"What's wrong with me, you ask?" she asked back. "You don't want to know."

Her lips came toward his. He thought their first kiss was on the way and reached for her face. It was a kiss and then it wasn't. She turned her head slightly and their mouths glided past one another's and their cheeks brushed.

"Tomorrow I hope to have a gift for you, Shane, perhaps from Iceland." She laughed as though she'd just played a savvy joke on herself, then quickly mounted the Tiger and gave it a jumpstart.

As she pulled away from Blinder's, she glanced back, knowing that if she'd been Shane, she couldn't have spared Talley, any more than she could spare herself for what she'd done to her father. She simply didn't have the strength. Strength. That was it in a word, strength, what she desperately needed but had no access to, the strength to put the past in its place.

Chapter Twenty

Back at The Oleander, Shane sat on the edge of his bed trying to wrap his mind around what had taken place at Blinder's. He didn't turn on the light because he didn't want to see Mel Ott smiling back at him. Nothing seemed to make any sense. If it hadn't been for Suzanne, he would have killed Talley. And yet Talley's confession stunned him. Had the bastard told the truth when he said he'd purchased a grave for Jesse and in doing so, saved him from Whitewash?

Shane had been a young boy in knickers the night his mother told him about the fates of Black people when they died. He couldn't sleep afterward and kept seeing the silhouettes of shovel-carrying gravediggers wandering the grounds of Blackberry Hill. Now, unable to break away from the horrible reflection, he closed his eyes.

Walking the uncontrollable precipice between sleep and waking, he darted from the graveyard to the ballfield, then to Blinder's and to Medic's and from there into a world where Suzanne, Jesse and Talley joined to harass him. He wound in and out of the unfinished nightmares unable to tell when he was awake or asleep. As his heartbeat slowed, time, fatigue and whisky brought him sleep.

When morning came and he surfaced into the daylight, he wanted to hold onto the belief that he was free from what he'd failed to do, but Suzanne was right, he wasn't. He had to remove Jesse from his conscience, but not his heart. He had to forgive himself in order for it to happen and he had no idea how that would ever come to pass. But if he could find a way, it would be a gift to the three of them. Where he had to start struck him like a smack in the face. He didn't want to go to Blackberry Hill, but he had no choice.

Two blocks after Hadley's Amoco, he turned down Dibrell into Almegro, the shamefully named Black village packed with shanties, several of them still piles of wood, reduced to rubble when Hurricane Enola came through years ago. In Almegro the pavement quickly dissolved into dirt and gravel. Shanties stood propped up in a long train of lean-to's that looked like jungle huts made of splinters. Even in the freezing cold, wash hung on the porch rails and on clotheslines strewn from house to house because there were no trees. The hardscrabble ground made it impossible to tell where one lot ended and the next one began. A rusty Dodge chassis lay flat on the ground with mustard weed growing in the door panels. In the yard next door, an old Studebaker with long running boards rested on cinder blocks. The hood was up and the engine gone. There were outhouses in front of some of the shanties, a few with doors missing or hanging ajar. In front of one house, with a half-dozen busted panes, a rail-thin dog was curled up in a hole. Shane hit the brakes and jumped out of the car.

Caked with dried mud up to its girlie eyes, the doggy looked as if she was inside a body cast. At the sight of Shane, her red eyes widened in fear. She shook and slurped frantically at the air as Shane scraped off the mud. The mutt had huge ears and big paws which made Shane think that she was a Bassett hound. She licked Shane on the cheek and scrambled out of his hands to run away, stepping on her ears, tumbling over and woofing as she regained her balance. Shane watched as the she scrambled up the broken steps of a shanty to the front door where she began to yap. The door opened and she scooted inside. As Shane got into the Rambler, he said, thank you, not to himself but to the heavens.

The entrance to Blackberry Hill was guarded by an ethereal Black angel whose wings were draped caringly over the corners of a tombstone that bore the name of Harriet Tubman, the resolute woman of bravery who'd led slaves and abolitionists through what came to be known as the underground railroad, her ninety-mile pathway to freedom, the very pathway that he and Jesse had tried to find several times by sneaking down the outdoor library steps into the stone tunnel that was rumored to have been part of her passageway.

The angel cast a scythe-like shadow over the tombstone, deepening the etching of her name. The heroine wasn't buried here. The monument had been built by the followers of Martin Luther King not long after he stopped briefly in Meridien on a journey through the South to speak for the freedom and equality of Black Americans. Using a bullhorn to project his voice, Dr. King spoke from the steps of the Southern Library, once a mansion that housed Jefferson Davis a month or so before the South surrendered. Whitewash and many other white protestors showed up, offering slandering and threatening howls as King spoke about the town and how, if Blacks could not be free in Meridien, they could not be free anywhere.

Whitewash was infuriated that Judge Aiken, in a surprising decision, had given approval for the angel. Aiken was outspoken on the matter, claiming that he allowed her to remain to avoid the attention of the reporters from The Richmond Times Dispatch who were closely following King. The judge worried that the reporters could influence the local politicians to shut down Meridien's mills due to the flotillas of poison dye the plants so often released.

"I will allow the angel, but it shall remain white," Aiken had ordered. But it was not to be. The night the angel was put in place it was painted black by Whitewash. Not wanting to rouse the attention of either side, Aiken let it be.

Behind the angel, leaning against her gown, was an elderly Black man with weathered skin. He appeared to be trying to stomp a cough out of his chest. He slipped a Mason jar filled with what Shane assumed to be whisky, from the pocket of his mangy wool coat, unscrewed the cap, took a swallow and coughed some more.

"Excuse me, Sir," Shane said.

The man didn't show any concern or surprise. "You know that saying. It ain't the cough that's gonna carry me away, but the coffin. To avoid going with me, keep your distance, young man," he muttered in a deep but hollow voice, shooing Shane away with his empty hand.

Shane waited until the coughing settled down. "Sir, are you the guard here?"

"That's me, the guard of a graveyard but not of all mankind. Any other question?"

"Just a quick one. I'm here to try and find the grave of someone I knew… a friend of mine."

The man's eyebrows lifted. "A friend of yours in a Black cemetery? Was he buried here by mistake?"

"His last name is Willip, Jesse Willip. Would you happen to know where he's buried?"

The man's eyes froze, staring at Shane, and after a moment they softened as he smiled with deeply stained teeth set in broken rows along his gums. "First of all, you're old enough to know that you should never call a Black man, 'Sir.' It could get you in deep trouble if certain white folks overheard you. Second of all, I know the boy you're looking for and where to find him. He was buried in a deep grave by a digger who bought the plot with coins that mighta been lent to him by Judas. Whitewash didn't send you here to dig him up, did they?"

The man's tone lay somewhere between sarcasm and worry. Shane was on the verge of asking if the digger had been Talley, but caught himself. "Jesse was a friend of mine. I've been away almost since the day he left us and I came back recently to pay my respects."

"To come here to pay your respects to a Black boy makes me think most likely you're the first white man ever to do such a thing in this town. You deserve a taste of this here. It's straight out of my nephew's oil can."

Not wanting to offend him, Shane accepted the offer but sipped lightly. The hooch was thinner than it appeared but tasted like kerosene. He didn't think he could get it down but grimaced and chugged up some spit to help it trickle through his throat. Coughing harshly, he handed the jar back to the guard.

"I know how it hits you," the man said, grinning. "It's like drinking from the Mal, but it'll clear out your bowels quicker than oatmeal."

"I appreciate it. Thank you," Shane panted while wanting to laugh. "But I'd better get on my way. Could you tell me where to find his grave."

"Every daddy knows how to get to his son's grave, or by Jesus, he should."

"Daddy? You… you were Jesse's father?" Shane said, stunned. He'd never met any member of Jesse's family because they'd always worried about what might happen if Whitewash found out.

"Not were his daddy, but still am," the man said. "And his momma, Elise, is still his mother. Include his brother, Jason, who lives out in St. Louis and refuses to come back to this town because of what happened to Jesse, and our family still numbers four, as it always has. We ain't about to subtract one just because he's living up high." He glared at Shane. "And who might you be, other than a white man taking his life in his own hands by spending time wandering in a Black cemetery. Here, give me your hand and close your eyes."

Shane hesitated.

"Just do it. I ain't gonna hurt you. You know what miasma is for a Black man? I know, it's too strange a word to know the meaning of, but give me an answer anyway."

"I don't have any idea."

"Some say it's a wounded soul afraid to return home due to the evil that's been done to it. Others say it's the shadow of revenge hovering over a grave until the wrong's made right. Sometimes, when the damp rises just so from the ground and mixes with the evening sun, you can get a glimpse of the shadow turning purple. Other times you might feel it as sort of a dry wetness, like moss at evening time." His grip tightened and let go. "There," he said, "feel that?"

Shane rubbed his fingers together. "They're wet," he said, amazed.

"Look a'there. You felt it. Now what you have to do is figure out how come?"

"Either the wet air or sweat from your hands, I guess," Shane said.

Jesse's father opened his hands. "Dry as a bone," he said. "It'll come to you when you're most in need of help. By the way, my name is Saul. I come from Tarsus. What's yours?"

"Peter, from Galilee," Shane said, smiling. "Just kidding, I'm Shane, Shane McCauley."

The look of surprise on Saul's face rivaled Shane's when Saul told him that he was Jesse's father. "When something's so hard to believe, you can be sure it's true," he said. "Once, Jesse told us that you were his new brother, given that his older brother got married and has forever refused to come back to Meridien." Saul bowed his head, then raised it slowly. "Jesse loved you, Shane McCauley."

Shane's heart filled with gratitude. "I loved him and I always will. I think about him every day." The tone of Shane's voice was an octave above a whisper as he searched for a way to say what he wanted to keep inside.

"Don't hold back, son," Saul said. "Worrying about hurting somebody's feelings shouldn't ever get in the way of speaking the truth. What was it you were about to say?"

"I was on the mound the day…" Shane glanced at the angel and swallowed the word, killed, but it wouldn't stay down. "The day Jesse was killed."

Saul didn't flinch. "I know you were because until that day he'd never been to one of your games, but that day he came right out and asked us if he could go. We knew the rules here in town, so we said he couldn't, but he was so excited he wouldn't stop begging us. When he told us why it meant so much to him, Elise said, 'all right, then go.' While I wasn't so sure he should've, I went along with it."

Saul stopped to take a swig before looking over Shane's shoulders with distant, unfocused eyes. "If we'd just said no and stuck to it… if only we had, but there was so much more in Jesse's voice than just wanting to go to a baseball game. Momma and me both could hear it. On one level I imagine it was love, love for you, his white brother, and on another level it was his love for the game. Then, too, it was excitement and pride for what you'd let him teach you. Put 'em all together and we've managed to leave blaming ourselves behind, though sometimes, I admit, it's hard."

Shane didn't know what to think. Were Jesse's parents to blame or was he, or were they both? Saul and Elise had the chance to stay their ground and keep Jesse home. How then, how in Christ's Name, had they put it behind them?

"How did you and Mrs. Willop…"

Saul answered before Shane could finish. "Because Jesse had to see if you could throw that baseball a hundred miles an hour. He'd learned how it was possible from his brother, who some said threw even faster before his arm gave out. Jesse wanted to see if he'd taught you the right way. Now, I've been yearning to find out ever since. I tried but couldn't find nobody who clocked it. There weren't any Blacks at the game, of course, and everyone knows we folks can't tell time. Did you hit a hundred?"

It took a moment for Shane to find his way back to the cemetery. "I did, at least that's what I was told."

"Somebody clock it?"

"Not exactly, but… Saul, you're going to think I'm out of my mind…"

"The whisper," Saul interjected. "You heard the ball whisper?"

The very moment Shane heard the sound, Toby had shouted, "Time out, ump!" and went running out to the mound to ask him the same question.

"Yes, I did, Saul, I heard it whisper and so did Toby, our catcher."

Saul's bloodshot eyes filled with tears. "I'm so glad to hear another heard it as well. No one I know ever has, just you, Jesse, Jason and Toby. Oh, and the man who raced Bob Feller's fastball in that Oldsmobile. Others say it was a motorcycle that raced him, but it don't matter, he beat both of them."

Saul handed him the moonshine. This time Shane took a bona fide swallow and was about to sit down beside him, when Saul pointed up the hill. "Look yonder. See that cross on top? That's where you'll find your brother."

The base of the huge cross was hemmed in by a cluster of untrimmed boxwoods, but the crossbar and the upright intersected in a silhouette far above them.

"Shane, just so you know, this huge, whisky-bloated white man who looks like a rhino comes every Sunday evening to pray over Jesse's grave. Sometimes, he passes out up there and I have to help him make his way home the next morning. He's been coming for a long time. He says that he made the cross himself, out of a phone pole he stole from the Power and Traction Company. He sawed it into six-foot logs, chugged them up the backside of the hill in his pickup and put it together. It's countersunk in a sleeve of cement, so it'll stay 'til the Day of Reckoning."

The confirmation of Talley's story brought a surprising sense of release to Shane. Saul's eyes turned inward as though he was watching the memory play out. Shane knew there was more and had no intention of interrupting.

"I showed up one Sunday about three years ago and saw the cross for the first time. I was shocked. As I was making my way up to Jesse's grave, I heard somebody crying like a child. The same guy was hugging the cross. There was an empty bottle of whisky on Jesse's grave. I inched over toward the fellow, got as close as I dared, and all of a sudden he dropped to his knees and started praying.

"I had no idea who he was. I thought maybe he was just some drunk who'd lost his way in life, but I wasn't about to mess with him, so I rushed back down to the angel, wishing I had a gun in case he'd been sent by Whitewash to dig up Jesse. I waited and waited. He stayed up there until the sun went down. I was about to go back up just to make sure nothing had turned wrong, when he came stumbling down the hill. He staggered over and told me he was sorry, but every time he went up to pay his respects — always in the middle of the night, so nobody would ever know — he had to drink hard to blot his memory of the last time he smacked Jesse with his gun. I asked him who he was. He went pale and started shaking all over. I had no idea what was going on. He looked up at the cross and told me that he was Roland now, but that he was part lying because underneath the lie his real name was Talley, Barnes Talley, the used-to-be cop who killed Jesse and brought him here to be buried.

"I wanted to kill him right off, but my heart and soul grabbed onto me and wouldn't let me move. He said that he was sure I didn't recognize him because he didn't look at all like he used to. Now, he was carved up, half-blind and fatter than a pregnant sow. He went on to say that he'd been away for a time, trying to hide out from what he did and that he came back because, as he put it, he couldn't bear not facing the lowest part of himself and had to be close to my boy to do so."

Saul stopped. His mouth hung open. He raised his hand to let Shane know that he was okay and that there was more.

"Saul, please don't feel like you have to go on."

"Forgive me, young man, but I do. Talley said that he dug the grave that night, with Jesse's body in the trunk of his car. When he was done, he came down for Jesse and carried him up to his grave.

"He stood there shaking and went on to say that he knew there was no way I could forgive him, and that he understood and certainly respected that. He said if I'd go up to Jesse's grave with him, he'd kneel down on the grass and let me beat him to death with a shovel. He'd bought the plot next to Jesse's in order to be side by side with him when the day came, hoping to find out if The Almighty had forgiven him because, as it stood, he'd never forgive himself. I told him that I felt what was in his heart but wasn't about to do such a thing. Now I know what I didn't know then and am so glad I stuck to my heart's leanings."

"My God, how did you?"

"As I'm sure you know, better than most, there's a certain kinship, a certain kind of love between the living and the dead. Elise and me didn't have any idea how wonderful such a thing could be, until we forgave ourselves for letting Jesse go to the game. Stop worrying, young man, and get on up there. If I'm passed out when you come back, and there's any whisky left, be sure and help yourself."

The attempt to laugh stuck in Saul's throat. When things settled, he tilted the jar to his smiling lips, took a mouthful and flinched. Stretching his lips wide as if trying to make sure his face still worked, he looked up the hill.

"If someday I go up there and find Talley hanging on that cross, with crows pecking at him in the morning and bats feeding on him at night, maybe I'll ask God to let him down so I can tend his wounds." He smiled, took another swallow and smacked his lips. "See here, young man, get on up there and I pray that you find what you're looking for."

Shane was at a loss for words. Finding what he was looking for had suddenly become much harder than killing Talley. "Saul, I don't know what to say, only to thank you for your kindness."

"And you for yours, young man."

Chapter Twenty-One

Shane climbed the hill slowly, reading the names on the headstones as he passed by. The hill was steep and packed with footprints, cigarette butts, and slabs of cement or white stones, rounded like a scattering of prehistoric eggs. Graves without cement or stones were marked with crosses made from broom handles and the slats of Coca-Cola and orange crates to mattress frames and lengths of chains wrapped tight around crosses of copper tubing to hold them in place. Those with small wooden crosses made of sticks or pieces of branches were bound at their intersection by shoestrings, rope or leather strands. A few headstones lay crumbled in piles. Names, birthdates and dates of passing were chipped and etched, often erratically, into the surfaces.

He stopped when he saw a rusting American Flyer locomotive, the same type of electric train he'd had as a child. There was no stone and the plot was tiny, about the size of a shoebox. Shane bent over to touch the engine and with blurring eyes he continued up the hill.

As the slope steepened, his heart picked up steam. The clouds were welding together in a seamless canopy. Breathless, as if he were slogging up a jungle stream with a fifty-pound knapsack on his back, he stepped out onto a ridge and clutched his knees to catch his breath. He straightened and looked out over the town. Even though some of the letters were missing, he could make out the blue Meridien Refrigeration sign on top of the ice plant.

At last he reached the top. Talley's red cedar cross stood stout and tall. Its rail-thin arms stretched out like those of a fairytale witch. The ground was soggy with dew. Jesse's name crawled out from the shadow of the cross. Painted in black on a weather-beaten square of wood the size of a small pillow, his name was written in the same confusing spirals Shane had seen etched in the ground where Jesse was killed. He remembered thinking that in its strange shape maybe Suzanne had drawn it, but now he knew she hadn't.

The shadow crept from his shoulders, easing the temptation to run that was swelling up inside him. He knelt on the marshy grass and traced Jesse's name with his fingers.

"Come back, Jesse. Please come back," he said, longing to see those huge dark eyes that smiled even in the rain. He wanted to watch his brother hurl a football half the length of a football field, wanted Jesse to take him once again to the Army-Navy store as he did when Shane was fourteen to see what a gas mask looked like. He wanted Jesse to walk him downtown past Whitewash's Almighty Men's Club, and more than anything he wanted to hear Jesse tell him over and over to practice, practice, practice until he could throw a baseball a hundred miles an hour.

He and Jesse had been on the fringe of the Clayton Swamp, where they went to practice in isolation, so that no one could see them together. The Swamp was once an old, rutted, ballfield where the Black team from Langston High played until the field was flooded by Enola and converted into a nest of crippled ash trees and sinking ponds draped in ghostly Spanish moss.

Today became yesterday. Shane remembered raking the shimmering slime from a root so that he could push off with force. He planted his foot on the root and straightened, staring at Jesse who was kneeling sixty feet away with his mitt open.

"Throw the ball!" Jesse shouted.

He dug in with the toe of his cleat and rocked into his wind-up. He raised his left knee level with his ribcage and reached back, as Jesse had taught him, until the ball was almost touching the muck. At the tipping point, with more thrust than he'd ever mustered, he lashed his arm forward as if it were no longer a part of him. His wrist snapped and the ball shot out of his hand. When it slapped his catcher's mitt, Jesse winced.

A moment passed before Shane realized that he'd never thrown a baseball that hard. The astonished look he and Jesse cast at one another overwhelmed the silence. "Did you hear it?" Jesse called out, jumping to his feet.

"Hear what?"

"You must be deaf, Shane. You don't have a clue what you did, do you? As God is my witness, the ball whispered, just like Jason said it would." He looked at

Shane with suspicion and took the ball out of the mitt to balance it on his fingertips like a trophy. "A ball has to travel a hundred miles an hour to make that sound!"

The excitement in Jesse's voice was wrapped around a tone of pride that Shane had never heard from anyone, except maybe his father the moment he thought he'd found a cure for his mother's cancer.

"Come on, Jesse, that's nonsense."

"It's a fact, Shane! They took Bob Feller out to the Erie Canal where the water was still and smooth, just like here. They told him to rear back and throw for all he was worth. Then they mashed the pedal on a fifty-four Bonneville and roared past him at a hundred miles an hour. He let go of the ball, and it raced ahead of that car for better than sixty feet. The driver said it carried a humming sound, like a whisper riding on a secret."

Now Shane scraped the snowy dirt out of the roughly etched letters and below them, the dates of Jesse's birth and death, set in parentheses, as though his life had been confined to a span of time no wider than his hand. Shane let his breath out and felt the words pass over his lips.

"I love you, brother."

The shadow of the cross was stretching into the valley of gravestones. Shane heard the fading bark of a coyote and began to sob, something he'd not done since Payne was killed on the riverbank. "Forgive me, Jesse, please forgive me." There was no whisper from the cross, no relief from the grave, nothing in the wet air rising from the winter's grass. He watched the dampness mix with the sun. The sheen through the clouds created a fake sunset, so pure that the rising air turned purple. What had Saul called it? A miasma, yes, and what exactly did he say it was — a shadow of revenge that hovers over the grave until the wrong's been made right. It was Shane's shadow and the color purple was hovering inside it.

When he got to his feet, the miasma lingered. It came to him that he could never remove Jesse from his conscience because he would never be able to forgive himself if he did. Without question, there were some sins that could not be forgiven.

It was a long slog down to the entrance. Saul was still there, leaning against the angel's cloak. The empty mason jar lay at his feet. When he saw Shane, he reached into his jacket, took out a matchbox and slipped it open to reveal a number of small bindings of curly black hair, tiny dark haystacks, each bound with a string.

"That's all my boy left behind, right there, curls of hair, but they might as well be spun gold." Gently fingering them, Saul's voice broke. "God bless Roland for clipping them off Jesse's head and binding them for Elise and me."

Shane touched the curls and sniffed them. Without a doubt they were Jesse's. His orchard smell had become a staple in his house, even when he wasn't there.

Saul closed the matchbox and looked up the hill. "Roland said that he went back to the field where he beat Jesse. He said that he cried and prayed but that wasn't enough to let him feel forgiven. So, he took out his gun and slammed it against his head until he fell over in his own blood and laid there, almost happy that he was going to die. He came to in the night and thought he was in Hell. He got to his feet with his head splitting and said a bolt of lightning struck over the scoreboard and because it didn't strike him, he felt God hadn't forgiven him but just might, if he would live the rest of his life helping others live theirs. He tried by visiting his Calvary Church every Sunday, drunk and when the service was over, preaching to the flock but the Reverend reported him and he was ordered out of town by the Judge. Somehow he found his way down to the Smokies for help.

"After he told me all that, he went quiet. I thought he was about to leave when he reached into his coat and pulled out a pistol. 'Here' he said, 'This is the gun I beat Jesse with. It'd be easier than using a shovel. It's loaded.' I could tell both by his eyes and his voice that he meant it. I took the gun but I couldn't do it. There was just something… something in his voice that… I knew that Jesse had forgiven him, and I told him so."

Shane stood watching, wondering what he should say. "Bless you, Saul," he said but there was no reply, only the look of faraway eyes staring at the past.

Chapter Twenty-Two

Back home from Blinder's, Suzanne went out on the veranda unable to get the chokehold out of her mind. Talley's sputtering struggle to ask for forgiveness and the outright confession for what he'd done had taken her beyond disbelief. Though Shane had spared Talley's life, she now knew why he'd returned to Meridien and hoped that his determination to kill Talley had been put aside forever.

The veranda's ledge seemed adrift over what appeared to be a wide lake veiled in fog. She heard the distant sound of the chimes, their frozen rings brooding and dull as though they'd been forced to travel against their will over time. It brought to mind what See-Through said about the endless tunnel of darkness that the blind carry in their heads, that love was felt, not seen, and when the lights come on, we are no longer hidden in the mind's darkness.

And yet, she reminded herself that if she could resolve the enigma, maybe she'd be able to parse the twin feelings in her heart, the love she felt for him and the love she felt for her father, so that either choice she made would allow her to live or die in the arms of love. If only she could find the strength to make the choice that would allow her to live.

That she stood even a remote chance struck her like a bolt of lightning when they were leaving Blinder's and compelled her to plead with Shane to meet her at the ice plant.

She spent a good part of the night attempting to implant in her mind's wilderness the exact image of Jesse she'd seen in Shane's photo, hoping that Jesse's twin would find his way from her heart through her hands at the ice plant.

When the sun began to rise, she worked her way out of The Lilly, threw on a pair of freshly washed jeans, a hand-gilded sweatshirt, a smattered smock and tennis shoes, then hurried into the garage for a hammer, a chisel, an icepick, and the pair of tongs that Stavros had given her father to help him pry ice cubes from their trays to chill his bourbon. She laced the supplies into the saddlebag, climbed onto the Tiger and headed to the plant. Along the way, she rehearsed the lies that she hoped would allow her to wangle her way inside.

Three stories high, long ago painted deep blue as a reminder of the sea, the turn-of-the century brick building sat deep in its own shadows, as if taking the measure of all who entered. The blue color had weathered into azure, accenting the inset windows that had been cemented over and painted white, as a warning to ocean bound birds about to fly into the building. The words on top of the building, Meridien Refrigeration, were cracked blue, reminding her of broken nest eggs. Two empty, canvass-roofed delivery trucks were backed up to the loading dock, their sunken tops looking dreary in winter's off-season.

She met Samuel, the plant's yawning, middle-aged manager, at the door. He had a long nose with a strange upturn at the tip that opened his nostrils for all to see the hairs sprouting inside. He apologized for his grogginess and with a deep southern accent asked what he could do for her.

The accent prompted Suzanne to ask where he was from. Without hesitation he told her that he'd migrated north from Alabama to Virginia because here the seasons changed, whereas, in 'Bama he'd been forced to work nonstop because it stayed summer year-round and the demand for ice never ended. "That said, young lady, how can I help you?"

The rehearsal she'd primed for while driving to the plant became her audition. She told Samuel that she was studying art, majoring in sculpture and had been assigned a difficult project which overwhelmed her. She was home for the semester break and had to practice sculpturing before she returned to school or she risked failing the class and possibly losing her scholarship. She waded into her thin version of the truth, telling Samuel that in addition to the school's demand, her need to make the sculpture was a tribute to her father who'd passed away and had loved playing baseball as a young boy.

She asked Samuel if he'd ever played and his eyes lit up. In a way he'd played baseball all his life, he said, starting in high school down in Opelika, and even though when he finished high school and had to find work — not only for himself but for his struggling parents whose small tomato farm had been devastated by the heat — following the Atlanta Braves was now his daily obsession.

"Hold on, Miss. I'll be right back," he said and rushed into his office to bring out a skull- cap and a pair of thick leather gloves.

"Put these on," he said handing her both. "You can stay up in the room we call, The Artic, for as long as you like, but be sure to wear these and step outside the room every half hour or so. This here's a picture of me and my dad back in the day."

Suzanne slipped on the cap and gloves. "May I see it?"

"Of course." He handed it to her. She stared at it, absorbing young Samuel's glove, uniform and smile, as well as the wrenching flow of pride in his father's loving eyes. The picture reminded her of Jesse. What Medic had said about coincidence came to her, that it was God's way of showing He cares.

"The first day of Little League. I was ten."

"That must have been a wonderful day," she said, giving the picture back.

"To this day I remember the feel of my dad's arm around my shoulder and the sweet smell of chewing tobacco that always clung to him. Here, young lady, zip that jacket up to your chin and follow me. You've come to the right place. Spend all day if you need to but please take a break every thirty minutes or so."

"Will do, and thank you so much."

Thrilled, Suzanne quickened her pace to keep up with him as they headed down a long hall with a ceiling lined with red water pipes. As they approached the door, she suddenly remembered to let him know that a friend of hers, Shane by name, might stop by.

Chapter Twenty-Three

Later that day, Shane drove to the ice plant, feeling the weirdness of Suzanne asking him to meet her there even as he grappled with the despair that had overcome him at the Jesse's grave. Left with an emptiness so crippling, he wondered if he'd ever find true forgiveness. As Saul said, there was a certain kinship between the living and the dead, and regardless of whatever that meant, he and Jesse's mother had freed themselves from blame. Why couldn't he?

Having no idea what to expect, he got out of the Rambler feeling a stranger to himself.

A man met him at the door, said his name was name was Samuel, asked his name and smiled when he heard it. "Suzanne came by this morning and told me that you might be coming. She wants you to see what she's working on and asked if it would be okay. I said it would be just fine. She's in the freezing room upstairs."

"The freezing room? What's she doing in there?"

"Working on a school project of some sort. You'll see. Not to worry. I gave her a pair of gloves and a skullcap and told her to take a break every thirty minutes or so, and she said she would. I went to check on her twice. She seemed fine. She told me she was immune to the cold. I laughed and she just stared at me like I'd insulted her. When I apologized, she laughed!" Samuel looked at his watch. "Whoops, I've got an order to fill, so let me point the way. If you know your left from your right, it's second-nature."

Samuel pointed down the hallway. "Go all the way to the end. You'll see some red waterpipes overhead. The stairs'll be on your left. Take 'em up to the second floor and follow the pipes all the way down to our storage room otherwise known as The Artic. You'll know you're there when you spot the porthole in the door. You won't be able to see through it on account of the ice fog. When you knock she might not hear you because the door's thick, so knock like you're trying to beat it down. When you get in, make sure to shut it tight and drop in the beam. If you have any trouble, yell and I'll come help."

"Will do and thank you," Shane said and headed down the hall. Just when he reached the stairway Suzanne came rushing down. Stunned, she stopped a few steps above him. Her coat and hair were dappled with ice. The fissures in her frozen lips cracked open. "Shane, I'd almost given up on you. I was running down to see if you'd come and gone. Thank you so much for being here! I promise you won't regret it. Follow me!"

"Hold on, Suzanne. Samuel said you were supposed to be wearing a skullcap and gloves."

"I did for a while but when they started to interfere I took them off."

"Interfere with what?"

"With my sources! Now, come on!"

She grabbed his hand, led him up the stairs and down the piped hall to the freezing room. She rammed the door open with her shoulder, ushered Shane inside and slammed it shut. On the far side of the enormous room, stacks of ice lined the wall, standing like columns studded with glitter and colored crimson by the amber lights overhead. A maroon fog swirled around the rafters, dipping and jerking like a flock of tortured souls. Suzanne bolted the door and turned sharply, pointing her finger toward the end of the room. "There!" she declared. "There! He's been waiting for you."

When Shane saw the figure standing in an eddy of mist, he halted. For a second, he thought he was looking at a young boy frozen to death in a cage of frosted glass. But when Suzanne took his hand and moved him closer, his impression of the figure shifted from that of a young boy dressed in a baseball uniform to a life-sized ice sculpture of Jesse.

There was no mistaking him. His sleeves were rolled up his arms and his pants were tightened just below his knees, showing his taut calves. The thumb and index finger of his right hand griped the bill of his baseball cap while his gloved hand hung by his side. Jesse stared at him with huge shining eyes.

Dazed, Shane glanced at Suzanne.

Her lips cracked into a crooked smile, and her breath hung in the freezing air. "Samuel wet the bottom of a bunch of thirty-pound blocks of ice and set them on top of one another so they'd freeze together. Responding to my lie that I needed help to practice for a sculpting contest at Pratt, he said that it was my grade-stone to carve."

Shane's eyes were fixed on Jesse. "It's unbelievable!"

"I did it for you and for me. Watch and you'll see."

She unreeled a hose from its spindle in the corner of the room, dragged it behind Jesse and climbed up on a crate that raised her to his height. She adjusted the valve to turn on a trickle of water and let it run onto his cap and shoulders.

"Suzanne, don't!" Shane said.

"No, Shane. He wants to leave now, to disappear before your eyes, so that he can remain in your heart forever, but not in your conscience. You must let him."

"What?"

Jesse gleamed like lighted crystal. His eerie, translucent face became human. His bulging eyes, tinged with cinnamon from the lights, roamed across Shane's face, searching, wondering if Shane understood why he was there and why he was leaving. As his cap thinned, Suzanne's face began to blend with Jesse's until Shane couldn't tell them apart. Suzanne increased the flow of water.

"No, no, Suzanne, let him stay!"

"You can turn off the value or grab my hand and take the hose, but whatever you do, it won't change the fact that he's going to disappear. It's his way of telling you that there's nothing you can do to stop his leaving, no more than you could have done to prevent him from coming to the game."

The brim of Jesse's cap gradually sank to his forehead and then to his eyes. His mouth became a brief smile, as if reminding Shane that he, Jesse, had made the right choice in coming to the game. Warm tears slipped down Shane's cheeks.

"Love is in the goodness he left behind, and the realization that no matter what you did, then or now, nothing could have changed that," Suzanne said.

Her face replaced Jesse's as his chin lapsed to his chest, and into the slowly turning earth, his arms, shoulders and chest gave way. When his wrist weakened, the glove dropped to the floor and shattered. Gradually, his legs vanished as they melted over his ankles and cleats. He was gone and yet he stood taller than ever in the auburn pool of his water.

"What do you see now?" Suzanne asked.

Shane held his breath and let it out slowly. "I still see him."

"Is he smiling?"

As if a gas lamp were being turned down, the lights went low, yet the reflection in Shane's eyes brightened as he recalled what Saul had said, that there was a kinship, a special kind of love between the living and the dead. The cold tightened around him and his teeth started to chatter. He hunched his shoulders to force the collar of his jacket against his ears. Jesse's smiling image rose from the water. There was no blame in his eyes, only joy. Shane's heart and conscience began to part.

"Yes, he's smiling," Shane said.

That he couldn't have prevented Jesse from coming to the game made no sense to Shane, but in his heart, it did. The room began to undulate. He thought he heard the floor creaking in the turbulence. He became dizzy, the same dizziness that overcame him on the trestle. And then the earth slowed, his balance gradually returned and what had been missing all these years came to him.

Pent-up somewhere in his soul he'd always known the truth, but like a criminal confined to a cell of silence and self-hatred, he couldn't find the key until Suzanne handed it to him. As he stepped into the shallow pool of water and knelt, the whole of it came down to just a few words, without a tinge of regret or shame, but with a sense of reconciliation. "Jesse, if I could return to that day, I would have asked you to come," he said, knowing it was the truth.

Suzanne not only heard him but knew Jesse had as well. She wanted to break with herself and admit the underlying truth about why she'd done such a weird thing as sculpting a statue of Jesse. Yes, its purpose was to help Shane put the past to rest, but beneath that, there was more, the inevitable paradox that she so often found in herself, the familiar contradiction that that haunted her — living was dying and dying was living. The selfish side of her had sculpted Jesse not only for Shane, but for herself, hoping that if Shane found the courage to free himself from the past it would give her the strength to stand up against what she'd done to her father and free her to fall in love.

It was snowing lightly as they left the plant. When she mounted the Tiger, Shane thanked her from the bottom of his heart. She wanted to escape her timid smile by jumping off the Tiger, throwing her arms around him and insisting that they return to Medic's driveway.

Instead, they stood gazing at one another, wondering if there was any possible way to verify the revelations that had just come to them? Though neither said a word, the answer came to each. Without sharing, they headed separately to the ballfield with no idea that they were traveling together.

Chapter Twenty-Four

When Shane arrived, the flurries were dotting the desolate field. He leaped over the dilapidated fence and went to where Jesse had fallen. The strange letters spelling out his name were thinner now, on the verge of disappearing. It was as though he and Jesse stood at the intersection of two worlds with the past having receded and the present having caught up, canceling time and erasing the shame that had filled it.

Shane wondered if a piece was missing. It had never entered his mind that Jesse might want forgiveness for coming to the game, for the aftermath, the suffering that those who loved him had gone through.

Jarred at the awakening, he stared at the markings in the dirt. Time was overcome by a feathery stillness, the same calm that threatened to thicken when he and his mother ended their nightly prayer. He crouched, folded his hands and closed his eyes. "I forgive you, my brother, we all do," he said, pausing to let his heart verify what he said at the ice plant. "God bless you, Jesse, for coming to the game."

Shane thought he could feel their thoughts and feelings and possibly their heartbeats passing back and forth from one brother to the other when suddenly Suzanne materialized out of the snow-peppered trees. Her face seemed to float in the overcast. With the snow dampening her cheeks, she seemed more mysterious than ever.

Shane jumped to his feet. She threw her arms around him. Even in the cold, he could feel the warmth of her body.

"You knew I had to come here, didn't you?" Shane said.

"I didn't know for sure but hoped you would. That's why I came, to see if you had."

He wanted desperately to kiss her, and she wished desperately that he would, but she stepped away, afraid of giving fate a chance to wreck the day.

Disheartened, he took her hand and walked her to the curb. "How about dinner?"

About to give in, she gathered herself. A white lie came to her rescue. "I'd love to, Shane, but I'm so exhausted I don't think I could make it through a dinner. How about tomorrow evening, after church?"

"You're going to church on Tuesday?"

"I've got a four o'clock meeting with Reverend Bradley. Toward the end of my father's life, the two of them became close friends. They talked a lot about the sufferers' line and the face of God. I've got a few questions that only he can answer."

"I'd be happy to take you and wait for you."

"It might be a long wait. My father told me that sometimes the Reverend would rattle on and on and that their meetings always went longer than planned. We're supposed to get together about four o'clock. I don't want you to feel that you have to sit there until midnight."

"How 'bout, if I pick you up at three-thirty?"

She straddled the Tiger and came down on the kickstart. Shane thought she hadn't heard him, but before he tried to shout through the noise, she backed off on the throttle. "I'll be out on the curb. Look for a woman in a black habit and hood. Oh, with a pectoral cross as well. If you happen to see two of us just know that they're both me."

It startled him for a moment. When he thought he'd grasped the humor he said, "I love you."

The words were as shocking to Suzanne as they were to him. She instantly forgot that she was on the Tiger and it started to topple over. She trapped it between her legs, clutched the handlebars and steadied it. It took her a moment to come out of the silence. She heard herself tell him in a voice that cleared the grunting motor. "No, Shane, not now."

"Not now?"

"Especially now," she said.

Even in the shadows, he could see the alarm in her eyes.

Chapter Twenty-Five

The following day under billowing clouds they drove to the church with their voices suspended in yesterday's memories. Suzanne's happiness in Shane providing evidence to See-Through's unforgettable definition of love had given way to her own unyielding trap. Despite what she'd seen, she couldn't summon the strength to tell him that she'd fallen in love with him, fearing that it might delay, or even prevent her from leaving, which she had to do on the rapidly approaching anniversary of her father's death.

Bewildered and on edge, her mind moved into overdrive. On one level, her situation wasn't all that different from Shane's, and yet, on another, it was. Just as nothing would have stopped Jesse from coming to the game, nothing would have stopped her father from trying to hang himself — the exception being the intervention of his daughter. Yet, she'd kept him alive to suffer the worst pain of his life, equaled only by the agony in his eyes when he demanded to know what she was doing up on the ladder beside him. But there was more, much more, buried in the treasure of her father's urn.

Before reaching the church, Shane tried several times to start a conversation, but ensnared by her driven mind, she heard nothing. Despite her silence, a sense of relief came over him when he thought about how Jesse, of all ironies, had brought Suzanne into his life in a way he could never have foreseen. Maybe that's what Saul meant when he said there was a special kind of love between the living and the dead.

They passed through the eerie, stone octagon of the Meridien Train Tunnel and pulled up in front of the twice-steepled church where a huge bronze replica of Jesus-on-the-Cross stood on a rocky mound with its emerald eyes gleaming as it rotated round and round.

"My father told me that the knoll represents Golgotha," Suzanne said, "where Jesus was crucified. His statue is hinged at the waist and breastbone to allow the transept to rotate round and round, but slowly, like a weather vane in a weak wind.

Every day before his lunch, Reverend Bradley throws a switch and Jesus starts His twenty-four-hour count of six-hundred and sixty-six revolutions. Bradley came up with the idea, saying that the unstoppable orbits stand for the ineffectiveness of the Evil One's attempt to impede Christ's journey into the heart of his parishioners."

"Maybe that's what Talley was trying to do when he got drunk and sat out on the steps of the church to give his sermons," Shane said, expecting Suzanne to weigh in, but she sat immobile, stifled by the question that had risen in Christ's eyes. What was she doing there?

She knew why, exactly why. She'd told Shane that she wanted to meet with Bradley to hear more about the sufferers' line, to make sure she understood it, but the real reason lay side by side with the contrived reason she'd given Shane for her leaving school and her story about the urn. She'd betrayed her father, not just once, but twice and couldn't escape the memory of her mother's last words to her, that Judas had invaded her soul.

"Wish me well," she said, reaching for the door handle.

"You'll do great."

She started to open the door and hesitated. "Shane, yesterday you asked me why I was coming to see Bradley. I gave you an answer but left something out that you should know."

"Tell me," he said, hoping that she was about to say those precious words.

"It has to do with a terrible friend of mine, a friend who's stayed by my side for years."

Shane went on alert, scrambling through his hope. "Who would that be?"

"Judas Iscariot."

"Very funny."

A tongue-in-cheek smile played around her lips. She opened the door. "Oh, by the way, there's something exciting to look forward to."

"What's that?"

"Tonight, if I survive this meeting and you're willing, I'm going to take you on the ride of your life."

"Crazier than the ride to the trestle?"

"It's not on the Tiger."

"The Pontiac, then. You must've filled the tires."

"It's not the Pontiac or the Tiger."

He hoped that her whimsical comeback suggested that the ride would be on top of him.

"It's on life's cycle," she said.

Her answer gave him hope but he asked anyway, "What do you mean?"

"You'll see, but I've got to go now. I'll be back soon, maybe."

Suzanne headed toward the church. Watching her, Shane felt that a huge portion of his life had been lived in the few days since they'd met. Every time they'd been together he'd been drawn closer to her perplexing character. Sometimes a line between normal and insane was hard to draw, but in truth, it didn't matter which side she landed on. When she disappeared around the corner of the church, he switched off the engine and waited under the silent watch of the Savior.

She'd never met the Reverend, although he had visited several times in the narrowing last weeks of her father's life. Her need to speak with Bradley began as an afterthought when she went off to Pratt, but over time, as her guilt weighed heavier and heavier on her heart, the afterthought progressed into a mandate. She called Bradley the day she returned to Meridien, but he delayed meeting with her because Thanksgiving was fast approaching and his obligations to the Channel of the Apostles were many. A half-an-hour on Wednesday was the only time he had available.

Bradley was known by his parishioners as the "Anointed One" because of the story he'd brought to his ministry. It went this way. One night when he was a child, he died from the flu, to return only hours later from the afterworld that, according to his recollection, had been "adorned with sunrise."

Suzanne's father loved Bradley's story and often told her that he couldn't wait to move ahead in the sufferer's line, so that he could see the same sunrise over the Pearly Gates.

She followed the brick path to the rear of the church, stepping over a patch of gold-painted, broken bricks where the church's cross had fallen from the spire in the wake of Enola, leaving the path shattered but fortunately harming no one. Bradley shared with the worshipers that the sparing of life and injury was undeniable evidence that Christ had been looking out for His children, and in gratitude, he'd adorned the bricks with the color of sunrise.

A set of stairs led up to the detached rectory that sat high off the ground like a tree house. Suzanne climbed the stairs but before she could knock, the door opened. Bradley's enormous body clogged the doorway. The bone-chilling copper eyes of a ferret stared down at her. His face was smooth and powdery white. His complexion seemed to absorb the light. He had a full head of white hair swept back in neat wire-like gullies. He was wearing a broad gold tie with a clasp in the shape of a fish.

"George de Ville's daughter, dear Jesus. A prayerful moment, indeed. Please come in, Suzanne." He opened the screen door, but before she could enter, he pivoted into the parsonage.

The room was walled in cedar and lined with bookshelves stuffed with what appeared to be dozens of Bibles. In the middle of the room, stood a card-table with a stack of collection plates. Dollar bills sprouted over the edges. Piles of loose change lay spread on the table. Suzanne wondered if he'd turned the church into a casino. Silhouetted against the stained-glass window was a life-sized statue of Jesus on the Cross. The tilt of His head and the painful look in his eyes reminded her of the expression on her father's face as he hung from the rope with his head stretched toward the attic, trying to see if he'd made God angry or proud.

"Suzanne, would you have a seat in the ancient choir chair and kindly come forth with your concerns? As I mentioned the other day, my time is quite limited."

She climbed into the tall chair and grasped the arms to keep from slipping out. "I remember what you said, Reverend Bradley, so, let me get right to the reason I wanted to see you. I should start by making sure I have this straight. You told my father that under God's watch he, my father, stood at the rear of a long line of sufferers, those who were experiencing far more pain than he, and until his pain became greater than theirs, he would not be allowed to enter the Kingdom of Heaven because he'd be taking away a space from someone more deserving."

Bradley raised his white eyebrows. "You are correct, Suzanne. The very first time I visited him at your house, I feared that what I saw in his eyes and detected in his voice suggested he was determined to end his life. So, I sought help from The Father, whose answer came in the form of the sufferers' line. The Lord instructed me to explain its meaning to your father, in hopes that it would squelch any thoughts of suicide, for just as you said, despite his pain he was not at the head of the line and stood to be abandoned altogether if he took his own life. Suicide is the ultimate betrayal of The Almighty. God doesn't approve of such under any circumstances, but at times Satan has a way of entering a beleaguered body and a tortured mind. Such, I'm afraid, was your father's condition. In his confusion, he came to believe that the pain he would experience in committing suicide would be so severe that in the last moment of his life, God would allow him to move to the head of the line."

Removing God from the picture for a moment, Suzanne thought of Plato's lesson of the cave, which her father said was taught in virtually every law school — who commits the lesser crime, who the larger? Had she committed the lesser by saving her father or the greater by filling her story about the urn with a lie and hiding the truth in a tiny alcove in her heart? The dilemma had to be Plato's worst nightmare. She took a deep breath and, in her father's prosecutorial demeanor, put aside the idea that Bradley had made a legitimate attempt to prevent her father's suicide and went straight to the underlying reason she'd come to see him — to find out if she was truly Judas' minion and had not the strength to stand up against him.

She shoved the confusion aside. "Reverend Bradley, did Jesus kill Himself?"

Bradley's eyes widened and his voice spilled out. "Of course not, child. One of His apostles, a man whose name it chafes my lips to utter, Judas Iscariot, betrayed Him for a handful of silver."

"But didn't Jesus tell the apostles that He would dip a piece of bread into a dish and give it to the one who would betray Him? He handed the bread to Judas, didn't he? Who then committed the greater sin, Jesus or Judas?"

Bradley's cheeks ballooned into those of a saxophonist and after a long moment they deflated. "Listen, young lady, Jesus laid down His life for you and me. His death was an act of magnanimous courage unmatched in these modern times. He was fulfilling the scripture, not justifying murder."

"Either way, He set up his own death, didn't He?"

"He set up no such thing. He was fulfilling His mission on Earth. What you refer to as death was but a brief waystation in The Messiah's life. He died to prove there is no death, for each of us has been given a return ticket to life. Think of Judas as the one who accompanied Christ to the ticket booth with enough silver to purchase the Savior a round-trip ticket. Judas was complicit in helping Jesus destroy death, though he knew not what he was doing. Thus, Judas's ticket was but one-way."

The confusion coalesced around Suzanne. "You mean Jesus was asking Judas, whose name would forever be a synonym for betrayal, to buy Him a return ticket to life while buying himself a ticket straight to Hell?"

Bradley sighed and raised his hands to pat the air for calm, but Suzanne paid no attention.

"Reverend, you seem to be saying that the betrayer wasn't Judas but Christ Himself. He could heal the multitudes, the sick, the blind and the downtrodden but instead, He chose to have Judas do what He didn't have the courage to do, all the while shifting the blame from Himself to Judas for all eternity. Reverend, I've done my homework. People who commit suicide usually make several attempts in order to work up enough courage to overcome their fear of dying. Maybe Jesus didn't have the courage or strength to even try, and as a solution, He had to turn the job over to someone else and with it the blame."

Redness crept up Bradley's neck like mercury rising in a tube. He rocked forward and gripped Suzanne's hand. "We, who are truly schooled in the Bible and baptized in the name of the Holy Spirit, know better, and so should you, though I understand and forgive you for shaming both Jesus and your father in such a way. The devil's playground is often a child who feels betrayed, but you needn't blame yourself, for the Heavenly Father just came to your rescue. Listen to His words."

She jerked her hand from Bradley's and cupped her ear. "Is He whispering, Reverend? I don't seem to hear Him. Oh, but wait a minute, there is a voice," she said, remembering when Medic expressed the opinion of John Donne when it came to Jesus taking His own life. "Reverend, the poet, John Donne, said it best when he wrote that suicide was justified when done in the glory of God. In that reverence it would seem that Christ not only planned His crucifixion but allowed it by voluntarily taking His last breath when He of all people had the power to survive."

The redness deepened and overtook Bradley's forehead. "The contrived words of a poet aren't those of our Father. Even with such a burden on your shoulders as your father's death, you must listen to me as I repeat the Lord's words, for I hear Him without confusion." Bradley closed his eyes and raised his chin. A muted hum followed, flowing in a long count, followed by two short measures, pausing and continuing lyrically, as if God were sending down a poem. The meter slowed and his eyes popped open.

"In an effort to heal your broken heart, the Father is speaking through me directly to you. Suicide is a sin against God, an abomination, a surefire way to shutter your soul in eternal damnation. It is the ultimate affront to the Father. We do not have the right to pre-empt His will."

Her rejoinder came seamlessly, riding both the seen and the shrouded. "Reverend, my father had ever-worsening rheumatoid arthritis and unstoppable guilt for losing the trial against Talley. It crippled him to the point where I had to help pry his fingers open so he could hold a glass of water. He couldn't lie down without curling into a knot. No drugs could take away the pain or shame. Shouldn't I have done something to help him?"

"The one who agrees to help in such a way as suicide is guilty of a monstrous betrayal. That I can say with certainty."

"Here's what I know for certain, Reverend. My father committed suicide," she blurted out in an edited version of the truth. "Maybe God did reach out and give His approval after all."

Bradley's jowls quivered. His left eye twitched. "You are bitterly confused, young lady. You're placing blame on the Lord for something you aren't old enough to understand."

The branches of a tree tapped on the window as if telling her to speak louder. "And you think that you understand?" she exclaimed. "Maybe it's Satan who's whispering in your ear. This isn't about my father's suicide. It's not about what he did. It's about what I didn't do!"

Bradley rose abruptly. "You are making no sense. I'm an ordained minister and your elder by five decades!" He took a drawn-out hesitation before the words lurched out. "With a child like you, it's no..." He clamped his mouth shut.

She looked at him with alertness. "It's no what? No wonder? No wonder that with a daughter like me, my father committed suicide? Is that what you were about to say?"

"Those are your words, child, not mine."

She felt that his tone of evasion confirmed that she'd finished his sentence accurately, word for unspoken word. Tempted to unleash every slanderous term she knew, her face flushed. She took the temptation as a warning, slid off the chair and pointed at the shelf of Bibles. "You ought to start reading those, Reverend." Unwilling to listen to anything he might say, she jerked the door open and rushed down the stairs.

At the spot where the cross had fallen, she reached down and forced out a chunk of brick. She ran toward Golgotha and with every ounce of strength she could summon, she hurled the brick at the statue. It was as if she'd taken a hammer to a porcelain doll. The spinning stopped. Fragments of Christ's head flew everywhere. Wire springs spooled out of His neck and bounced on His shoulders and chest. One of His eyes hit the ground in front of her. She bent over and grabbed it. With hands on her hips, she stood defiant, watching The Savior's face come apart.

She started to run but suddenly pivoted toward the statue. It appeared to be a monument to tragedy. She couldn't help but feel sorry for Him. She realized that one of His eyes was in her hand and looked at it. Unlike her father's, it possessed no anger, only loneliness. Tears came to her eyes.

"Please forgive me, please, please, please," she repeated, louder each time, as if she felt that Christ was no longer capable of hearing. But the plea wasn't only to the figure of Christ. It was to her father as well. She'd betrayed him in more ways than one. "I'm so, so, sorry... for who I am."

She rushed to the mount and placed Christ's eye at His feet. She was about to take off when she saw Bradley standing in shock at the bottom of the vestry steps. Torn between begging for his forgiveness or screaming, "It's your fucking fault!"

she braced and bit back the words. Plato came to her again. Who'd committed the greater crime, who the lesser? She or her father?

Bradley trudged toward her. She was about to flee when he stopped to stare at the statue. He put his hands beneath his chin in prayer. Suzanne wanted to go to him and apologize but she couldn't move and shouted instead, "I'm sorry, Reverend, I'm so very sorry!"

Bradley came out of his prayer and wiped his eyes to stare at her. "Jesus has been sacrificed yet again, but The Son of God has a round-trip ticket back to this very place, while you, this hostile young woman, a minion of Judas, is destined to pay for her sins."

"Reverend, I'll find somebody to fix Him. I promise."

Bradley's chest rose. "I am that somebody. There is no one else. I built His image with the help of The Almighty and by His Grace I will restore it. But you, you must restore yourself before Judas snatches you from the earth. Be gone and never set foot on this sacred ground again."

Suzanne began to back away. Stumbling, she caught herself, pivoted and ran toward the ponderous tunnel. As she got closer, the garlicky stench of creosote used to bandage the fractures in the walls slowed her down. She considered trying to climb up over the stone arch that supported the tunnel and cross the train tracks when Shane pulled up beside her and rolled down the window.

"Get in!"

She jumped into the car. Her eyes were glazed and tenderly demonic.

"Have you lost your mind?"

"I lost it a long time ago," she said.

"What happened back there?"

Realizing that she most likely had to answer his question before he would answer what she was about to ask him, she glossed over all that had transpired in the vestry and focused on Bradley's piercing implication that with a daughter like her, it was no wonder her father had tried to kill himself.

"He said that to you? Bradley said that to you?" Shane responded and mashed on the accelerator.

Suzanne's head bounced against the back of the seat. "He cut himself off but yes, that's what he said." Her mind was in turmoil. She was bound to eternity, and it gave her an eerie sense of relief to realize that there was no return ticket. Nothing she did or said could change a thing.

They shot out of the octagon on the wrong side of the road. A wide-hooded Buick was heading straight at them, its horn blowing in one long honk. At the last second the Rambler hit a pothole and swerved into the right lane, barely avoiding the car. Shane whirled the steering wheel to straighten out but couldn't help notice that Suzanne's dress had moved up her leg to expose her thighs. She made no attempt to cover them. The strange look in her eyes, whether bathed in remorse for what she'd just done or sequestered in the joy of victory, couldn't tamper with her beauty.

Despite all that had happened and all that Shane may have suspected but didn't know for sure, Suzanne wanted him to pull over and put his mouth within an inch of hers. She wanted to feel locked in the invisible mist of their breath and stay there entranced and forgiven, until she fell off the edge of the earth.

She wanted to spend the night with him but feared that whether by accident or intent, the very words she had to suppress would find their way out and the ultimate betrayal of her father would be impossible to avoid. Now, as Shane's fingers massaged her thigh, the temptation to tell him all that was going on in her soul began to swell, so she sought a way out in the form of a favor, as she would put it. But it was far more than a favor. It was another of the instincts she could not avoid. She had to go to the fair. She had no choice, no more than she'd had in climbing onto the ledge of the veranda or going to the trestle. These hadn't been choices. They were instincts she had to act upon if there was any hope of keeping time from running out. Shane would probably mistake it for refusal or idiocy. Either way, to say it was incongruous with the moment would be one of the most obvious understatements she'd ever made.

"Shane, remember, I mentioned the ride of your life?"

He glanced into the side mirror and muttered with hope, "Yes, I do."

"Would you take me to the fair?"

"The fair, you mean the Harvest Fair?"

"It's the only one in town."

"Now? After all you just put yourself through you want to go to the fair?"

"Especially after all that. I need to be in another world for a while, and I can't be alone there."

The car was silent, the space between them still. She was tempted to wade in and tell him that her father had always taken her to the fair. He loved it, especially the Ferris wheel. Even when he was no longer able to go, his spirits rose every fall, when the fair came to town. Her mother had always refused to go because of what she labeled, "the freak shows." "They are satanic," she said, to which he always replied that those who were hobbled were there to remind us of how fortunate we are, and, in truth, that they see themselves as far more fortunate than we.

Suzanne was convinced that asking Shane to take her to the fair was the last thing he'd want to do. She needed more than a simple break. She needed a complete distraction but would only take the risk if he accompanied her, for she knew that her father would be there. And there was another reason to go, a reason that she hoped would entice Shane. It had to do with his love of baseball, a bizarre sideshow that Medic told her about at the party but had been lost in the turbulence of the day.

Medic had remembered the story Suzanne shared with him about her father's take-away from the sideshows. He'd never forgotten the story because her father's interpretation of what many, including her mother, referred to as freakshows, gave an entirely new meaning to those cruelly and judgmentally thought of in such a way. Medic told Suzanne that this year there was a special show, a tribute to her father's ability to find good in just about everything. It reminded her of Ascot at Blinder's and what Talley had done for See-Through.

"But the preacher, Suzanne, and what you did to the statue?"

She put her hand on Shane's. "Not to worry. Judas has got me covered."

Chapter Twenty-Six

Because Shane didn't immediately respond to her request to go to the fair, she wanted to ask him again but fought the inclination and instead tossed him a softball. "Shane, do you still love baseball?"

"That's certainly out of left field," he said, instantly recognizing the unintended pun and smiling to himself. "Of course, I do. Overseas, I lost track of the standings but I love the game. Why'd you ask?"

"Well, Medic went to the fair the first night it came to town, and at the party he took me aside to tell me about this one particular sideshow, called 'The Dream Team,' that has to do with baseball. He loved it but wouldn't go into any detail because he said that he didn't want to ruin the surprise, if I chose to go. All he'd say was that it reminded him of a story I'd told him about what my father had said about certain sideshows, those that almost everyone, including my mother, called freakshows. Now, knowing that the love of baseball is still in your soul, I thought you might want to see it."

When they pulled up at the stoplight by the Catholic Church, a surprising sparkle burst from his eyes. "You bet, I would!"

"Shane, if you'd made Christmas come tonight, it wouldn't have thrilled me as much."

They took Riverside Drive along the river, over the Robertson Street Bridge and past Pleasant Hill cemetery. He was tempted to ask Suzanne if she'd ever wished that she'd buried her father rather than cremated him, but he kept the question inside as the tombstones flew past and the anticipation of the fair returned.

They drove to the parking lot in the pastureland high above the fairground. Jammed with cars and pickup trucks, a few vehicles toed the line at the edge of the cliff. Shane settled the Rambler next to them and they stepped out of the car into the loud, merry noise. He took her hand and they headed down the side road toward the glow of a thousand lights. The closer they got, the faster they walked. Suzanne felt her spirits lift with every step.

As the sights and sounds flooded over them, she remembered how her father always held her hand as they walked down the same slope into the excitement below. She caught glimpses of the rides they'd taken together: the salt and pepper shaker, the tilt-a-whirl, the round-up and the matchbox, but nothing equaled the majesty of his favorite, the Ferris wheel, whose top seats were swinging in the rich haze, which was now turning gold in the setting sun. It looked for all the world like the wheel of a giant chariot. With Shane as her protector, she wanted to tempt fate immediately, as she'd done at the trestle, but before they rode the Ferris wheel, she wanted to go to the sideshow, in hopes of postponing what she feared would take place on the ride.

Before she knew it, she was tightening her grip on his hand and rushing towards the far corner of the midway where a collection of sideshows stretched the length of the fairgrounds. Sounds of bells, whistles, and barkers competing for attention surrounded them. The laughter and cheers were pounding in her ears as they pushed their way through the crowd. She stumbled into Shane, setting up a chain-reaction of folks banging into one another. Shouting, "Sorry!" over and over, she lurched ahead.

Shane called out for her to slow down, but she lunged ahead, plowing into the largest crowd, which had gathered before a hanging marquee boasting the words, "The Dream Team." The barker was touting the incredible skills of a pair of twins from Tennessee, joined at the hip from birth, who could wind-up and throw two baseballs at the same time, both for strikes. Suzanne took the lead and wedged her way to the ticket booth. In one motion, she slapped down a dollar, grabbed the tickets and with a huge grin shouted, "We're in!"

They passed their tickets to the gateman and entered. The tent was filling up fast, mostly men of all ages in coveralls, lined denim and Sherpa jackets, boots and brogans. Young sons sat perched on fathers' shoulders. The smell of whisky was as thick as the crowd but stale, like the lingering smell of liquor in the trenches of Vietnam, when after a grueling mortar fight Shane's platoon would take to the bottle, along with a few joints. They justified the escape by telling themselves that if the enemy was duping them with deadly stillness and the platoon woke up dead, they'd never know.

They made their way down to the front row where they found two seats eye-level with the stage. The canvas curtain was covered with a painting of a distant, bases-loaded game being watched through the binoculars of a grandfatherly spectator sitting far back in the mezzanine on stage right. He was bending forward with a fist raised in joy. The runners were off their bags headed home. Shane squinted. The dot of a baseball was soaring high toward the fans behind the right-field fence. His heart bounced. He leaned toward Suzanne and whispered that they'd won. Unexpectedly, with questioning eyes, she pecked him on the lips and turned quickly toward the stage.

"We ain't got all night!" someone shouted.

Others joined in, clapping and calling for the show to begin. A minute later, a young man stuck his head through the curtain, yoking it tight around his gaunt face. He wore rouge on his dented cheeks and a baseball cap boasting a capital M above the bill. Just when everyone started to get uneasy with his muted stare, he announced that his name was Bugle and informed them that the M on his cap stood for Mudville, not Meridien. Then he began to recite "Casey at the Bat."

Shane knew the poem by heart and even though a few impatient folks groaned, Bugle kept the rhythm alive. His voice rose and became more dramatic. Shane found himself whispering under his breath, "...when the dust had lifted and the fans saw what had occurred, there was Jimmy safe at second and Flynn a-hugging third." The exciting, anticipatory lines always got to him because they signaled the soon-to-follow, disappointing letdown and even so, he always felt something encouraging in the outcome:

"The band is playing somewhere, and somewhere hearts are light.
And somewhere men are laughing, and somewhere children shout,
but there is no joy in Mudville — mighty Casey has struck out."

With a flourish, Bugle took a deep bow, yanked the curtain open and waved the twins from the wings. "Ladies and gentlemen, please welcome the most magnificent pitchers in the history of the game, Gates and Harper." Bugle rushed offstage and the twins marched on, arm-in-arm.

Long-legged, raw-boned and pink-skinned beneath scruffy red beards, they looked to be in their late twenties. Each gripped a baseball in his outer hand and a glove in the other. They wore putty-colored uniforms with a big red M over their hearts. The jerseys were loosely cut over the bulky rise of their joined hips. They bowed together and as they straightened they glanced at one another, each feigning surprise at discovering a mirror image of himself.

Harper took over. "Today we're going to perform a feat of magic, except it ain't a trick. It's real as a badger's breath. We're gonna throw two baseballs, pretty much at the same time, only one's coming from me and the other from Gates. It took us years to work it out, so we wouldn't fall all over ourselves, but I can tell you proudly, with help of the Lord, we nailed perfection to a post. Even if Casey was manning both sides of the plate, he wouldn't stand a chance."

Gates nodded to Bugle who'd slipped a catcher's mitt onto each hand and was squatting deep in the left wing of the stage. "What you're gonna witness is the impossible turned possible," Gates said. "It's a gift from God. We've been blessed to come into this world as we did, from our mother's womb connected by love, and find such mercy in the hands of people who always fill the room with applause and, if I may add with a smile, they're prone to filling the stage with quarters when we're done."

At that, the twins went to the opposite side of the stage and climbed up onto what appeared to be a wooden pitcher's mound covered with plastic grass and possessing two pitching rubbers side by side.

"Catcher ready?" Harper called out.

Bugle braced. "Ready!"

The twins began to helicopter their throwing arms, speeding up until their arms were a blur. Simultaneously, they jerked the balls down into their gloves and raised their kicking legs chin high. Dual shadows rose up the side of the tent and merged together, blurring as their spindly legs straightened abruptly and thundered down on the edge of the mound. The baseballs shot out of their hands toward Bugle, who caught them both, but Harper's rubber cleat slipped out from under him, crimping his leg. The brothers crashed into a heap. The crowd gasped.

Gates and Harper were trying to scramble to their feet. A couple of stagehands ran to their rescue, shielding them while promising to give the crowd its money back.

It wasn't until the curtain closed and the tent went dark that the astonished, murmuring crowd started shoving toward the exit. Then, unexpectedly, the curtain opened to the sight of the twins smiling and taking a bow. They wore maroon robes tightened around their chests. They straightened and stepped to the edge of the stage. The crowd went still.

"We've fallen many times and we've had to rise above it just as many," Gates said.

Harper nodded, smiling. "Our misfortune is our fortune. When you wake in the morning, please get down on your knees and thank God for who you are, a human being born with the strength to overcome all of life's misfortunes and see them for what they are, opportunities for discovery! As is said, 'When someone throws a brick at you, pick it up and build a castle!' Thank you all and goodnight."

Suzanne thought of what See-Through had said about Ascot playing the pinball machine at Blinder's. He, too, had found the strength to overcome his troubles and take on a new way of life, "Bless you!" she shouted.

The silence became chatter and chatter the gasoline that fueled applause. The sound of coins clinking on the stage encouraged Suzanne and Shane to dip into their pockets for spare change and follow the enthusiasm of the crowd. Holding hands, they made their way out of the tent where the midway lights went off like a flurry of fireworks in Shane's dazed eyes.

"The hotdog stand! I'm famished!" Suzanne shouted. Yet, at the sight of the Ferris wheel, she let go of his hand and halted. Cast into the spell of blue lights strung around the ride's staggering, globular frame, her heart leapt at the memory of her father taking her thin, twelve-year-old body by the waist and placing her in his lap to calm her fright when the wheel started to rise.

"Life's cycle, the Ferris wheel," she murmured.

Shane overheard her and realized that was what she'd meant when she told him that she was about to take him on the ride of his life.

"Let's get a hotdog first," he said.

"No, no. You don't want to ride on a full stomach. It's like being in a bouncing boat. Believe me, I know. Come on. It's slowing down. Let's get in line. Then hotdogs."

"Okay, okay."

They hurried to the ticket booth and slipped into the line. The Wheel came to a succession of brief stops to let the passengers off and welcome others. Suzanne felt her father's spirit join them. When they climbed into their chair, his presence eased into the narrow space between them and put an arm around her shoulders. She slipped closer to Shane.

Her father had told her countless times that he loved the Ferris wheel. He believed that it gave folks a chance to put life in perspective because as the moonlight enlarged while it rose, we begin to wonder if, in the next spin of our lives, we'll need to change anything in order to fill ourselves with contentment and satisfaction. Or, he questioned, always with wet eyes, were we doomed to keep spinning, blinded by our unwillingness to adjust to wherever life had taken us, when one opportunity after another had fled, leaving us stuck in despair, always blaming others for our fate. If so, were we turning our backs on the will of God? He always concluded that we must be grateful for the chances we've been given to overcome our obstacles, or we would never know who we were meant to be. The memory reminded her of the message delivered by the baseball twins.

The chair rose haltingly as more folks climbed aboard. Shane leaned over to Suzanne. "You're so quiet."

"I'm listening," she said.

"To the noise?"

"No, to my father."

As they edged upward into the moonlight, she gripped the guardrail and moved against closer to Shane. When the ride peaked for the first time and began to coast down, she glanced at him and wondered how she could possibly feel such love for anyone other than her father. Who, in all of Meridien or beyond, would have gone with her to the trestle, Blinder's and the church and still come with her to the fair? She felt eternally grateful, reminding herself that the word, eternally, wasn't misused.

When they reached the top of the world on the last spin of their ride, the Wheel unexpectedly halted. The seat jerked back and forth prompting them to grab onto the bar. Suzanne wondered if her father had abruptly stopped the ride to give her one last moment to look inside herself and declare that she was prepared to repent. She clutched the bar and leaned forward to peer into the shining steel center of the Wheel. She began to inch out of her seat, hoping that Shane would throw his arms around her, pry her away from her duty and tell her that her destiny had changed forever.

As if he'd partially read her thoughts, he grabbed her by the arm and jerked her back into the seat. A man's voice blasted through the speaker, enthusiastically announcing that even though the electric power had shut down for no apparent reason, not to worry because it had just come back on. They descended.

When they stepped off the platform, the midway lights reflected in her cheery eyes. She caught sight of the hot dog stand and jumped in front of Shane, so he'd have a good look at her backside. Suddenly, a woman's terrified scream pierced the air.

Suzanne glanced back at the Ferris wheel, shocked to see a Black lady in a bonnet hanging over the edge of a seat clutching the foot of dangling young boy and struggling to pull him back inside the chair.

"Shane, look!" Suzanne cried out, but to her astonishment, Shane was sprinting toward the ride. A moment later the toddler slipped from the woman's hands.

Frantic, Suzanne shoved her way through the swarm of shocked onlookers to find Shane sitting on a mound of sawdust, hugging the motionless boy to his chest. Shane's face was stark and ravaged. He pivoted onto his knees, placed the boy on the ground, pinching off his nose and clamping his mouth over the child's while puffing quick breaths into the child. The boy's little chest rose, quivered and then flattened.

"Is he alive?" someone gasped.

Suzanne knew the boy wasn't. Silence settled over everyone.

The woman in the bonnet broke through the crowd and fell onto her knees next to the boy. She tried to take him from Shane but when he refused to let go, her mouth opened in a frozen scream and after a moment, erupted. "Give him to me! I'm his mother!"

"Lay him on his back! I'm a nurse!" Suzanne shouted, grabbing the boy.

The mother loosened her grip.

Suzanne didn't have to call on her memory to tell her what to do. Her response was instinctual and immediate. She ripped open the boy's jacket and shirt, spread her fingers and started pressing into his ribcage.

As if Death itself had arrived, a thin young priest wrapped in black clerics appeared. He seemed as panic-stricken as everyone. With a trembling hand, he raised a silver cross over the boy while madly crossing himself. His lips were quivering. Suzanne couldn't tell if he was praying or just searching for words, but she had no time to waste and stroked the boy's chest ceaselessly.

At last, the priest began to speak, but in Latin, and immediately caught himself. Embarrassed, he translated in an apologetic voice, "Child, may the Holy Father open the gates of paradise for you and welcome you to everlasting joy."

"He's gone! My baby boy's gone!" the mother screamed.

The priest bent over Suzanne. "Nurse, you may relent, for his soul has been called away by his true Father. This boy is needed in heaven. You've done your best within the boundaries of life on Earth, but there's no more to be done."

As if in defiance, the boy began to shudder. Looking at Suzanne, his eyes blinked frantically and he started to cry for his mother. Petrified that her mind was playing tricks on her, she pleaded for Suzanne to let her hold him.

Suzanne handed her the boy. His mother held him to her cheek and gave him a dozen kisses. If it hadn't been for the sawdust clinging to his cowboy pants, one would have thought she'd just lifted a newborn from its crib.

"What happened, Mommy?"

"A miracle, plain and simple," she sobbed.

"Praise God," echoed through the crowd until it became a chant.

People started patting Shane on the shoulder and blessing Suzanne.

Ethan's mother stared at her, transfixed. "Nurse, you are a saint, an unfettered saint."

"I'm but a hatchling," Suzanne said.

An ambulance crew made its way through the crowd. The leader looked up at the motionless Ferris wheel looming overhead. "The sawdust must have cushioned him just enough. One in a million, I tell you."

An elderly man sporting a straw hat stepped out of the crowd and pointed at Suzanne. "I didn't see the boy fall, but that girl there in the green dress brought him back from the dead. As God is my witness, it was her who done it."

With a free hand, Ethan's mother fumbled to open her purse. "Here's five dollars, nurse. It's all I have," she said. "Take it, please take it."

"No, thank you, ma'am," Suzanne said, "Ethan is my reward."

The woman reached up and touched her cheek. "You were guided by God," she said softly. "Only He could have known that such a thing as you just did would bring about a miracle."

"He was in shock," Suzanne said. "Like a little bird who'd fallen from a branch. Here, let's close his shirt and jacket."

Ethan yawned and rubbed his eyes with a chubby fist, then rested his head on his mother's chest and looked up at her. "Can we go home now?"

"Yes, my child. In a moment."

That Ethan could even make a sound so soon surprised Suzanne and added to her joy. Years ago when she and her mother met with Chelsea to discuss Suzanne's birth, the nurse had explained that chest compression caused sharp soreness and weakness throughout the body, often cutting off the patient's ability to even murmur until the soreness cleared.

Shane and the priest helped Ethan's mother to her feet. Folks began to clap, gently at first, and then they began to cheer. The applause grew louder and louder, searching for a high.

"I'm Sally Hooper," the woman said, looking gratefully at Suzanne before turning to the priest. "Father, I'm sure it was at your praying that these wonderful folks were sent here to save Ethan. Thank you and God for seeing to it. Can you imagine, a man of the cloth and a black cloth at that," she said, smiling.

"I was wrong to give up on our Lord so soon," the priest said. "It's a lesson that will stay with me forever. Please forgive me for my failure to do what I should have done."

"There's nothing to forgive, Father," she said. "God's telling you that through my heart."

"Can we give you a ride home, Mrs. Hooper?" Shane asked.

"Thank you, sir, but we got an old DeSoto with a holey canvas roof." She smiled and looked at the priest. "Forgive me, Father, I wasn't trying to smart-talk you."

The priest chuckled and took Suzanne's hand. He knelt before her and kissed her knuckle. Smiling, he stood up. "It wasn't me who had anything to do with God's intervention, nurse. It was you. The Almighty performed the miracle through you alone. I must go make amends now. By the way, I'd love to see you at church. We're on the corner of Clarendon and Main."

"Thank you, Father, but I'm sorry, I'm not Catholic. I'm not sure I'm anything," Suzanne said, looking past him with regret. "It's just been a long day."

"Given what you did here tonight, it would have been a swipe at The Almighty had I taken any offense."

Suzanne took Shane's arm. The cheers trailed behind them as they made their way up the hill to the parking lot. When they reached the car, they stopped to look back. The lights were fading into a cloud of golden dust, increasing the fair's supernatural presence. The Ferris wheel slowly began to roll through the aura like the paddlewheel of a huge boat.

They got into the car. "Shane, it was like you knew ahead of time that the boy was going to fall," Suzanne said.

"I couldn't get my friend Payne out of my mind."

"Who's Payne?"

"A private in my platoon in Vietnam." And he told her more.

Private Payne, lovable Payne, the oldest private in Shane's platoon. Enormous private Payne, who took up the space of three, so that two comrades had to sit on his spread knees when the Sikorsky brought them in from the troop ship. Payne, the West Virginia man-child with aptitude scores so low that he had to be shown almost daily how to break down a rifle. A coal miner at thirteen, moonshiner at fifteen, Marine at seventeen, Payne, with his buffalo head and puppy disposition.

And always with a smile, even when a branch smacked him in the mouth causing him to swallow an uprooted tooth.

Payne who, when they were camped on the banks of the Mekong River, saw a young Vietnamese girl fall from a low wooden bridge, and against every rule in the war-book, he slammed his huge frame into the water, reached the child and brought her ashore. When her mother came running from the bridge, Payne handed her the baby, tore off his jacket and tried to give it to her to wrap around the boy, but she didn't understand what he was doing. Payne pointed to the baby and to the jacket, whipped his arms across his chest and rocking back and forth, hugged himself. She then understood and stripped the little girl of her wet clothes and wrapped the jacket around her. After a moment, the baby stopped shaking. The woman took Payne's hand and kissed it and with the baby in her arms, she walked away, crying.

"Dear God, what are men like you and your friend Payne made of?" Suzanne sighed. Was courage a synonym for strength, or vice versa, or did it matter, she wondered?

"Shane, please stay with me tonight?"

Chapter Twenty-Seven

On the way home, Suzanne took Shane's hand from the steering wheel, and allowing passion to overcome fear, she guided his fingers slowly up her inner thigh. She could feel the heat start to build between her legs, and given how often Shane shifted on the seat, she suspected that something similar was taking place in him. She reached across the armrest to verify her hopes when, to her surprise, the Rambler took a sharp right turn and they were speeding up the moonlit driveway to her house.

They rushed out of the car and ran inside. Not even thinking about closing the front door, she led him down the hallway to her bedroom.

The room was barely lit by the moonlight, stretching the bed's shadow wide. Shane was tempted to grab her and throw her onto the bed, but despite his unyielding desire, he conceded that it was hers to will the night, not his. He followed her closely across the room. When they reached the window, she opened it to a gust of chilling wind.

"My… my escape route," she said, tripping over her tongue, which caused Shane to tense, wondering if she was about to jump through the window, but he hoped that the quick puffs of her breath was desire making her lungs stutter. He reached for her silhouette.

"He who follows Me will not walk in darkness, but will have the night of his life," she said, offering a surprising, though personalized quote from the Book of John. Their chuckling ended as she opened a dresser drawer.

The burst of a small flame startled Shane. His momentary blindness gave way to a shimmering glow from the wick of a capped lamp. She held the lamp and moved across the room. When his eyes adjusted, a wall covered with her sketches appeared. They included a building that carried the name Brooklyn Art Museum, the front of the Chelsea Hotel, whose name was broadcast on a marquee she'd placed on its roof, a bleak but all too familiar view of the River Mal as seen from a bridge and Jesse's name swiveled in the dirt behind the right field fence. Next to his name, a thin, young boy stood on a pitcher's mound, taking a sign from his catcher.

Inching along the wall, Suzanne said nothing until she reached a large painting of her father whose enormous eyes crept out of the shade. She leaned toward the painting. Over his shoulders sat vague images of the rogue jurors with smiles on their otherwise nonexistent faces. Her father wore a black coat and tie. She'd tightened the tie around his neck and extended it alongside his ear. The end of the tie disappeared into an imaginary attic opening. Lines like flumes ran down his cheeks carrying gold tears. His purple lips spoke to his death.

"I painted it the day after I got home, the same day I called Reverend Bradley," she said, raising the lamp to her father's eyes.

"He seems to be crying," Shane said.

She wanted to say that she was as well, but the moment wouldn't allow it. The emptiness in her heart that she could not hide nor even attempt to repress, showed in her eyes. Lamp-lit tears, gold like her father's, laced her cheeks.

Shane reached for her, but before his hand could touch her shoulder, her arms were around his neck. She clung to him so tightly that he could feel the warmth of her breath on his neck. He clutched her face in his hands, wanting to immerse his being in her breath, but before their lips could meet, she dropped her arms and pivoted to the painting.

She stared at her father and felt him returning the stare. She trembled and Shane stepped behind her to massage relief into her shoulders. As he pressed his thumbs into her clavicles, her father's eyes escorted him back to the courtroom, into the moment when he testified that he and Jesse were brothers. It caused Aiken to smile, for as he said, he'd just been given a gift by 'Master Shane,' a gentle, sarcastic feeling that Aiken twisted into a wink-and-a-nod at the all-white jury, suggesting the possibility that Jesse and Shane were in a relationship that was too close.

"What do you see in his eyes?" Suzanne asked in a voice that sounded like it was thrown over a great distance.

Shane left the courtroom with his answer. "Sadness... and love."

Suzanne stepped aside. "Now look closer."

He moved toward the painting and squinted. To his astonishment, he saw a tiny young girl in each of her father's retinas. Shane glanced from eye to eye. She was a perfect copy of herself, her own twin. She wore a white petticoat and held a bouquet of white lilies below her chin. "That's you, isn't it?"

"It was and still is," she replied with an eerie ripple in her voice.

It came to him. He'd seen the duel image before, when she stepped out on the trestle and instantly switched from the person she seemed to be into someone else.

"Here, Shane, hold the lamp while I get you some blankets. You can sleep on the living room sofa. There're some logs by the fireplace, but you'll need some blankets."

"I thought you wanted me to spend the night with you?"

She couldn't answer with the whole truth, whose wholeness lay in the admission that she'd fallen in love with him. She'd asked him to stay for the same reason she'd asked him to go with her to the trestle. She'd found strength in him, enough to get her through each day as the feeling of time running out hounded her. Without question, she'd led him to believe that sleeping together was her intention, but as hard as it was to turn him away, she slid again into the rabbit hole to explain away her lie with a half-truth.

"I asked you to stay with me, Shane. That's not the same as sleeping together. I have to sleep alone in my father's presence. I shouldn't admit this, but his image reminds me of what I did and the price he paid for it. That's why I want you to stay with me, why I wanted you to go with me to the trestle, to protect me. The irony of all ironies is this: I love my father beyond the meaning of what we call love, but I have to resist him in order to live. Yet, I'm not strong enough to do it alone." She paused to take a breath. "I know that it makes no sense to you."

"But Suzanne, like you said the other day, it's the same with me and Jesse. Your dad's gone but he can survive in your heart, without grief or worry, without living in your conscience. And you made me see that with Jesse."

"But with my father, it's not what I failed to do, but what I did."

"Keeping his ashes in the urn rather than scattering them at sea, the way he wanted? That's what you failed to do?"

She wanted to tell him that wasn't it and that there was more, but her voice trailed off. "He's gone but he isn't, and never will be unless…"

"Unless what, Suzanne?"

He waited as she lingered. Speechless, she became this beautiful, remote young woman who seemed to have slipped into another world.

Her eyes returned to the painting and she shook from her head to her toes. When she took off her tennis shoes, her bare feet appeared to be standing on top of the lamp's glow.

Shane felt trapped between disappointment and despair. She seemed much too far away to return anytime soon. He wondered if it was like the moment just before his father was sent away to the asylum, when that which had been on the way for some time, arrived at last? In case she needed help getting oriented, he would stay the night. And then, her lips moved.

"Shane, please stay."

She'd come out of her depths, but he was concerned that at any minute, she'd sink back into them. He didn't know what to say or how to feel about her request.

She went to her dresser, gathered three blankets from the bottom drawer and handed them to him. "If you think you'll stay, take these and make yourself comfortable on the living room sofa." She reached for the matches and the lamp and handed them to Shane.

Grateful for his response, she walked him into the living room, where she thanked him and headed back down the hallway.

He stacked a few logs into a triangle, lit the paper, and watched as the flames set in and the wood began to crackle. He stretched out on the sofa and pulled the blankets over him. The cushions gathered around him as though they knew the contours of his body. He had no idea that he was so exhausted but he wasn't surprised given the journey they'd taken — from morning to night, from the broken Jesus to the fair, from The Dream Team to the Ferris wheel and on to Ethan. It reminded him of a day in the jungle where the enemy and venomous snakes and giant insects kept the soldiers at the ready until the fear gave way to exhaustion and sleep overcame them.

Gradually, the flames settled into a glow that hovered over the bare floor like moonlight. He lay with an arm crossing his forehead, wishing the day had ended differently but admitting that he was glad he'd stayed. There was something strangely inviting about a place that felt forbidden.

He began to see the speckle of stars on the wall. He closed his eyes. The image of the gyrating Jesus floated across the darkness and exploded in slow motion, creating a maze of symbols that caused his eyes to open. A thin layer of smoke was rising above the mantle, masking Joan's image as it headed across the sea of Achelois. Wondering if the goddess was real, he felt the scar on his throat. There was no pain. He sank into the sofa.

Chapter Twenty-Eight

Suzanne hurried down the hall to take a quick shower. She hastily dried off, blotted her wet hair with a towel and twisted the strands to squeeze out as much water as possible. She glanced into the mirror to find herself staring at a medieval woman peeking out from behind a batch of coiled braids. She pushed them over her shoulders and hurried back to the bedroom to slip on a singlet and wrap a robe around her. She forced herself to climb into bed and stare at the moonlit painting of her father.

His voice was gentle and beguiling. "Suzanne, I love you and need you with me now more than ever."

Her heart started tripping. Nothing had changed. She'd lied again. The painting of her father was set at the trial, yes, but the look of sadness in his eyes wasn't just because of the trial and her mother's leaving. She threw back the covers and sprang out of bed.

What appeared to be the image of Joan d'Arc emerged from the smoldering fire and rose into the pain-free world. Gradually, the shadowy gold trusses of her hair deepened as she approached the sofa to lean over Shane. He tensed as her wet hair tickled his face. The distance between them was again defined by their breath. They moved through the barrier that had separated them in Medic's driveway. Their lips touched, slightly at first, waiting, hovering, trembling against one another's to gently force their mouths open. Their tongues met, flinched, softened and began to slide against each other like starving fish searching for food on a hook.

She could feel the desire in her breasts and below her waist. When she jerked the blankets away, Shane kicked off his boots and slid out of his pants. Suzanne yanked off her robe and singlet. There was nothing left to remove. She threw her legs over his pelvis and sank onto him. Given how fast time was fleeting, she felt that protection had no relevance.

She labored above him, her face and breasts streaked with sweat. She paused to raise her hips and slip back onto his thighs to coax him with her mouth. Then she returned flat and hard against his pelvis to finish what she'd started.

With every nudge she felt the urgency to climax. When she tilted forward to increase the pressure on Shane's pubic bone, he pulled her mouth against his. Neither of them could breath. The little shocks running from her vagina became lightning bolts throughout her body. She mashed herself painfully against his groin. Her body went numb and released a shivering, gasping pandemonium in the throes of a climax, the likes of which she'd never experienced. She screamed, "Love me!" and sank against him, embarrassed and contrite, trembling in the aftershock of her orgasm.

"I do love you," Shane said

The words lodged in her chest. She faced an abrupt fork in the road. Without a doubt, it was what she felt but could not, would not, say, for fear of ruining the night. Her body tightened. She tried to relax by telling herself that she didn't have to respond and in refusing to do so, she didn't have to admit that she was a coward or a liar and break the promise she'd made to her father.

She tried to collect herself. She nestled against his chest and touched his face with her fingertips. In her eyes the reflection of the fire from the floor lit the space between them.

Shane thought that maybe she hadn't heard him. "I love you," he said.

Shane felt a delicate sense of love passing between them, until she straightened and began to go on about her fear of impermanence, knowing nothing could possibly last, including time itself.

"We can't stay here," she said, scrambling to her feet to slip on a pair of soft sandals and her robe.

"Where're we going?" he asked, startled while belting his pants and hurrying to lace his boots.

Suzanne snatched up the blankets. "To The Lilly," she said in a rush.

"It's all right, Suzanne. We can stay here or in your bedroom. I'll be with you. You needn't worry."

"No, Shane. I can't stay inside, even with your arms wrapped around me. Come with me, please. I'll make room in The Lilly."

Attached to her nuttiness, he went with her to the veranda where they climbed into the boat and wiggled together as close as possible, with the narrowing stern pressing them into a V-shape. For a while they lay silent, staring at the sky. He put his arm around her and tucked her head into his chest. She told him how, when the fear of her father's spirit overcame her, she'd run out to the veranda, grip the ledge and with temptation pushing from behind, fight it by watching the color drain from the sea as the sun sank.

As the stars made their way from behind the moon's halo, Shane closed his eyes, listening to the tide recede while darkness seemed to ride in on it.

"You'll never know what this means to me, Shane, to have felt your love while our bodies became one. It's never happened to me before. I could just lie here with you until we came ashore on the banks of the Styx and be greeted by my father, who'd welcome you."

"Where?" Shane asked.

Her voice went into hiding. It came to her that she'd brought them all together at once: she, Shane and her father. She'd never thought it possible. Even at the top of the Ferris wheel when she felt her father's presence urging her to see the good in her life before she jumped. She lay still and silent in Shane's embrace, listening to the sea and watching the stars. "It gives me the… the courage to share something with you," she said.

"Please," he encouraged with an internal smile. Had the time come? Was she about to say that she loved him?

"Ever heard of a necrologist?"

"A what?" he said in disbelief.

"A necrologist, at least that's what this psychiatrist calls himself. He said that it's a psychiatrist who specializes in helping people gain a full understanding of death and how to put it in its proper place. Tomorrow I have appointment with one, a Doctor Rufus. I went to see him when I first got back from Pratt and my father's image started showing up. He sent me to this clinical psychologist to take a bunch of tests that Rufus said were necessary for his understanding. His helper called early yesterday to let me know that the results were in. Anyway, maybe afterwards, we could meet at Stavros for a drink. It was my father's favorite restaurant, and toward the end of his life, he and Stavros became close friends."

It wasn't what Shane had hoped, but he pulled her to him and looked into her eyes. "There's a quid pro quo," he said, running his hand under her robe to touch her breast.

She braced. "Maybe tomorrow," she said. "Please don't misunderstand me. I meant what I said when I told you that what happened between us just now has never happened to me before. It was like my body was coming apart, and I have to see if… I have to see if… if it gives me… I don't know how to say it, but if it gives me something I've never expected to have. I must give it a chance."

"I'm not following, yet again."

She smiled. "How could you? How could anyone understand a psycho? Will you meet me at Stavros for dinner, maybe early, around six?"

"Of course."

"I went there a few days ago to thank him for being so kind to my father," Suzanne said, wrapping her arms around a half-truth, or maybe better said, another white lie intended to both share and hide the truth.

"You mean, for the times Stavros went to your house and read Odysseus with him?"

Suzanne let it rest for a moment. She brought her lips to Shane's without touching them. What passed through her revealed something that said more than she wanted him to know, maybe even more than he'd want to know, that the missing part, the part she desperately needed but had no access to, lay tucked away below all the lies and wicked spirits that imprisoned her. At times with Shane, hoping to find it, she'd purposefully hinted at what she was talking about, and other times, the clues snuck out like gnats, but she'd swatted them away.

"It was for more than just reading Odysseus," she said

Their minds gave way completely, surrendering to the blissful confusion that each cast over the other and together, over themselves.

Chapter Twenty-Nine

At mid-day, Suzanne rode her Tiger out to the countryside where Dr. Rufus's office was located. The landscape looked like the end of the world. Where once there had been an orange grove, mounds of dirt now appeared on freshly scraped earth. Irrigation pipes and warming fans from a razed dye plant lay broken and twisted in a huge pile of abstraction, reminding her of a Jackson Pollack painting. The grey stone building was fenced in with barbed wire. It sat far off the road adjacent to the county prison. Mud had collected against the side of the building, making it look as if it was sinking into the ground.

The receptionist area was in an empty alcove walled in stone, cold and smelling of mold, as the dew clung to it.

A forlorn voice from an emaciated yet towering middle-aged man emerged from the darkness. "Miss de Ville?"

Suzanne tensed and tried to ease her shoulders. She was able to make out a thin face with eyes glowing like wet ice.

"Yes."

"I'm Adam, the receptionist who called you," the man said. "I'm also a patient of Doctor Rufus. He's waiting for you at the end of the hall. If you cannot see me, just follow the sound of my voice, and if you cannot hear me, just call out my name."

Trying to ignore the flutter in her chest, she wondered if she'd come to the right place? Had she gotten the doctor's name confused with someone else's?

"Miss de Ville," Adam said, "it's a fifty-minute hour and just to prepare you, every minute might well feel confrontational. The doctor has a kind heart but at times it isn't easy to feel. If you want to make progress, the goodness must be extracted from his demeanor and placed where it belongs, in your heart. Come with me."

As they started down the hall, a shrill cry pierced the air. Suzanne's eyes were drawn across the foyer. In a room showcased by two heavy glass doors, a pastel glow hung like a cloud above a hugging couple sitting in silhouette on what appeared to be a sofa. Masked by the somber light, they were as still as mannequins. Without warning, from the woman came another cry so full of pain that Suzanne and Adam halted. As she stood there trying to figure out which shadow had screamed, she was thrown off by another cry more piercing than the first.

"Miss de Ville," please let me explain," Adam said. "Those poor folks just saw Dr. Rufus and he asked them to take a rest before they left for home," Adam said. He clasped his hands and looked up at the moldy ceiling. "Take care of them, dear Lord." Without separating his hands he looked at Suzanne. "They lost their child, a young girl. Her name was Brahms. She was a violin prodigy who wrote classical music on blank sheets of paper that remained blank. She said that the notes rose off the paper to appear in her eyes, but she played the violin as if every note was really there. One day she brought her violin but would only play here, in the hall with the lights turned off. The music came through my ears straight to my soul."

"A piano savant. Just twelve years old."

A different voice broke through Suzanne's total understanding. She was greeted by a pair of eyes, blue and ringed with fatigue or illness. The man's body was stooped, bent at the waist, as though despair had invaded him like a disease. A stethoscope dangled from his neck.

"Brahms was simply no longer interested in living," he said. "Her birth parents had given her up for adoption and Brahms… she… she felt a deep sense of having been cast off unwanted, unworthy of love. She couldn't get beyond it." His moving voice faded. A moment passed. "I'm Dr. Rufus and my guess is that you are Miss de Ville?"

"Yes, I am."

"Very well, let's go to my office. Adam, keep me apprised of the couple's behavior."

"Certainly. Good-bye, Miss de Ville."

When Rufus closed the door to his office, Suzanne's sense of foreboding intensified. The room was small and windowless. Cigarette smoke hung above scattered pieces of clustered, oversized furniture. Two plump chairs faced each other over a round granite table. On top of the table sat a bowl stuffed with cigarette butts. The bookcases were packed with medical reference volumes and between them a framed, slightly extended version of the beginning of Medic's favorite poem: "Death be not proud, though some have called Thee mighty and dreadful, for thou art not so."

Rufus' desk was a block of rough stone. Next to his sagging captain's chair, a halogen desk lamp beamed light onto a folder. He picked up the folder and came out from behind the desk to sit into one of the chairs and ask Suzanne to join him.

As she sank into her chair, her rear dropped below her knees. She pinned her legs together and did her best to take only small breaths of the stale air.

"The little girl felt she had no choice," Rufus said. "The cloak of life became too heavy, and she suffocated under its weight." His lips moved again but no words came out. He shook a Camel from a mangled pack of cigarettes and lit it. He leaned back as he inhaled and let the smoke out slowly. "Death is like that, isn't it, Miss de Ville, ever-present and vigilant, yet it need not govern us. So why then do we make so much of it?"

Suzanne assumed he was drawing a parallel between her and Brahms and meant the question for her, or was it for him because he had no answer? She remained silent and shoved her hands under her legs. She sensed her pulse speeding in her hamstrings.

"Why do we make so much of it and in doing so, refuse to put it behind us?" Rufus repeated and waited for a reply.

Suzanne waited as well.

Snuffing out the cigarette in the bowl of bent butts and picking up the folder, he sighed, "Why do we?" The question disappeared as he flipped through the folder, stopping now and then to glance a page. He put the folder down, leaving it open while he sighed again. "Death for most of us is a troubling subject is it not?"

Suzanne felt caught off-guard, realizing that he was again expecting her to answer.

"Don't be embarrassed," he said. "It's troubled mankind since the beginning of time. Is it not what brings you here?"

She pressed her fingers into the chair but didn't respond.

Rufus scrutinized the open page. "According to what I see here, the answer is, yes. Meaning, that from the look of your Rorschach test results – by the way, Miss de Ville, the Rorschach is, in my belief, the most reliable of the tests Dr. Chapman administered – yes, from the results you live in a very different world than most of us."

"We all live in different worlds," Suzanne said.

She'd taken the Rorschach, which she learned afterwards, was considered by psychiatrists as fun game. It was described by some of the doctors as 'having fun with madness.' A series of inkblots had been placed in front of her and she was asked to study them and tell the amused doctor administrating the test, Dr. Chapman, what she saw. She thought that maybe he'd been playing a joke on her and was showing her works of what she thought had been abstract art. But she'd responded to the abstractions and continued to listen as Rufus read her answers.

"You referred to the images as a spinning wheel, a spaceship blasting off to the sun, a photograph of two islands, a beautiful ballerina, a log cabin on a cliff, my father's motorcycle parked in the living room under the spell of Achelois, the Cave of Heracles on the shore with its beaten pier."

She'd seen far more but wasn't about to share them. She'd seen a cloud with her father's face scrunched in agony, the piercing look in his red eyes, a pile of used condoms on her bed at the Chelsea, giving her mother the finger as she left home, the sight of the ocean as she plunged from the veranda, sitting alone on The Lilly with its lost engine, with the oars in her frozen hands.

"Who is this Achelois? I'm not familiar."

"The Greek goddess who rids us of pain."

"It wouldn't appear that she's done so you, Miss de Ville. Am I correct?"

Suzanne did not answer.

"What say you, Miss de Ville?"

"It seems she has."

Rufus' eyes were filled with frustration. "Let me read to you what Dr. Chapman, who interpreted your test results, made of them. And I quote, 'The patient's personality is in the process of deterioration… her ego strength is too weak to mediate the world of reality or cope with normal stress…' And here," Rufus dragged his finger down the page. "'Her basic affective controls are insecurely and tenuously maintained. She possesses a pessimistic, fatalistic and depressive view of the world around her and maintains a constant preoccupation with death.'"

"What do you make of that?" Rufus said, lighting another cigarette.

On the one hand she felt that it described her to a tee, but on the other, it was too mechanical, too scholarly for her to give it credence by admitting to Chapman's interpretation. "I believe the results of such tests can be made to say whatever one wants them to say, Dr. Rufus."

"Why then did you agree to take the test?"

Why had she? What the hell was she even doing here? Because she'd dipped far down to the bottom of the swamp and at last was able to admit that she needed help? But help for what? You know the answer, she told herself.

"Honestly, Dr. Rufus I'm not sure why I took the test. For the heck of it, I suppose. I had no idea."

He set the folder on the desk and tapped at Chapman's conclusions. "Miss de Ville, listen to what the doctor's saying and reach deep inside to be honest with yourself. According to this, the real world, that is, the norm — trees, homes, streets, love, hate, temptation and so on, is collapsing around you. You're replacing reality with a self-induced reality of your own, a reality with its own rules and order, which ironically produces no order whatsoever. It only creates loneliness and despair, sometimes even hallucinations, all designed to protect you, perhaps under the guise of your goddess, from pain in a world of fantasy and illusion you've created. It allows you to hide beneath your soul in a make-believe world that doesn't work under any circumstances. Miss de Ville, you are on the edge, and it won't take much to tip the scales in the wrong direction."

Her father's insurmountable ghost-whisper inserted itself with its warning — without repentance, she would lose his love. She clenched her jaw to prevent her teeth from shattering and disappeared into memories she hoped would bring her distraction. Closing in like jungle heat, she remembered Medic's voice introducing her as Van Gogh's granddaughter, her canvasses at Pratt laying in a junk pile and Shane taking her down from the ledge on the veranda. Then, somewhere deeper her memory's alleyway, she was up on the joists in the attic, fumbling with the remnants of the noose when she heard Shane calling for her.

"Sorry to interrupt your thoughts, Miss de Ville, but would you mind telling me where you were are at the moment?"

She winced at the sound of the doctor's voice. She'd been drawn off course by the passage of time, which abruptly filled the echo of Shane's voice with the memory of reprimand in her father's eyes. She struggled to collect herself.

"Nowhere important," she managed.

"Let me be the judge of that."

She pulled her hands from under her legs and slid her wet palms over the arms of the chair. "Some memories come to me in fragments, Doctor Rufus, memories that I don't try to recall because I don't want to. It's like I'm drawn to them by a harness," she said, wondering why she'd answered.

Rufus nodded, "And what does that feel like?"

She felt embarrassingly vulnerable, naked in front of someone who'd just barged into her room at the Chelsea. "It's like driving at night with no lights," she answered. "Being pulled along by something outside the car, some force that's chained to the past and unaffected by the passage of time."

"So you've created a world without natural law where things like gravity, sunshine and the need to hydrate have no consequence, no place in the scheme of things? A place where the thought of being happy is prevented from entering your mind. Forgive me when I say this but that sounds suspiciously like a fantasy world, a make-believe world created to shield you from yourself."

She wanted to tell him that her world wasn't a fantasy, that it was real. It was what her father had seen when his time was done, when the delusion of a wonderful, fulfilling life had been lifted to expose towering spans of hope lying in ruin. She hurtled past the destruction, wondering if time finally run out? Had the gateway opened? Had she, as had Brahms, earned the right to leave this world?

"How long have these delusions been going on?"

"They aren't delusions," she said. "They're as real as life can be."

"How long, Miss de Ville?" Exasperation lay heavy in his voice.

Suzanne took a deep breath, letting it out slowly. "Months, years… since time began, I suppose. I don't know."

"Did they start when your father died?"

Her father's image floated like soot through cigarette smoke.

"Miss de Ville, let me repeat. Did these feelings start when your father died?"

Died. She rubbed her jeans and griped her knees, wondering why he'd said it that way? So declarative, so final, hammer to steel, as if he thought that he had to jog loose the memory of her father grimacing and moaning while she helped him off the pier into The Lilly.

"I'm waiting for an answer."

What was her father's last thought? That she'd forsaken him not once but twice? Not only on the ladder…

"Miss, de Ville, did you hear me?"

Hear what? she mimed. Her father's gasps after she got him seated in the boat or hisses, scorning her for saving his life? She leaned forward, pushed against her thighs and rose to her feet.

"Miss, de Ville, by chance were you with him when he passed away?"

She stood wobbling as the question tore into her. Rufus tapped the desk with a knuckle. She was inside a box balancing on a teeter-totter. Someone was banging on the box with an axe. She had to get out.

"He died alone," she said, watching herself on the trestle, held in place only by Shane's presence. She shuddered, clasped her hands over her ears and closed her eyes. Echoes, explosions like the New Year's rockets, yellow moons and words burst around her like shrapnel. She was tempted to grab the lamp and bash Rufus's head in.

"Is it your guilt over not being by his side when that moment came that keeps him alive? Does your absence translate into feeling responsible for his death?"

Just when the chaos inside her was about to explode and shout out the truth, her voice, unexpectedly calm, but firm, emerged from the silence. "You're wrong, Doctor Rufus. Love is what keeps him alive," she said and headed for the door.

"Where are you going, Miss de Ville? There's time left in your hour."

She opened the door. "Thank you, Dr. Rufus, but our session's over."

"Hold on a minute. We need to schedule."

Hurrying down the hall, she slowed when she saw Brahms' adopted parents kissing. Love in the most difficult of times, she thought and felt a strange elation, heard stillness like never before, pure atoning stillness, not even a semblance of sound past or present, not a hint of loneliness.

She realized why she'd asked Shane to go with her to Stavros. Because there, she'd left a gift that couldn't be mistaken for anything but love. The gift was for Stavros, yes, and for her father, but it was more than that. It was an attempt to transmit through her father's spirit what she'd been afraid to tell Shane, that she was in love with him.

Chapter Thirty

Stavros was located on Weyburn Street, deep in Meridien's old tobacco district where the poorly lit streets lay somewhere between bustling on the weekends and deserted during the rest of the week. But even though it was Tuesday, the night was alive. A line of cars almost a block long filled the street. The robust sound of Greek music heightened the excitement as Suzanne and Shane pulled into the parking lot where years ago, a Black pool hall, named Holland's, had been set on fire and shuttered forever by Whitewash.

Several days before the fire, Jesse had taken Shane to Holland's where the staircase was filled with pictures of Jackie Robinson, Willie Mays and Hank Aaron. Unlike being in a poolroom of whites, he and Jesse were welcomed with smiles. It put Shane not only at ease but made him glad that he'd come. He'd never been in the presence of so many Blacks nor had he ever played pool before.

Jesse showed him how to hold a cue and position himself to take aim. As they played, Jesse virtually ran the table in almost every game. Gradually, a group of Blacks gathered around to watch. When Shane won his first and only game, they clapped and invited him and Jesse to join them at the bar where they were treated with handshakes and beer. It struck Shane much differently than a crowd standing to cheer for him after he'd pitched a winning game. It was more than congratulatory. It was welcoming, so much so that they stayed until midnight and downed a few too many beers bought for them by the patrons.

When Holland's was burned down, Shane told Jesse that it was like a friend had died.

As they climbed out of the Rambler, Suzanne clicked her fingers. "Got it, Shane! The song's from the movie, Zorba the Greek. Stavros gave the record to my father. He played it again and again. I must have heard it a thousand times, as well as the story of The Odyssey."

"That was some time ago."

"Oh, just to remind you, Shane. There is no some time ago. We, you and I, are breathing the same molecules that Homer breathed. And that's not all, not by a landslide. You are breathing Jesse's, which allows you to feel not only his presence but his love and I… I'm breathing my father's, whose presence…"

"Whose presence…?"

She wanted to end the sentence by saying that her father's presence allowed her to be in love with Shane but couldn't bring herself tell such a lie.

"Whose presence is lost in the excitement taking place inside the restaurant," she said, taking Shane's hand. "Come on. There's something special going on."

When they entered the bar, the party was in full swing. In the large dining area, raised a few steps above the floor where the bar was located, everyone was crushed together amid ear-splitting noise. Two young servers were in constant motion, filling glasses with what appeared to be white wine, but could have only been retsina, and rushing plates of souvlaki and moussaka to every diner who waved.

A waiter dressed in a blue apron with the word Charon printed across the chest met them at the door. He was carrying two full glasses. "A retsina for each of you," he said. "Stavros saw you crossing the street and asked me to rush this to you. He's at the grill making moussaka for everyone. You're Suzanne, aren't you? I've seen what you did, what Stavros calls 'his gift.' It's amazing. I wasn't here the other day when…"

Suzanne politely shushed him with a finger to her smiling lips. "Is your name really Charon?" she asked, wondering if her father's spirit was trapped in the excitement.

"Yes, after the ferryman of Hades or elsewhere, depending on your choice." Charon pulled an uncorked bottle of retsina from his apron. "Please hoist your glasses in a toast to Adrian. It's the night of his life, so to speak."

Unfamiliar with the honoree, she and Shane went ahead and raised their glasses. "To Adrian!" they chimed in lockstep.

"Bless you, Suzanne," Charon said. "Stavros cordoned off the barroom the day…"

Suzanne instantly mouthed a forceful, "Ahhhh!"

Charon smiled. "I'll say no more. The bar's open for the two of you. Sit anywhere you like. Wave for me, if you need anything."

"Wait a minute, Charon, who's Adrian?" Suzanne asked.

"You'll find out soon enough."

As Charon headed toward the party, Shane tipped his glass to Suzanne. "To you."

"Why me?"

"For being you."

"You mean, for being a whack job?"

With fun nudges, they made their way to the bar and seated themselves. They toasted again while the smell of moussaka drifted around them.

Suzanne's reason for bringing Shane to the restaurant was overwhelmed by the celebration. A thick gathering of partygoers was packed around an extended set of dining tables. The men and women were dressed in paradoxes. The men wore what appeared to be expensive dark coats without ties, and denims held up by narrow belts with large brass buckles. The women were dressed in shiny black and white dresses cut just above dark penny loafers.

Both men and women shouted as they raised their glasses repeatedly to toast one another and signal the need for a refill. Charon and two young helpers darted from guest to guest to fill their glasses. Several patrons helped a bald gentleman climb up onto the end table and braced him as he dithered. His face was partially masked with large, circular glasses that expanded his eyes into ping-pong balls. They handed him an ancient megaphone and he began to croon in slurred Greek syllables with a Spanish-sounding accent. Occasionally, his tongue seemed to catch behind his upper teeth to reconstruct the sound of the letter F into that of "sh" which combined with his accents to transcribe the word, fit into shit. When he made such sounds the deafening mayhem of laughter presented a barrier that Shane and Suzanne had to break so that they could hear one another.

The song ended. "A Greek homecoming for Adrian!" the singer shouted above the applause, followed by a woman's voice calling out, "May he live forever!" Feet began to stomp the floor, causing the seats at the bar to tremble.

In a cave-like cranny at the end of the bar, Stavros was hunched-over, his back to them, scraping the vast, black grill with a pumice stone the size of a brick. Sweat covered the grimy white shirt stretched over his round, Zorba-like shoulders. A sweaty fellow chef dressed in a smudged apron quickly filled the cleaned spaces with pieces of pork and skewered them for the Souvlaki.

The inseparable chatter sounded like a group of caged parrots. To try and get away from it, Suzanne and Shane moved down the bar to the last two seats. In the cobalt glow of the oven's burners, Suzanne's black leather jacket was shining like a wet seal. The chest and belted waist were studded with rows of glossy brass buttons. The lapels were laid open to expose a necklace with a dangling cross whose rosy glean carried into the sheen of the leather. In the reflection of the glass behind the shelves of whisky, Suzanne watched and smiled as Shane's eyes scanned the jacket.

Stavros glanced over his shoulder, dropped the pumice stone on the grill and hurried to the counter wiping his hands on his apron and smiling. I'm so glad you came, Suzanne. How grateful I am for…"

"Meet my friend, Shane," Suzanne said. "I'm keeping the secret from him for now."

"Shane, not Shane McCauley, the Jefferson High pitcher that Suzanne's father could never stop talking about?"

Shane smiled. "Maybe I'm still that person, but probably not."

"Suzanne your father would stop by for a beer or two after your games and tell me all about them, strikeouts, flyballs, hits, runs, the whole thing. Shane, he thought you were going to the big leagues, but if my memory still serves me, I believe you joined the Marines after… after the trial."

"You've got a great memory. I did join the Marines."

Stavros's placed his hand on Shane's shoulder. His smile gave way to an unmistakable look of pride. "Thank both of you for coming tonight. I'm sorry it's so raucous but a celebration's a celebration, at least by the Greek definition. Suzanne, is now a good time or should we wait until things die down? It'll be over by ten."

"Let's wait," Suzanne said. "By the way, Charon mentioned that the celebration was for a man by the name of Adrian. Is it his birthday?"

"Oh, were it so. No, 'tis a funeral. It's part of a Greek tradition that calls for death to be celebrated, not denied, because it is the celebration that rallies the gods around the loved one's soul to protect it from bereavement. They're striving to send a Greek brother, who just passed away, across a flowing river to the far side where the wicked are forbidden and he can wait for his loved ones without fear."

"In the Elysian Fields," Suzanne said.

Stavros nodded and pointed toward the partiers. "See that man, the singer sitting at the head of the table downing his retsina? His name is Staunch, Staunch Castellanos. He's Adrian's brother. Adrian fell while freeclimbing a beautiful but frightening pinnacle in Meteora, in the Ionian Sea, where they built the stone monasteries."

Suzanne leaned across the bar. "I'm sorry, Stavros, I don't understand. Maybe it's the noise. Why would his brother celebrate his death?"

"Your father never told you?"

"No."

"I'll try to explain. Your father was here the night we celebrated the death of a coal worker from Appalachia who was killed when the mine he was working caved in. George asked the same question you just asked. As his condition got worse, much worse, he asked the question every time I went to visit him. It wasn't because he mistrusted my answer. For a while, I must admit that he did have trouble getting his mind around it. But in time he did. It made him happy."

"Stavros! We're running on empty! More retsina!" The demand blared from the megaphone.

"Be right there!" Stavros shouted. "Suzanne my apologies for not telling you the other day, but I didn't want to interfere with what you were doing. I'll be back in a moment."

"No rush. We'll be here," Suzanne said.

"What's he talking about, Suzanne? Interfere with what?" Shane asked.

"The gift I brought him in appreciation for the help he gave my father."

"What was it?"

"You'll see."

Stavros grabbed several bottles of retsina from the shelf by the cash register and hustled to the party room where he set them on the table to applause. He brought his hands together in prayer and the room went silent. He prayed in Greek, lowered his hands to cross himself when he finished and then, he hurried from table to table bowing to each person and quickly sipping from the glasses offered by the thankful. When Staunch passed by, he took a cigarette from his lips and handed it to Stavros. They traded it back and forth until there was nothing left. Staunch fingered a small box out of his pocket, rolled another cigarette on the table, lit it and passed it to Stavros who took a deep inhale and coughing, let it out before wandering breathlessly down the steps with the cigarette between his lips. Stumbling, he grabbed onto the bar.

"Stavros, are you all right?" Suzanne asked.

He took the cigarette out of this mouth and cleared his throat. "You ever smoked a spliff? You know, paper rolled with skunk. It ain't the animal, I'm referring to."

Suzanne laughed. At the Chelsea, she'd used spliffs to take her mind away from the guy she'd most recently met who was always accompanied by her father's threat. "I know what it is," she said. "You're not hooked on it, I hope."

Stavros cleared his throat and chuckled. "No more than any man is to good medicine. It started back when I was a boxer on Crete. Smoked it to clear my head after a fight and settle the pain. Nowadays I take it for my nerves and stomach. A few drags check the desire to heave. You want a taste?"

He twisted the joint so close to Suzanne's mouth she felt that she had no choice. She knew not to lip it and dry-sucked it as far down into her lungs as she could. She let the smoke dangle in her lungs before letting it out slowly. The horrible taste lingered in her mouth. She wiped her lips and started coughing.

"Grab onto the counter and breathe deep," Stavros said.

The cough ended. Thankful she'd left the habit at Chelsea, she shook her head when he offered her a second drag. "I'm done, but thanks, Stavros."

Looking fondly at the joint, he smiled and heaved a sigh. "Some say skunk fell from the Tree of Life. Some say it's what Jesus gave to the Apostles at The Last Supper. Ever noticed that little smirk on the Savior's face? You ever seen the look in His eyes? I suspect He was stoned most of the time."

It took her back to Southhall and silenced her while Shane and Stavros laughed. She'd seen the look in Christ's eye when she held it in her hand. It wasn't from skunk or any such thing, but from sadness.

Stavros sucked the joint to a nub and stuffed it into an ash tray. He reached under the counter to retrieve an open bottle of retsina. "It'll take away the taste," he said, filling their glasses and leaving the bottle on the counter. "On me."

"Thank you," she said as the taste disappeared.

"By the way, Suzanne, I've been wanting to ask you something for the longest time, but give me a sec, the room's swirling." He grasped the counter, rolled his head around several times and shook it abruptly. "Better now. The whirl helps every time. "Ok, back to my question. The other day, when you were in the corners, did you see what your father saw?"

She replied immediately, wanting to keep Shane on the sidelines until they were alone. "Stavros, you knew him so well. What do you think he saw?"

"The same as Adrian."

"And that would be?"

"In one word, courage. Adrian was a free-solo climber, maybe the most dangerous sport on the earth, short of war. He was a metalhead with a total disregard for danger. When people would ask him how it was possible not to fear falling. He'd tell them that every fear can be overcome by challenging it at its core, which he claimed he did by practicing falling. He started low, falling from a height of five feet and worked his way higher until he was granted access to eternity. He said it was like climbing a rope to the clouds where God lived. Staunch, told me that Adrian once threw himself off a hundred-foot cliff and survived. That's how he mastered his fear and allowed himself to move to the heights above.

"When we started reading Odysseus together, your father thought it was a fable, but as the pain worsened, he saw that it was a truth designed to last the ages. One day toward the end of his life he told me, convincingly, that he was moving ahead, not in spite of his illness but because of it. I wasn't sure what he meant and became concerned, so one day he called and asked me if I would come to visit him. It was in November, about now, close to the day he passed away. I believe you were out getting him some food, Suzanne."

Stavros paused and with glazed eyes, looked into the corner of the room where the sharp angle of the window prevented the passing sunlight from coming in.

"He welcomed me and asked if I'd help him out to the veranda and sit him in The Lilly. I lifted him off the floor, took him outside and sat him in the hull. It took time for him to connect Homer's thoughts, but his grit assembled and he pieced them together as if Homer was sitting on the balustrade.

Suzanne's glass rattled on the bar. Shane reached out to steady her hand.

"Your father told me that Odysseus had discovered how to escape the grip of Calypso and fool the wicked spirits who were so intent on keeping him on this earth in the housekeep of pain. He said he'd discovered how to dismiss the threat of never being allowed to cross into the Fields. It had to do with the sufferers' line, as he called it. He came to the realization on what he considered to be the anniversary of Homer's death."

"From God's mouth to Homer's quill to my father's soul," Suzanne said.

Stavros grinned. "A message sent only to the few."

"The time has come!" the singer's voice blasted over the giant speaker. Amidst a cluster of earsplitting screams, everyone grabbed a plate and smashed it on the floor. The flinching sound swiftly devolved into an emboldened chant.

"Opa! Opa! Opa!"

Shane gripped the counter. "What's going on?"

"Have no fear," Stavros said with joy in his voice. "The breaking of plates is called Kefi, a Greek symbol of love, and more importantly, a gift of trust that hope will be realized. That given pursuit, the answers we're looking for will show themselves, as happened with Adrian and was abundant in your father."

"The answers we're looking for will show themselves," Suzanne repeated.

"If given pursuit," Stavros amended.

"And with the help of others?"

"Kefi teaches that we cannot clean up another's sorrow. When one's been brave enough to leave sorrow behind, it will disintegrate into forgetfulness so strong there will be no desire to recall it."

Suzanne glanced at Shane and tightened her grip. "And when is that?" she asked.

"When the broken plates are pieced together," he said and glanced at the disappearing crowd. "Mercy, I'm forsaking my duty folks and must leave you to stand in the warmth my guests leave behind, such as in the gift you gave me."

"Thank you, Stavros," Suzanne said, again remembering her visit to the attic, when Shane showed up and unbeknownst to him, saved her life. She wasn't sure what happened the moment she heard him call her name or what she'd seen in his eyes when he stepped through the front door, but it took no longer than the moment in Medic's driveway to realize that a chance to overcome her father's chokehold had entered her life.

"Turn around, Shane," she said, slipping off the stool and rushing to the end of the bar to flick on the overhead lights whose sharp violet beams reached into the far corners of the room. The fragments of the last few minutes vanished as the light was absorbed by the corner paintings whose depth not only stunned Shane but drew him off the stool into the middle of the room.

In the walled corner, a painting of a dirt road bound by Corinthian columns stretched into the third dimension. Headed down the road was an apple-red motorcycle, no doubt the Tiger, driven by a woman whose long hair was blowing in the wind. Behind her sat what must have been Suzanne's father wearing a dark jacket sprinkled from shoulder to shoulder with emeralds. He was leaning forward with his arms around her waist and his chin resting on her shoulder as if he were whispering in her ear. Shane felt he could run into the corner, jump on the bike and ride off with them into eternity.

"And look over by the window," Suzanne said.

Shane was barely able to pry his eyes away and shift to the other corner. There, the overhead light made its way through a bewildering jungle of painted branches that held a number of what appeared to be leaves shaped like books with torn and shaggy covers. Each bore the name, Odysseus, and under the legend's name, the word, s'agapo, the Greek word for "I love you" that Stavros had spelled out for her. Shane's eyes flicked from one impression to another, trying to convince himself that he wasn't seeing things.

"How did you do that? It's like a 3-D movie."

"It's an art form called trompe d'oeil," Suzanne said. "Paintings that deceive the eye, making you want to step into them and transform yourself into their reality. A painter from ancient times, ironically a Greek, with this strange name, Ouisix, invented the art. He painted a vineyard of grapes so that birds would fly to it so they could feast on their imaginations. So many artists ventured into the medium."

"It's like I'm seeing something I'm not seeing, like your painting in the living room. Is that a Greek word on the books or something you made up?"

"It's Greek for joy," she said, circumventing the true translation. "Things we think we see are often not the things that are, and the things that we do see often aren't. All of which is to say, do you think Mrs. Abernathy would mind if I spent the night with you tonight?"

In the gap between total surprise and laughter, Shane replied. "I'm sure she won't mind at all."

They thanked Stavros and shook his hand. When they were about to get into the Rambler, she told Shane that her palms were slippery wet. "It must be my nerves," she said.

"It's called a miasma," he said.

Chapter Thirty-One

On the way to The Oleander Suzanne kept the hidden takeaways from the paintings in her protected world of enigma. But as was true with Adrian, she told herself that maybe none of it mattered for now because she knew where she and Shane were headed and fed on the anticipation.

"Suzanne, should we stop by your house on the way?"

"What for?"

"I thought maybe you'd like to get some warm clothes, like your robe or pajamas."

Her smile was pleasantly sinister. "No, Shane, I won't need either of them because I don't plan on wearing any clothes."

Until their eyes met, they didn't laugh. There seemed to be a silent agreement that humor was welcome but not allowed to take over their desire. So, it didn't become laughter until their eyes agreed that wit could intercede. Their amusement rolled into a shared cackle so strong that Shane had to slow down. Laughing, they crept along the rest of the way. Chuckling, they pulled up in front of The Oleander and kissed, renewing the taste of retsina.

When they got out of the car, Suzanne gazed at the house. "It would make a haunting, Halloween painting," she said. "Looks like a dark cloud settled around it, giving permission for the ghosts to start flying out of the windows. Thank goodness for the moon," she said. "Is it hard sleeping in there?"

"Only if you're looking to light up a ballfield," he said, remembering his dream the night he returned from Dallas and imagined himself soaring over the high school's newly installed lights toward the moon. They'd defeated Martinsville, the toughest team in the county. His ball had reached one-hundred miles an hour. Jesse had been there.

He took her arm to climb the porch stairs. When they entered the living room, the yellow reflection of the evening's half-moon was shining down through the tall side window bringing an ashen light to the Persian rug.

"The not-so-harvest moon is on its way, just a couple more days," Suzanne said, wishing she hadn't. She moved into the light without a smile.

"Who might you be, my dear?"

Suzanne flinched at the sound of Mrs. Abernathy's voice, followed by the soft notes of a piano, which added to the sense of the mystical already in the room. Eunice sat across the room at the piano. An open bottle of whisky sat on its top. The moonlight turned the spokes of her wheelchair gold. She placed her fingers on the keyboard and began to play and sing "Auld Lang Syne."

"That was beautiful," Suzanne said.

"Nature has a basic note," Eunice said, without any reaction to their presence. "B-minor, always B-minor; most motors run in B-minor, telephone wires hum in B minor. Some people lie and cheat in B-minor, others leave home in B-minor and should be forgotten and forgiven if they never return, but such surrender can never happen because God answers your prayers, urging you to cling to your hope."

"What does it sound like when He answers your prayers?" Suzanne asked.

"A little voice in your head whispers in B-minor, like this," she answered, barely striking the note. "And the irony is this, it sounds exactly the same when you die." She looked at the two of them curiously. "Who are you?"

"I'm Shane, remember, the boarder upstairs, and this is my…"

"Mel passed away the other day," Eunice interrupted. "It broke my heart. I've been taking in the whisky to try and avoid a heart attack."

"I'm so sorry to hear that." Shane said, pausing for the sadness to pass. "Mrs. Abernathy, I'd like you to meet Suzanne."

"But Mel still talks to me when I'm out on the porch at sunrise. Is there anything you'd like me to tell him?"

"That I miss him."

"And he certainly misses you," Shane said.

She took a sip of whisky but offered none. "It restores my brain," she said, putting the bottle back and turning away from the piano. She and leaned over the edge of the bumblebee rug into the moonlight's hem, which colored her gray hair with a garnet tone. She capped her eyes to ward off the glare and took a sip from the bottle. "Young man, the lady standing at your side in the moonlight, is she real or an angel or both?"

An aura of orange framed Suzanne's silhouette. The gold in her hair was aglow. Eunice's comparison of Suzanne to an angel reminded him of the twins she'd sketched in her father's eyes. "She's both," he replied.

Suzanne gently nudged his arm with her elbow.

"Do you have a name, angel-lady?" Eunice said. "Oh, forgive me. First, I should ask if you speak aloud or transmit your omens through the air, like the angel Gabriel, who went to Mary without words to tell her about the forthcoming arrival of the Christ Child. She knew as he approached her that her womb had been pledged to the heavenly Father."

Suzanne answered with a smile. "I do both, Mrs. Abernathy. I speak and transmit my omens through the air. My name is Suzanne."

"Of course, it would be Suzanne. In the Jewish faith your name means love. Is it any wonder that the wandering spirit by your side is drawn to you? And certainly you to him. The two of you must be in love."

Suzanne remained quiet.

"I'd like to think so," Shane said.

"And how 'bout you, angel-lady?" Eunice said.

Suzanne hesitated. The words edged out. "I would like to think so as well."

"But not really? Is that what you mean? In other words, you can't look Mel's spirit in the eye and say, I love you?"

Silence came instantly and thickened as her question lingered in the awkwardness. Eunice rolled her wheelchair into Suzanne's shadow, where the spokes of her small chariot lost their gleam. She reached out, took Suzanne's hand and ran a withered finger over her palm, then joined Suzanne's hand with Shane's. Instantly, Helen Keller's quote about how the rapture of love can be felt when one's hand touches another's came to Suzanne.

"Something lost, something gained, and when we are lost, we are somewhere in between," Mrs. Abernathy said, hoisting her whisky bottle to Suzanne, "I sense such a conundrum in you, angel-lady, and I would imagine it's similar to what Mary felt in Gabriel's presence."

Shane was astonished at the change in Eunice. When they first met, she was a cigar-smoking, tough-talking woman with a waning mind, but now she seemed mystical, religious, and poetic and yet stayed on course with a sense of assurance.

He could feel Suzanne's fast heartbeat in her hand and wondered if she was about to let go and run out the door but, to his surprise, she squeezed his.

"Suzanne, perhaps the spirit told you, but in case it didn't, I feel I must," Eunice said. "My husband, Abe, lost his soul in the Battle of the Bulge. He returned home, well, not exactly home, but to the Smokies. Even there amid the rocks and storms, which you would think, being God's decorations, would help him find his soul, but he's never been able to. So, dearest angel, you're not alone. I, too, am caught in the helm of loss and gain."

Suzanne released Shane's hand. Hadn't Stavros been quoting Homer when he said that when one's been brave enough to leave their loss behind, it would disintegrate into forgetfulness a forgetfulness so strong there would be no desire to recall it? She was tempted to ask Eunice why, if she thought if such a thing was possible, hadn't she put the loss of Abe behind her.

"Mrs. Abernathy, thank you for your inspiration," she said instead and glanced at Shane. "It's been a quite a day. Could we please go get some sleep."

"Let's do."

"Sleep brings darkness of which we are not afraid. Why then, when we wake, do the sorrows cascade upon our hearts and minds to insure that we are afraid of the day ahead?"

It begged the question. Suzanne wished she had an answer. "I don't know that poem, Mrs. Abernathy. Who wrote it?"

"Abe. He wrote it after the battle was o'er and sent it to me by way of a raven, as was the way during the War. One day when I was sitting out on the porch watching the rain pour down like sorrows upon my heart, the raven landed on the railing and left the poem there. How the bird had flown so far, I've never known, but it gave me confidence that Abe was on his way, no matter what. Sleep well, angel."

As they moved toward the staircase, Suzanne watched as Eunice rolled farther onto the rug, taking their place in the moonlight. She hunched forward, silent and still. Rainbowed tears slid down her cheeks. Her mouth didn't move but her voice found a way. "Abe will be home soon," she called after them. "Thanks to an angel whose name means love."

Suzanne's breath raced, preventing her from saying what she wanted to say. Eunice was right when she told them that they were caught in a conundrum. The only advantage of being handcuffed in such a place was that it was a paradox, but only for those who could understand it, and while understanding was no guarantee for escape, it was a reason for hope. As Stavros put it, that given pursuit the answers we're looking for will show themselves, as happened with Adrian.

Suzanne felt that listening to Mrs. Abernathy was weirdly insightful. The whole concept of nothing lost, nothing gained was frightening, for, caught in her own wartime trench, Suzanne had no way out. To climb out and run from the shelling would mean her death. She had neither the strength nor the courage.

Her purpose for coming to The Oleander was another test, a challenge to try and determine if Shane did have access to the very things she didn't, things that her father also had access to but used as a way to control her destiny. She knew that it made no sense, but when she stepped into Shane's bedroom and saw the deep, arcane allure of moonlight across his bed, it gave a different meaning to the idea of spending the night with him. It bordered on a heating compulsion to stay with him. She took a deep breath, gagged at the enduring warmth of retsina in her chest and wished she'd brought a bottle with her.

Chapter Thirty-Two

The smell of retsina made an even stronger comeback when they turned toward one another and kissed. Suzanne wanted desperately to put her instincts aside and tell Shane what he wanted to hear. She wanted to climb inside his desire to make love and at the climactic moment, scream, "I love you!" The time of her exodus was two days away. She had one day left with Shane, one day. If only she could bring herself to leave the past behind, she could treat their time in bed as making love with love.

If only, the phrase of the misbegotten, the last thought before dying.

She glanced toward the moonlight and, feeling its pull, she felt the passion in her body, the yearning below her waist and realized that when matched with such cravings, the mind has no chance.

As Shane hurried across the room to yank the covers down, she dropped her dad's jacket on the floor and without delay undid her blouse. Shane whipped off his pants. She slipped off her skirt. They stood looking at one another until, in one sweeping motion, they were naked on the bed swapping tongues. Overcome with desire and without a care that she might alert Mrs. Abernathy, Suzanne shouted unashamedly, "Make love to me!"

Though her voice was loud, her father's incessant mandate rippled through her cry. She heard it every time she switched from the person she'd made herself out to be, into the person she was, both a liar and a betrayer ashamed and haunted by guilt. Every time she'd been with Shane she'd had to deal with her mental subterfuge. Every time she felt guilty as hell for betraying both him and her father, but she could do nothing less.

She wanted to be honest, to fill in the details, to tell Shane that she'd used him over and over to attempt to shun her true commitment — the day they went to the trestle, when she'd leaned over the abyss into the windstorm, hoping to see the face of God, the night they'd gone to the fair and he'd put his arms around her when the Ferris wheel jolted to a halt and her father seized the opportunity to beckon her into oblivion, the day at Southhall when Shane had come to her rescue, and the first moment of escalating hope, the day on the veranda when he grabbed her ankles and guided her down from the railing. Hope jumped from the outer limits of her subconscious into her heart.

As if she were mounting the Tiger, she swung a leg over Shane and came down on his manhood. Gasping, she began to rub back and forth, causing soft waves of pleasure to wash through her. Her ribs contracted until she could barely breathe. Tiny shocks originating at the tip of Venus fired into her nipples in an unbroken stream. Shane's lips grabbed onto them like a thirsty baby. Her staggered moan rose to a cry. She tossed her head from side to side as she arched her back to force her pleasure spot even harder against him. They made love faster and faster until the minutes it usually took to bring her off became seconds and then the uncontainable storm of sensations erupted, coalescing into a scream.

"Forgive me!" she cried. Instantly stunned and embarrassed, she sank her head onto Shane's chest, scared that he knew what lay beneath her scream.

He groped for his breath. "Forgive you? For what?"

Still trembling, she scrambled for an answer. "For yelling like an idiot. I'm sorry, I couldn't control myself. I've never felt anything like that, not even on the sofa." She hesitated. "Shane, what does one have when a lie and a truth are parts of the same answer? Guess what? You have deceit."

"Jesus, what's that got to do with anything?"

Relieved, she sought his breath and they kissed.

"I love you," he said.

He lifted his head slightly for her reply.

She teetered on the fence, knowing that the distance between them had narrowed. More than anything, she wanted to return the words, but she went still and mute instead. The harvest moon was beginning and, with it, the shortening of time.

His now softened penis quivered and came to life. He rolled onto his side and started kissing her neck and cheek and working his way to her breasts.

Venus began to warm again, insisting that she slip under him, but her second orgasm was always more powerful than the first. If she spun out of control and screamed again, she had no idea what might come out of her mouth. Though more than vulnerable, she was strongly tempted. Beyond the temptation, there was nothing she could do because the jailed reasons for keeping Shane at bay found their way between her legs. He slipped into her and sensations throughout her body began to shriek, raising the fear level that she'd lost all access to the ability to refuse him.

She fought it as long as she could, telling herself that she had to separate her conscience from her body or risk losing her father forever. She bit her lip, clenched her teeth and tightened her jaw, fighting to keep herself to herself and climax apart from Shane.

When he began to gasp, her imagined twin arrived. She was Suzanne's age now. They had no business straying from their father. They joined hands. The distraction momentarily sidetracked her body's rush to detonation and allowed her to forge the explosion by moaning as Shane released. She lay there fallow, but panting. She hoped her father was relieved.

In an attempt to cover the awkwardness, she began to cough in a long chugging breath, but when she ran out of air, she could see the anticipation of what he hoped she'd say in his eyes.

"If only we could live here together… forever," she said. It was as close as she dared.

Unexpectedly, he smiled. "We could become Mrs. Abernathy's apparitions," he said. "Mel and the Angel."

"Sleep tight," she said, sighing in relief as he pulled the blankets over them.

Chapter Thirty-Three

She turned on her side toward the window and Shane put his arm around her. As their hearts calmed and the mattress went silent, he sighed and his arm sagged against her waist. She stared at the moonlight watching it creep across the window and slowly inch down the narrow, shingled walkway that stretched along the roof and led to the widow's walk.

She blinked when she noticed the stiff plank poking out over the front yard like an ironing board. She told herself that she was seeing things, while knowing full well she wasn't.

The widow's walk was often a fixture on the homes build by the tobacco barons. At The Oleander it made more than perfect sense, for as was well-known, the walk was made for women whose husbands had gone to war and failed to return. The widows would go out on the walk to watch and wait for their husband to come home, refusing to believe that his ship home had been hit by a submarine and had disappeared below the coral reefs. Suzanne wondered if Mrs. Abernathy had ever been able to go out on the walk?

Perhaps a woman's heart-wrenching hope that the love of her life would return from war wasn't far from her own situation. Would Shane believe that she would return when she left? Would he go to the trestle and look out over the ocean certain that she was on her way back? Would he go to Blinder's or to Stavros or Blackberry Hill or even to the streets around the Chelsea to try and find her? Or if he stayed at The Oleander after she left, would he go out on the widow's walk, assured that one day he'd find her running through Hook's Alley calling for him?

Suzanne lay on the bed staring at the moon until her father's spirit beckoned her. She tensed and tried to make him go away by shaking her head, but his directive held steady, demanding that she obey, giving her yet another chance to atone for her mistakes.

In the off chance that he would let her, she wanted to shout again, "Forgive me!" but the words clogged in her throat and devolved into the sound of a suppressed cough. She started to wake Shane up and halted. Unlike the other times when she'd managed to sneak him past her father's watch, this time her father was not just on duty but seemed keenly vigilant. Her plea remained silent, resonating only in the corridors of her mind. She stayed in bed as long as she could, hoping that her love for Shane would keep her nestled in his arms despite her father's ultimatum, but love had taken a break.

"Shane," she whispered to make sure he was asleep. When he didn't respond, she softly lifted his arm and set it between them, then crawled out of bed and cautiously raised the window. She worried that she might disturb him if she put on her clothes, so she climbed naked over the windowsill onto the walkway. She stood shivering as the freezing air enveloped her. She thought about the possibility of the cold blowing in and rousing Shane, so she eased the window down, watching to see if he'd wakened. Thankfully, he remained asleep.

With the air biting at her skin, she stood looking down the narrow walkway. Because Shane had been with her at every opportunity, she'd not been able to keep her promise to her father, but now, though Shane was nearby, she had to try and disregard him completely. As Rufus said about suicide, taking one's own life was so frightening that leaving this earth usually required three attempts. And as in Adrian's situation, with each attempt one gains more strength and eventually becomes able to put fear aside. She wasn't sure if this was her third or maybe even her fourth try, but it was the last chance to free herself from her father. Day after tomorrow, on the fifth anniversary of his death, she'd sworn that she would join him. There would be no give and take, no tearful plea and no chance of forgiveness. Shane would be far away, far too far for unrequited love to travel.

The cold was unbearable, reminding her not only of the ice plant but winter at the Chelsea, painting in her unheated room, fully clothed and a blanket wrapped around her. Her nipples hardened as she looked down the walkway. Banisters on both sides of the gangplank had been crushed by the fallen tree limb that lay over them. Getting to the widow's walk would be a balancing act, yet if she died by accident and not by purpose, it would be like sneaking onto the train with Judas without a return ticket. To keep her promise she had to die by resolve. If so, maybe she didn't have to consider it to be death at all. It might be as the Greeks deemed it, a lone crossing to the far side of the Styx and then, if granted a ticket, to the Elysian Fields where the miracles of love and forgiveness flourished, converting Death into an emboldened cause for celebration.

Her fingers trembled along the clapboard siding as she edged down the walkway. She moved carefully toward the corner of the house where the walkway became a path that funneled onto the widow's walk.

She made her way to the thick bough and climbed over to the edge of the plank. She looked down at the moon-shaded willows. Everything she could make out seemed to have been still forever, the sprinklers by the gate, the string of stones along the alley and an old boot crumpled by the bird bath. The silhouette of a cross appeared on the horizon and evoked the sight of Christ's porcelain eye in her hand.

When she stepped onto the plank, the vortex of the past began to spin in the trees. Lightheaded, she spotted the faint letters of the ice plant's broken name and remembered standing behind Jesse's melting sculpture staring into Shane's bewildered eyes.

Her legs began to shake and the board creaked faster. She glanced at the bedroom window. It was closed. Had the last chance to break from her father run its course? She'd vault as high as she could to find out. Her years of diving at the Lake had taught her how. It was called the five-step hurdle. She would gain her poise at the rear of the board, then take three quick steps, followed by a skip and a hop on the fourth step, when she'd lift her leg to her hip and shove it into the board to gain as much height as possible before she came down on the end of the board and vault into eternity.

When she aligned her heels with the edge of the board, heat rose in her chest. It had been years since she'd taken a dive, but what difference did it make now, she wondered? She'd leave this earth no matter how flawed the dive. She rose to her toes and dropped her arms behind her and rushed into the hurdle. When she jammed her leg into the board on the fourth step, the plank screeched like an ally cat. Suddenly the words, "I love you!" lanced her ears. Had they come from Shane or her?

Her instincts answered instantly. She twisted her hips and shoulders toward the house. When she came down on the middle of the board it wailed and began to crack but her momentum yanked her off. She stumbled onto the pathway and toppled over the branch. Gasping, she came to her knees with her heart racing and her head spinning. She took a quick look at the window. It remained closed.

When the dizziness started to wear off, she got to her feet, pressed a hand against the side of the house and crept back to the bedroom. She leaned close to the window. She could hear Shane snoring and as far as she could tell, he hadn't moved. She raised the window, inched into the bed and nestled beside him.

He rolled against her and flinched. "You're freezing," he said.

She took a deep breath. "I… I'm sorry. I crawled outside for a minute to see the moonlight."

When the explanation replaced what was screaming to escape her heart, she knew that the spell wasn't broken. So, in her damaged world it made perfectly good sense to ask Shane if he would meet her at the Cave of Heracles tomorrow, Friday afternoon about five, when her father's vision of the harvest moon would be in the sky, the day before the anniversary of his death.

Chapter Thirty-Four

She'd put off telling Shane about the Cave of Heracles because she had no idea that their relationship would ever get this far or that it would turn on this moment, but because it had, there was no other choice. She'd run out of time. After all, she told herself that when an imposter works so hard and long to cover-up the truth, her chance at honesty is reduced to a moment, and if the opportunity is lost, the moment becomes oblivion. Even so, against all odds, she pleaded with herself to enjoy her last full day on earth and know that her joy would endure forever once she crossed the river.

In reality, the beach was named The Crystal Cove, but to her father it was known as the Shore of Heracles. With his penchant for Greek myths and customs, he'd come to believe that inside the cave, located at the far end of the beach, his hero, Odysseus, had conjured up the spirit of Heracles from the underworld. Once done, Odysseus allowed the survivor of the Twelve Labors to wait on the banks of The Styx for Charon who would deliver her to Psyche, the muse with whom he'd fallen madly in love and agreed to have her take the deserving souls to the welcoming Elysian Fields. The myth, pieced together by the winds while he suffered on the veranda, strengthened his belief that when Suzanne came to join him in the afterlife, she would find his soul waiting for her with outstretched arms on the same riverbank.

She asked Shane to meet her at the entrance to the cave, which was set inside a cliff of ancient stones whose multi-colored striations of gold, green, red and blue mixed to turn the stones into perplexingly beautiful waves. Despite her knowledge of paints, she was mystified, unaware that such color could not only be stirred by time but could endure its ravages.

It was just a simple cave, until the day she rolled her father out onto the veranda in a wheelchair and he seized the ledge with both hands, his fingers locked. When Suzanne tried to pry him loose, he told her to stop because she was interfering with his memory.

"The cave. Something about that cave," he muttered. "Remember when we were in Morocco?"

Suzanne sighed. She'd never been to Morocco and, to her knowledge, neither had he.

"I knew it!" he bellowed, clearing the relentless clog in his throat. "It's the Cave of Heracles, where he went to rest before... before... cleaning the stables."

Excited, he tried to stand up, but his hands were stuck so he could only lift his haunches a few inches out the chair.

"Odysseus loved Penelope as much as I loved your mother," he said, easing his way into the seat and starting to cry. Knowing that his emotional pain was far more hurtful than the pain in his hands, Suzanne pried his fingers from the railing and took him into the kitchen for some whisky. From then on, they would go out on the veranda every day to view the shore and repeat again and again how much he loved Elaine.

Shane showed up at the cave before Suzanne. The waves were chest-high, rolling over and crashing upon themselves in crescendos that were too magnetic to be called noise and too deafening not to be. It came to him that the sound might be the ocean's resonance of joy, its own deja-vu that dated back to the beginning of time. It crossed his mind that he was beginning to think like Suzanne and his smile expanded.

The sunlight shining through the cave's opening faded as the grotto narrowed. Shane could only make out the shadows of the hollows in the walls, which according to Suzanne's father, once housed ancient beasts. With little more to be seen after staring at the paintings, he returned to the entrance to look for her. What he saw brought him to a standstill.

Wearing a white terrycloth bikini, Suzanne stood ankle-deep in the water, looking out to the sea. She'd changed into the likeness of a strange and beautiful seabird, thinner than the ballerina he'd imagined her to be when he first saw her at Medic's. She appeared thinner than at the Oleander and yet more beautiful and mysterious than ever. Though sunset clung to her body, enhancing her beauty, her sensuousness repelled any worry that she'd taken ill. Her face seemed to float in the faint light. Her thighs, bared to her hips, and barely covered rear shivered in the cold water. The brine foamed around her ankles and licked at her toes.

"Suzanne!"

She glanced at him and waved. If only he knew why she was there, she thought, feeling guilty that he didn't, but realizing that if she told him what she was about, she would drown in guilt. Yet she was tempted. It was why she'd asked him to meet her there, to see once again, if not for the last time, he could save her before tomorrow arrived.

She put her hands on her hips and, after a moment, slipped off her bikini, tossed it toward her winter coat and sweater, her jeans and boots she'd laid over the rocks. Her undies and her watch with no hands lay on the coat.

As she moved deeper into the water, he watched, both worried and fascinated as the water rose to her thighs. She splashed the freezing water on her arms and breasts before slowly advancing until the water touched her chin. Shane jerked off his boots, quickly rolled the legs of his jeans above his calves and rushed out of the cave.

Her head bobbed on the water as if she'd been decapitated. Then she dipped below the surface and breast-stroked farther out. Shane was about to rip off his clothes and go after her when she flipped onto her back, floating on the tide toward the shore with her arms planted against her sides. She remained motionless until she washed into shallow water. Gasping and stumbling to stand up, she found her balance. Relieved, Shane sloshed through the foam until he was beside her, and she smiled. She grabbed his hand and led him to her clothes where she dropped his hand to pat her chest. "Good God, my skin's burning."

He grabbed her coat, which was heavier than he expected. "Here."

"Hold on," she cautioned. "I'll put it on in a minute. I want to see just how long it takes for the stinging to stop."

She touched his cheek with the back of her hand. The distance between them narrowed but she stopped before their lips could touch. It was the moment she'd been praying for, but the words "I love you" hung in her mouth. The hypnotic energy in Medic's driveway passed from her heart to his and they kissed gently. Abruptly, she turned away to face the sea.

"Shane, don't you just love the ocean, how the water sloshes over your feet and ankles, how you hold your breath when diving into a wave just before it breaks, but more than anything, how the water in your eyes doesn't prevent you from seeing the truth. To stand in the water at nightfall, looking above the sea to the islands, you are alone, except for those you love and have left. I used to come here for just that reason." She smiled at the statement threaded with contradiction and truth, contradiction and deceit.

Shane thought of Blackberry Hill, when he lay on the dampness beside Jesse's grave in the miasma and listened for his brother's heartbeat. He'd heard nothing but he'd felt the closeness, reminding him of what Saul had said about a special love between the living and the dead. He wondered if it was something like opening a suitcase that's been closed for years and feeling that you knew the person who packed it by the things they cherished, or was it more like putting your head to a gravestone and hearing their heartbeat?

Suzanne turned her probing eyes to his. "What if I can't stand another storm. Can't raise my fists daring lightning to strike them? What if I don't have the courage to lift my head toward the heavens and scream, "Fuck you? What if, Shane? What if?"

"What if, what? I have no idea what you're talking about, but regardless, what if you can?" He draped the coat over her shoulders.

"Then I'll know. I'll know that pain's irrelevant, ephemeral, a temporary channel through which true love passes," she replied, nodding as if trying to convince herself.

She threw her arms around him. The coat slipped off her shoulders. She pressed her goose-bumped flesh against him.

With a kiss so rousing, they had to adjust their breath to taste the wetness of each other's tongues. They clung to each other until they lost all awareness of where they were. Nothing mattered but the moment and they were happy to be at its mercy. It lasted until their bodies gave out and their mouths separated. They stood panting as the forgotten sound of the sea came back accompanied by the loud, squeaky whistling of a gang of sandpiper plovers landing at water's edge.

"My God," Suzanne said, still trying to recover. "I don't know what just happened. Maybe that's what it's like to die."

"Or what it's like to live," Shane said.

Her eyes seemed to agree, but she remained silent. She slipped on her clothes, picked up her coat and tightened the cloth belt around her, then shook the sand out of her bikini and stuffed it into a coat pocket. While the clouds gathered in her eyes, she pulled a bottle of retsina from the other pocket and handed it to him.

"I stopped by Stavros on the way here. Let's have it in the cave."

At the entrance Shane popped the cork and offered her the bottle.

"No, no, you first," she said. "You've more than earned it just by coming here. It made my father smile."

Shane took a sip, Suzanne a swallow. "This is where I launched The Lilly to take my father's urn out to sea. To this day I've felt so guilty that I didn't save it. Every time I go into the living room, I picture the urn on the shelf between the Bible and Odysseus. I've wanted to paint it forever but couldn't bring myself to. Why did I say it would be okay to cremate him, to jam his ashes into the likes of a huge jelly jar?" Her head tilted slightly, as though she was listening to what her thoughts were about to say. "Shane, now you know the entire story about what makes me so strange."

Under the restrained passion in her tone Shane thought he detected a plea for him to understand whatever the moment had whispered to her. Whatever she meant, he knew only that something, a current, a flow, a wave of such a message had passed between them unheard.

"Ok, Suzanne, enough bullshit," she said. "Let's go into the cave. I want to show you something."

He followed her inside and almost ran into her when she suddenly stopped to place the retsina into a hollow and take out a box of kitchen matches. She struck one and held it toward the wall. Gradually, she moved ahead while lighting a long line of murals that went deeper into the cave than he'd ever gone before. There was a painting of an old Pontiac with the figure of a Tiger on the hood. Beside it, the faraway trestle replete with winds, and within the winds the ghostly face of what Shane took to be the face of God. He recognized the thin snakelike letters of Jesse's name and her father's image sketched in a wheelchair. As the cave narrowed, a painting showed a naked couple standing and kissing with a hint of the young man's erection pressed between them. And last, a sketch of her standing offshore in The Lilly with her hands cupped around her mouth like a small megaphone. The words "I love you" swept from her mouth, forming a path to the wings of Achelois lifting the muse toward the roof of the cave.

"I do this when we aren't together, sometimes even late at night or early in the morning, before sunset, like today," she said. She blew out the match and reached into the last hollow to retrieve two halves of a plate. She handed Shane one of the pieces and fit hers against it. "Opa," she said. "They came together perfectly, as Stavros said they would. Now, you keep my half and I'll keep yours."

They traded, but Shane couldn't so much as glance at it because his eyes were glued to hers. Neither of them moved. He didn't know what was about to come out of his mouth but he knew what he wanted to say more than anything. It arrived with a passionate glitch in his voice.

"Suzanne, will you… will you marry me?"

Without a second's hesitation, she responded, "Of course, I will…" and seemed to drift far away. "When I return," she said.

Disappointment tore through Shane's excitement like a rush of ammonia, until it dawned on him that a short gap in time wouldn't change a thing.

"A cause for celebration," she said, and reached for the retsina. "Here."

"You first," he said, elated.

"No, you."

Instead of answering, she reached out again. "Make love to me, here, now."

In a heartbeat, her mouth was on his and in one movement they were on the wet stone floor. Neither flinched at the cold. His knees slid as he pinned her arms to the ground, biting at her nipples through the singlet until she whimpered. He slid back and pulled at her panties until they were between her feet. He sank into her and she yelled, "Yes!" tossing her head from side to side and squeezing her breasts with her hands, arching her back and pushing against him as their pelvises chafed. He exploded, screaming her name and jabbing wildly inside just to feel something, anything.

"Yes!" she yelled again, forcing him against her, with the stiff edges of her feet clawing at his legs.

Her heart was going wild. Her mouth was wide open, gasping for air, and she went rigid. A low, staggered moan rose to a cry and suddenly she was on her feet with tears streaming from her eyes. She'd done all temptation had bade her do.

"I have to go," she said. "The time has come and I can't do anymore to put it off."

"You're leaving now, right now?"

"Yes."

"Please, stay."

"If you allow people who love you to come to you, they will. They'll find a way."

He'd never heard such resolve in her voice. "I believe you," he said.

She stroked his face. "No, you don't, but you will."

"When are you coming back?"

She straightened her clothes and feigned a smile. "Soon, and when I do, you'll be happy to know that I won't be coming with me. I have go now." She kissed his cheek and hurried out of the cave. He started after her, but stopped. What more could he have hoped for? She said that she would marry him.

Chapter Thirty-Five

The anniversary of her father's death arrived. Suzanne barely slept. The night had vacillated between fear of what she was about to do and a determination to put fear aside. She got up before sunrise and went to her father's desk to write Shane a letter to explain why she was leaving. After struggling with the letter for the better part of an hour, she reduced it to a note and put it aside. The words were weak on paper, but it was all she had. If it was a letter of consolation, it hadn't worked.

Before sunrise she went to The Oleander to leave her farewell in the mailbox. She was about to slip it inside when the door opened. Eunice glanced at the envelope and her eyes widened.

"Angel, is it from Abe?"

Suzanne's heart sprinted. "No, I'm sorry, Mrs. Abernathy, it's not from Abe, but I know he'll be coming home soon," she said. "It's for Shane. I'm going away for a while and I want him to know how much I'll miss him. Would you give it to him late this afternoon, at sunset?"

"Sunset?"

"It'll mean much more then."

Eunice reached for the envelope but suddenly concerned that the note might never get to Shane, Suzanne pulled it away.

"I see the worry in your eyes, angel," she said. "Here, give it to me. You have no reason to be worried. A letter from an angel to a spirit is Heaven sent and must be delivered."

"It just came to me, Mrs. Abernathy. It would be better if it came from a living voice rather than a piece of paper. Would you please tell him that I love him. Put your heart into it and say it with meaning, this way, "I love you!" Suzanne said, emphatically.

"I certainly will. See you soon."

As Suzanne got into the Pontiac everything was a blur. Time had run out. No need to ever remind herself again. She'd made a decision that couldn't be altered. She'd calculated the day down to the hour and the hour down to the rising of the moon and that to the image of her father's welcoming arms when she reached the River's bank.

She wanted to row out to sea at the coldest part of the day, at high tide, so that the water would do its best to harness her pain and put her to sleep as she read it would. She'd taken the time to thoroughly research the process of drowning. How long did it take? Between eight and ten minutes. How to avoid coming to the surface? Let the water stream into her lungs. What to do with her arms to prevent them from instinctively fighting to the surface? Either fasten a cement block to an ankle, as her father had done, or pinpoint her toes, slap her hands firmly by her side and refuse, against every natural demand, to reach out and shove to the surface.

Worried that a weight tied to her ankle would rush her to the bottom and slam her into a pile of rocks, she decided against bringing a concrete block, though she suspected that her father would want her to leash her determination to one. She packed the pockets of his jacket with gravel from the driveway.

With no engine on The Lilly, she knew that rowing out was going to be tough, so she researched it as well and learned that when the tide was high, the ocean worked with the moon to make the flow stronger and faster, helping one to get through the challenging breakzone where the waves gathered and mounted before breaking and coming ashore. She knew that she had to coast the waves, to angle The Lilly in order to ride the swells, and once mounted she had to take advantage of any remaining tailwind to lever the boat into the calm and make her way to the place where she'd betrayed him for the last time.

When she'd taken him to the pier that evening, the moon was rising and so was the tide. On wet, flat sand, she'd backed the The Lilly into the water and helped him out of the car. She sat him on the pier with his legs hanging over the edge, and unleashed the boat from the trailer. As it eased from the shackles, she gripped his wrists, which were locked at the elbows and edged him off the pier into the boat. He wobbled as his feet hit the hull, causing The Lilly to rock from side to side. Just when she thought that they were going to fall into the water, his muscles locked and he tumbled into a knot before collapsing on the hull. She'd felt terrible but his fall gave her plenty of room in the transom to jerk the three-horsepower Johnson to a start. She rotated the engine and they headed out.

With waves slapping against the boat, they plowed through the incoming waves and reached his imagined destination. When his body had gradually relaxed, he made her unhook the engine and let it fall into the water. "The motor won't allow the wind to choose its course, so be done with it," he'd said. "When we're gone, The Lilly will float to God's destination and Death will welcome us with celebration."

Chapter Thirty-Six

To have the tide at its highest, she had to be there just before sunset, when the moon challenged the equinox and the waves were ebbing and flowing rapidly.

Wearing her father's leather jacket and the same jeans she'd worn the day she took him to sea, she backed the Pontiac to the edge of the veranda. She strained to latch the trailer to the car and then went into the living room to kneel in front of the fireplace to plead with Achelois to watch over her. In case the pain of drowning became severe, she wanted to ease into the afterlife without giving her body any chance to betray her.

Had she gathered the strength to do such a thing from the most paradoxical of all sources, from Shane? Never had she any idea that the very strength she sought from him in order to deny her father's presence would be the same strength that would allow her to join her father. She'd made beyond the customary three attempts. Now, she'd reached her last, though it wasn't an attempt. It was a feat, an accomplishment achieved.

She'd done her due diligence and was ready. Her only lingering worry was Shane. Would he, as did Romeo, end his life to be with her? It delayed her for no more than a moment because she'd convinced herself that despite his love for her, he was too strong to even consider such a thing. Rather, he would choose to play out his natural life. He would find someone else, hopefully with her still locked his heart, and someday they would meet again, on the River's bank or in the Fields.

She took the highway to the turn-off to the shore and sidled past the rotting wood guardhouse down to the sand. A moment of relief came when she realized that her timing was exact. The tide was beginning to rise, yet there was still a stretch of wet, flat sand that should keep the Pontiac from sinking. Cautiously, she inched the car to the pier and backed the trailer into the water alongside the ruins. Through the rear view mirror, she could see the winch lines tighten as the water began to buoy The Lilly.

Relieved, if not encouraged, she shut off the Pontiac and made her way around one of the two remaining pylons onto the creaking wood where she unlatched the lines. She gripped the side of the boat and in one motion, grabbed onto the rower's seat, hoisted a leg over the side and pulled herself onto the seat and slipped the oars into the locks. With her back to the sea, she pulled away from the shore.

In the breakzone the incoming tide splashed hard against the aft, drenching her, but when the water receded she leaned back to get the most thrust she could from the oars. As the tide reversed itself, she pulled herself together and rowed into the sunset. As the ocean's mist trimmed her vision, the shore faded from sight and the cave became a dot. How long had she been rowing? She had no idea. She began to wonder if she'd passed the site of her father's death. And realized that it was a fool's question. How could she have possibly known exactly where they'd stopped?

The cold clung to her back as she sat idle to catch her breath, but she was now warmed by the joy in her father's eyes as she imagined him greeting her and telling her how proud of her he was and how much he loved her, but when he followed with, "Death is a cause for celebration," she almost lost the grip on the oars.

Exhausted and fighting to breathe, she swung the oars into The Lilly. No need to go any farther. It came to her that exhaustion was a good thing because when she sank into the ocean's vacuum, any instinct to fight to the surface would be overwhelmed by her weak muscles. She would do her best to open her mouth and smile, to inhale as much water as she could. Her lungs would fill, shutting down her body. She would turn ice cold. Her brain would fly into the stratosphere and her heart would collapse. No longer would she be stalked by the anger in her father's eyes. She would be with him in a matter of seconds.

She held onto the sides of the boat and came to her feet. The darkening sea was frightening. She took deep breaths and widened her stance. A wincing, crying sound escaped her mouth. Her chin shook reducing the sound to a frightened stutter. Shivers covered her body. She told herself steadfastly that the time had come.

Chapter Thirty-Seven

Shane awoke late in the morning dizzy from the retsina but buoyed by Suzanne's vow to marry him. He was climbing out of bed when he heard a gentle rap on his bedroom door. He threw on a wool shirt, wrapped a towel around his waist and cracked the door open to find Eunice standing there, seeming embarrassed. Her mouth began to twitch.

"I was out on the porch this morning waiting for my Abe when your angel stopped by. She said that she'd parked at the end of the nook so she wouldn't wake anybody up. She told me that she was about to leave town for a while, then put a finger to her lips and asked if I would pass along a message to you. She stammered and had to clear her throat before asking me to tell you that she loved you, but to say it from the bottom of my heart, so you could feel her voice speaking to you, through me."

Eunice closed her eyes and crossed herself. It appeared to Shane that she was whispering to someone inside when the words, "I love you," came out in a key so passionate that his spirits were raised.

"Did she say where she was going?"

"No, but it was somewhere she didn't want to go. It was written all over her face. She promised she'd be back soon, and she meant it. I can assure you that. By the way, I almost forgot. I don't know for sure but she might have left a note in your car. Maybe it says where she went."

As Eunice started down the hall, Shane didn't think to close the door. Hoping Suzanne had spelled it out at last, he threw on his clothes and boots, ran out to the car and jerked open the door. At first glance, no envelope. He looked on the floorboard and in the back seat. The glove compartment was locked. He checked the trunk, nothing.

His heart was riveted to his lungs. Terrified, he started the Rambler and took off.

If she'd set out to commit suicide, it would be by drowning. She'd inasmuch as admitted that at the cave. She hadn't been looking for her father's urn. That much was clear now. Why else would she have been wondering about the effects of the depth of the water and how, at a certain level, the cold would put a person to sleep so they could die without remorse or pain. But it wasn't as she'd said, an effort to understand what her father had gone through when he drowned. It was to understand what she was about to go through. It was clear to him now; why hadn't it been then? Because she'd said that she would marry him.

Glittering lights and windblown tinsel chattering like static swarmed back and forth across the street from lamppost to lamppost. There were so many that they seemed to draw the buildings on each side of the street closer together. It took just a moment before Suzanne's street sign, Woodlawn Drive, flew across the window. He almost missed it and spun the steering wheel so abruptly that it almost threw him out of the seat. He halted in front of her house.

The Pontiac was no longer in the driveway. She'd left the Tiger on the side porch. The bare branches of the elms where she'd housed The Lilly resembled a group of skeletons. He could see through them to the clouds hanging over the ocean. The Lilly was gone.

A truck packed with lumber sailed past. Even the normal sound of huge tires peeling over the asphalt was siphoned off into the immense solitude.

He rushed down the narrow road to the shore's empty parking lot. The Pontiac was parked on the flat, wet sand by the pier. It faced inland. The rising water was level with the car's rear fender and the trailer was underwater. The Lilly was nowhere in sight. He jumped out of the Rambler and ran toward the car.

"Suzanne!" He yelled and splashed through the ebbing tide. The driver's window was closed but an envelope with "Of course, I will!" written on the face was taped to the steering wheel. He jerked the door open and grabbed the envelope, but with his heart in his mouth, he couldn't bring himself to open it.

Instead, he scanned the sea. The islands came into focus but there was nothing in between, not even a buoy. As he searched the beach in fear that her body had washed ashore, hope became despair, and as the despair boiled over, he glimpsed a bottle of retsina at the entrance to the cave.

He stuffed the envelope into his jacket and sprinted through the foam. Was there any chance that at the last minute she'd chosen to stay?

"Suzanne!" he shouted at the entrance. The only reply was the echo of her name. The setting sun gave light to her murals. Then a sudden leap in time to a fresh sketch of herself standing nude, offshore in The Lilly, her hands in prayer as the words "I love you" rose into the cloudy image of Achelois's wings.

"Suzanne!" No reply.

The bottle was half-empty. Was it left over from yesterday? Or had she come this morning, he wondered? He gulped at the retsina until there was only a swallow left. He imagined her refection rising from the shore, her excited eyes blue as the sea, her long hair as wavy as the tide and her fragrance as unique as the salty smell of the water. He reached out for her and she tentatively asked if he happened to be Shane McCauley and, if so, would he marry her?

He stumbled into the water and sloshed to the Rambler, started the car and turned the heat vents toward his legs. The muscles in his calves started to shudder. He never suspected that love could be so devastating, so unyielding.

He took the envelope out of his jacket and stared at it. He didn't want to open it but now he had to. Her words came off the page.

Shane, I pray that you've gone to the beach to find me. While I'm not there in person, I am in spirit. I started this letter last night, intending to leave it at The Oleander, but I couldn't find the strength to finish it until this morning. You might consider it my letter of consolation. If you choose to throw it away or burn it, I understand. But if you choose to keep our love alive, as you have your love for Jesse, I promise that when we do meet again we will be inseparable.

In Medic's driveway pure love showed itself for the first time in my life — and scared the hell out of me! For a while I wondered if that's how love really felt. To be so rapidly and unexpectedly drawn to someone, even without so much as a kiss, was more than an eye-opener. See-Through put it together for me — love surfaces the moment our hearts realize that the other person possesses the very traits that we have but have no access to. In my case, I saw them immediately on the veranda the day I met you. They are strength and courage. Both are hidden somewhere in my soul, while you carry them in abundance.

I hope more than anything that you will never question my love for you, despite what I'm about to do. I'll never forget what you shared with me, that there is a certain love between the living and the dead.

The trip I'm about to make speaks to my major weaknesses, the lack of strength to stand up against my father and the lack of courage to stay with you. How close did I come to throwing myself off the veranda or the trestle or the Ferris wheel or the widow's walk? I was tempting fate with each but your presence coaxed me off the ledge and allowed me to stay with you, at least for a while.

The truth and the irony behind all this is that I shouldn't have saved my father when he tried to hang himself nor deceived him by promising that I would row him out to sea and that he and I would drown together. When I told him about my plan, he repeated joyfully what he'd taken from Stavros, that death is cause for celebration. Each of my mistakes, disregarding his pain and deceiving him, was the right thing to do and each the wrong thing to do, the inescapable enigma whose code I could never break. I am Judas, seeing myself as a savior and a savior seeing myself as Judas.

Shane stopped reading as the irony of it all settled around him, resonating as though he and Suzanne were still in the cave together. As Medic said, creativity was often mistaken for insanity and at times it was the other way around. And yes, he'd fallen in love with the person she was and the person she wasn't, a mesmerizing enigma that came together in a bizarre, yet magnetic individuality, a quality that he'd had no access to since the day Jesse died. It resulted in years of single-minded revenge, girded by shame and guilt, forcing him to abandon his soul, until he met Suzanne. He steadied the letter.

Shane, what follows is my deception, for which I could never find forgiveness. When my father and I rowed out, I took along two cement blocks, one for each of us, and when we could no longer see the shore, he told me to stop the engine. I helped him off the floor of The Lilly onto the stern and strapped one of the cement blocks to his ankle and the other to mine. His fingers knotted around my wrist and he jerked me toward him. 'The time has come,' burst from his lips. I started crying. "Together, my darling, to the Fields," he said with pride.

I've never known how it came to me, but I wrenched my wrist from his grip and shoved him into the water. My first impulse was to try and rescue him but instead, I dropped his block into the water and just before it jerked him under, he reached out for me but I didn't take his hand. His fingers knotted into a fist and he went under. I unfastened the block around my ankle.

If only Judas had seen fit to set me free, but he didn't and I cannot betray my father yet again.

I should tell you that I left you a memento with Saul. He'll be at Blackberry Hill this evening and will give it to you, should you choose to go. If you do, please take it up to our grave before you open it. I made a wooden cross and stuck it in the ground to signify our marriage, yet in another world.

By the time you read this, I will be far, far away, but by the time you get to the Cemetery, if you choose to go, I'll be on my way back, for I love you in a way over which eternity has no hold. Let me say it one more time, hoping it jumps straight from the letter into your heart, I love you!

Shane stared at the cave. What had she left him? Was she somehow her own memento? He had to know, if only to hold her breathless in his arms.

Chapter Thirty-Eight

Suzanne wobbled to the stern, sat down on the slat that once held The Lilly's engine and eased a foot into the freezing water. Repeating to herself that the time had come, she grasped onto the edge of the hull with one hand and cringing, slowly lowered herself until her shoulders were just below the surface. The gravel in the pockets of her jacket almost broke her grip but still holding on, she let the water rise to her chin. Her jeans and jacket briefly repelled the cold, but as the jacket filled with water, she shuddered and raised her eyes, hoping that even a distant distraction would soothe her. As if her father had already begun the celebration, the sunset had overcome the mist and was now an alluring conflagration of red, yellow and orange striations like the stones that formed the cave. Stars were coming out. As beautiful as the evening appeared, it failed to calm her.

"I'll be there soon, Father," she said. Her heart pounded as she closed her eyes and slowly released her grip.

Fighting the pull of the gravel, she paddled to stay on the surface a moment longer. She squeezed her mouth shut and took in a deep breath through her nose. The inhalation swelled her chest, causing her clothes to tighten around her. The cold water nipped at her skin. She opened her mouth and exhaled. Tempted to stay afloat a breath longer, she gave in and closed her eyes. She'd taken her last breath on planet Earth.

Planting her arms by her side, she stiffened her legs and went under. As she sank the sunset faded into a dome of darkness and pressure poured into her chest. Terrified that her lungs were soon to burst, she straightened her arms to slow her descent and retrieved her last memory. Shane was looking at her with eyes as immersed in the moment as were hers and asked her to marry him. "Of course I will, but only when I return." The words sped through her memory, opening a bare slot for the finish. "And when I do, I won't be bringing me with me." Her response to his plea had been a lie embalmed with hope, but the underlying truth remained buried in her heart.

A confusing paradox swept through her mind. All those times with Shane, when she'd evaded her father's demand to join him in death, hadn't she found moments of strength, that elusive quality she'd not been able to access? The pulse of hope vanished when it came to her that while she might have found the strength to escape his demand, it counted for nothing because she'd not been able to access the courage to put it to work.

She brought her arms to her side and descended faster. Her lungs began to fill. Darkness enveloped her. The biting cold went away as her body began to anesthetize. Death would come in seconds, she thought just before her feet rammed into a flat reef of bedrock. The impact jarred both her body and her oxygen-deprived brain. Hieroglyphics swarmed across her eyes. Spasms grabbed her legs. Her throat closed. In the last moment of her life, the most jolting enigma she'd ever experienced hit her — there was a certain love between the living and the dead. Her heart opened its gates and begged her to start swimming toward the surface.

She wanted to peel off her jacket but she was barely able to extend her arms. As she thrusted her hands into the pockets in an attempt to jerk out the gravel, her legs gave way and the words returned, "I won't be bringing me with me."

In less than a moment, all that she'd known and all that had escaped her came crashing down. Betrayal, guilt, and cowardice combined with hope in a paradoxical effort to make sense of her confusion and turmoil. Immediately, the pieces fell into place. If she were alive tomorrow, she'd run to Shane, throw her arms around him, and scream, "I love you!" again and again.

Love had accompanied her to the reef but wouldn't let her stay. A surge of adrenaline coursed through her body and gave a round of strength to her heart. Infused with a burst of energy she yanked the gravel out of her pockets and thrusted her arms through the darkness into an increasingly colorful layer of the sea whose beauty rose with her. When she surfaced, she started throwing up the water in her lungs, diminishing the pressure in her chest. She bobbed, weaved, and paddled to hold her place in the water while she searched for The Lilly. It had drifted out of sight.

The moon was rising and the tide was growing stronger. She reached with both arms to flatten out on the water and start breast-stroking. With help from the tide, she rode the waves, knowing full well that she couldn't ease up until she was at least waist-high in the water. It rattled her to think that if she didn't make it Shane might find her pasty-white body on the shore with her eyes frozen open, staring at him.

The current caused by the harvest moon carried her within several yards of the shore, where she was able to touch bottom. The simultaneous ebb and flow of the water rocked her back and forth but even so, she was able to struggle to the edge of the foam. She dropped to her knees just below a group of plover sandpipers sleeping on the sand.

Transported into a world whose existence she'd denied. She found herself in a domain of churchlike stillness where life wasn't bound to the trauma of the past but gave way to the present in a wave of hope that could carry her into a tomorrow where guilt, regret, and fear gave way to promise. She was inside that moment, neither cloistered nor afraid, but filled with a sense of joy. She'd been freed from weakness by summoning the courage and strength to live and to love. She felt the thrill of freedom, freedom to do as she wished and as she was driven.

Playing off the energy she'd marshaled, she made it to the Pontiac. Her letter was gone. She unhitched the trailer, started the car and mashed the gas pedal. The wheels spun and whined, sinking the car to a stand-still and alerting the flock of birds. She tried again but the car didn't move.

Before she could jump out and run, she heard a thump on her window. She opened the door to find a small, unmoving plover lying on the sand. Suzanne wanted to take-off but couldn't. She knelt, picked up the little bird and watched its chest for a heartbeat. There was none. She fingered its chest, stroking and compressing both sides, but no response. She was about to lay the little bird down when its chest suddenly throbbed. As its heart started to race, the tiny wings inched from the sides and began to flap wildly. It spun from her hand and took flight.

Suzanne watched, thrilled. She started running toward the cemetery. She ran into love's energy that not only permitted her to run on empty, but fueled her to run through the past and through the present, and like the little bird, into a tomorrow of her making. Could it be that her father was watching? Could it be that he was smiling?

Chapter Thirty-Nine

Alert to the misbegotten idea that Suzanne might be her own memento, Shane headed to the cemetery trapped in a world replete with confusing memories. They merged into a silent movie of ghostly excerpts that brought together moments that could not be separated from reality, any more than the idea that Suzanne was alive.

He saw her on the widow's walk and sitting in the stands and perched above him on her living room sofa. He saw her in a museum that featured Achelois floating on the wall above Joan d' Arc and at Blinder's dancing on the table with her bikini underpants showing under the swirling hem of her dress. He saw her waiting for him at the old train station and running toward him the moment he showed up to throw her arms around him. What was real and what wasn't?

Unable to answer the question, conviction came to the rescue, affirming that her love for him was alive and would never end and that her spirit or maybe her body was waiting at the grave. He tried his hardest to make something out of what was happening and then saw the moon in the windshield. Its glow filled the Rambler. He sped up with time outracing him.

At last, the cemetery appeared and guarding it, the black angel with its shadowed wings hanging over Saul who was kneeling under them. When Shane got of the car, Saul grabbed one of the wings and pulled himself to his feet. He hustled over to Shane and handed him a large, scroll-like tube wrapped in tinfoil. "Something from Suzanne," he said. "She asked me to beg you not to open it until you're up by the piece of earth that Roland gave her."

"Bless you, Saul," Shane said.

"Shane, there's more."

"More?"

"When Roland offered Suzanne his grave, they stared at each other for the longest time. Neither said a word. It was as if they were trying their best to find something in each other, something each of them lacked but wanted in the worst way. It was like a puzzle they had to solve but couldn't admit that they saw no way to go about it. I know it doesn't make any sense, but it was there, something so thick that it just hung in the air until they left. I got no idea what it was."

"I do," Shane said. "It was forgiveness."

"Wait a minute. When it comes to Roland, I understand, but Suzanne? What does she need forgiveness for?"

Shane hesitated. The day was coming to an end and he had to get moving, but his heart gave in. "For falling in love with me."

Saul's eyes widened. "For falling in love with you? That don't make any sense."

"It's her world. What often makes sense to her, doesn't make sense to anyone else. Saul, I have to get going."

Saul reached into his coat and handed Shane a small felt box. "Please take this. It's a gift from me and Elise. Now, keep your head up and move on, young man. You haven't lost Suzanne. Don't let her lose you."

It made no sense to Shane, but knowing the world Suzanne had lived in, maybe it did.

Shadowed headstones were spiking against the hill where the slope took away the wind and made a serene trough that cast the shadow of Roland's cross down the hill like a scythe. When Shane reached the crest, the fog was beginning to crawl over the ground carrying a thin veil of the moon's glow.

As he approached the gravesites, the wind picked up. He could taste the sea salt. The clean smell of ocean air replenished his lungs, but within a few yards of the graves, the smell of freshly turned earth jarred him. He wiped his face to clear his eyes, but the scent clung to his hands. Suzanne's voice vanished the smell. "Life and death are one and the same. Promise me, you'll go to my grave."

Silence surrounded him. Not even the sound of the wind came to him. It was more than the absence of noise, more like some strange substratum of stillness where everything was completely inert, suspended in a cold and seamless void. As if they'd been in hiding, the graves appeared before him. It was too late to betray her.

In the middle of the plot next to Jesse's, stood a make-shift cross, about a yard high made of trimmed pine. Suzanne had painted Shane's name on the arm and her name on the staff. The names intersected at each A. He knelt onto the cold, wet ground and leaned forward for his lips to touch the nexus of the cross.

He'd seen many graves, but never seen or felt anything this overwhelming. He wanted to believe that she wasn't there. How could she be, this wandering artist with insights, feelings and a mind so advanced that the world of coincidence bowed to her wishes?

As he bent closer he felt a faint miasma hovering over the grave. His hands were damp. Saul had told him that the mossy wetness was a sign that the grave possessed a wounded soul afraid to leave home due to the evil that's been done to it. Was Suzanne somehow there after all, deep in unplowed ground, waiting to foil her father and escape him? Whether or not, she was in the pit of his stomach, in his tear ducts and heart.

As the Reef melted into the colors of her father's cave, Shane heard his nervous voice asking her to marry him and her stunning answer whose sincere tone rode on his. He shivered as the fading howl of a wolf pled for the moon to rise faster. Cautiously, he unwrapped the tinfoil and unrolled the canvass.

She'd drawn a charcoaled sketch of herself and signed it, "I love you." Her penciled, smudged face made her smile seem to be behind a thin curtain, not so much in hiding but as a ploy, challenging him to reach into the paper and touch her, while coyishly buried in a cloud. He brought the drawing to his lips and briefly touched hers in what was not so much a kiss as an act of forgiveness, saying that he understood what she'd done and why. He spread the drawing on the ground and lightly traced her face with his fingers. He placed his ear against the surface, listening for her heartbeat. He heard a pulse as faint as wind through bamboo. Afraid to breathe he held the sound in his temple, only to realize that it was his heartbeat. He let his breath out slowly and felt the words collect on his lips: "I will always love you."

"Hush," her image whispered.

"I'm in love with you," he said, looking into her eyes when they were lying on the sofa.

"Please, don't be," she replied in an imagined but serious voice.

"But I am," he said, watching his tears drip onto her portrait, as though her image was crying.

He reached into his jacket, took out Saul's tiny felt box and pinched the sides to force it open, then tapped it on the palm of his hand to find thick sprigs of curly black hair bunched into dark little haystacks, each bound with a string. He opened Saul's note.

"God bless Talley for clipping these from Jesse's head. That's all my boy left behind, curls of hair, but they might as well be spun gold. These are yours to keep, for you are his brother. Eline and me have the rest."

Stunned, Shane touched the curls and brought them to his nose. The familiar orchard smell of Jesse's skin became a staple in his house, even when Jesse wasn't there. Shane untied one of the tiny stacks and sprinkled the hairs on the sketch. Tragedy on top of tragedy like the layers of a cake baked with formaldehyde, he thought. His life lay before him on a piece of canvass. He wished he'd brought his pistol.

He remembered Medic's reply to the student who asked him if he'd ever been in love. "Yes," he'd said, "but it wasn't with the living."

Thoughts struggled to form but there was no coherence, only the pounding of his heart drowning out any attempt to reason, to make sense of anything.

Her voice was implanted in his head. He would hear it forever.

"When are you coming back?" he whispered.

"Now, and you'll be happy to know that I didn't come with me," she said, placing her hand on his shoulder.

He thought he'd lost his mind as he pivoted to see her kneeling beside him, shivering. "Suzanne?" he gasped.

"Suzanne, no longer. My name is Fortune." The moon lit her stringy wet hair, shading her face with tones of red, orange, peach and yellow. "The colors of the cave," she said, "the colors of love."

"My God, I thought for sure you…"

"Weren't me, and you're right. I'm not the person I thought I was, the sister of Judas. I left her in the ocean, never to return. The other side of me, the side that you gave me, is who I am and forever will be."

For the first time, their kiss was exactly what it had been in the driveway, only this time their lips came together and the barricade she'd built around her soul crumbled. When their lips softened, she whispered.

"…when we shall die,
Take us and cut us out into little stars,
And we will make the face of heaven so fine
That all the world will be in love with night
And pay no worship to the garish sun."

"Romeo and Juliet," Shane said.

"Let's go to Stavros," she said. "It's time to celebrate life."